Segue House Connection

Regarding Hayworth

Book III

L. P. Suzanne Atkinson

lpsabooks
http://lpsabooks.wix.com/lpsabooks#

Cover Design by Adam Murray
Cover Photography by David Weintraub
Editing by Lesley Carson

ISBN
978-0-9949-5909-6 (Paperback)
978-0-9958-6960-8 (eBook)

1. *Fiction, Contemporary Women*
2. *Fiction, Psychological Suspense*

Distributed to the trade by the Ingram Book Company
Printed in the USA

Table of Contents

Trust no one, tell your secrets to nobody, and no one will ever betray you.
—Bigvai Volcy

Whether we appreciate it or not, we live out our lives surrounded by an intricate pattern of social connections....We're all embedded in this network; it affects us profoundly and we may be unaware of its existence, of its effect on us.
—Nicholas A. Christakis

The world does not have tidy endings. The world does not have neat connections. It is not filled with epiphanies that work perfectly at the moment that you need them.
—Dennis Lehane

Other works by L. P. Suzanne Atkinson

~Creative Non-Fiction~
Emily's Will Be Done

~Fiction~
Ties That Bind
Station Secrets: Regarding Hayworth Book I
Hexagon Dilemma: Regarding Hayworth Book II

For David

Thank you to Pauline, Wyneth, Kat, Marguerite, Barb,
and my editor, Lesley Carson.

Chapter 1

~

Ronny

Avoid panic. Assess your situation. Assess your injuries. Assess your surroundings. The personal-protection mantra, repeated over and over in her self-defence classes, finally penetrates her fear. Ronny keeps her eyes closed. She is on her back on a bed. Her hands are by her sides. The rough blanket beneath her scratches her arms. Her feet are without her sandals. Her sleeveless blouse and capris remain on. Her ever-present neck scarf is gone. Why is her shoulder sore? The air rests against her body like a warm towel on a hot day.

She listens and analyzes. There is no sound except the drone of a fly nearby. She opens her eyes a fraction. If he is there watching her, she is certainly not ready for him to know she's awake. She sees the inside of a shed or cabin, and the framing lumber of upper walls and ceiling. There are horizontal boards but no insulation between the studs.

She focuses on her breathing. *In and out. In and out. Avoid panic. Maybe he won't hurt you.* Finally, she opens her eyes. She is not tied up or held down, but flaked out on a rusty cot with a wool blanket—blue, scratchy, and certainly not needed today—underneath her. No one else is there. As she struggles to sit up, her head spins. She tries to remember what happened. *Time for recollections later. Keep assessing. Keep assessing.*

The room is about as bare as any prison cell, but still geared to sustain life. There is the cot. There is a piece of wide and rough-hewn lumber nailed with spikes to the vertical studs of the opposite wall. This is what serves as a

"

make-shift counter. It holds a plastic jug of presumably water, and two large bags of potato chips. There is a jar of peanut butter, a box of Ritz crackers, and a plastic knife. There is a paper cup.

One window and two doors break the flow of interior walls. The door across from the bed has bars, like jail bars you see in the movies. They're installed on the inside. The window, on the adjoining wall, is barred as well and has a small piece of wood in the bottom frame. She is able to fit her fingers through the bars and lift up the slat to reveal three holes. More hot, but fresh, air drifts into the room. She tries to rattle the bars in a futile attempt at escape. She knows better.

The view is of bushes—a high, leafy tangle of branches. Ronny guesses what's concealed behind the second door located on the same wall, because of the smell of lye oozing out from under the rough lumber threshold. The space is a lean-to outhouse, protruding through the wall just to the left of the bushes. She opens the door with caution. Her hand trembles. He might be hiding inside. The one-hole privy has a toilet seat and cover screwed to the top of the aged wooden bench. Rolls of toilet paper are stacked in the corner.

She is confined in a cabin somewhere beyond Hayworth. They will know something is wrong because she was a no show at her meeting. They'll know when they find her car; when she fails to appear for work tomorrow morning. They will search for her. Surely someone noticed what happened. Her head aches as she tries to remember. *What did he give me?*

✳✳✳✳

Her alarm rang at six. The drive to Carter River takes a couple of hours and she wanted to get an early start, permitting time to stop at the Petro-Can and have coffee. She likes to break up the two hour drive, but still be at a meeting in reasonable time. Today, she was scheduled to sit down with her provincial counter-parts in Northern Alberta—other counsellors from women's shelters. The focus of the meeting was to be funding sources and local statistics of women and families served in the first six months of 1984. Her successful fundraising efforts in the name of Segue House served to grace her with a spot on the agenda.

She left Hayworth at about eight that morning in her second-hand sedan—a black Buick Regal, two-door V-8 with rear wheel drive. The previous owner was one of the undertakers at the local funeral home. The car is a monster and not worth a damn in the winter, but great fun to drive when the weather is good. Today was glorious in the way August can be with a cooler morning but a promise of a hot and sultry afternoon.

Traffic was light on the west-bound highway to Carter River, a town about three times the size of Hayworth. Carter River has benefited from the oil boom. There are plenty of jobs, even as business has slowed down a bit with the rise in interest rates. There are all kinds of shops, new subdivisions, and no shortage of opportunities for people in the trades. Hayworth has never seemed to catch on in the same way.

The scenery between the two communities consists primarily of canola and wheat fields, sprawling farms, and cattle pastures. The hay is being cut and fashioned into square bales dotting the field like some kind of random board game. The azure blue sky meets yellow canola fields in straight lines along the horizon—vivid, stark, and endless.

Halfway between Hayworth and Carter River is the Four Corners Petro-Canada, a diner and gas station perched in all its glory at the junction of the highway and a cross-road leading off to farming communities in both directions. It has been there ever since Ronny moved to the area back in 1981, and has served as a stopover for much longer. She pulled her Buick into the gravel parking lot peppered with potholes. Blowing dust sucked into the air vents—relentless and inescapable. Five eighteen-wheelers were parallel-parked in the over-sized side yard. All the cabs faced forward, with windows down and big dogs ensconced in every driver's seat. Ronny remembers she waved at them when she navigated her way inside the restaurant as the five attentive dog faces turned in unison to watch her. Big dogs—huskies, shepherds, labs—all employed to guard their rigs. They reminded her of her landlady's dog, Martha, a husky and blue heeler mix.

The front window of the restaurant was hazy with grit from the parking lot. On the inside, three dusty and dirty philodendrons pressed themselves against the glass in search of scraps of sunlight they would need for today—a neglected jungle. Ronny assumed it was an attempt, likely by the restaurant manager, to inject a homey quality into this barren and wind-swept place.

The rattle of metal chairs on a linoleum floor emphasized the hollowness of the large open restaurant. The atmosphere was neither cozy nor quaint. Ronny approached the counter as a waitress in a tan shirt dress with a red apron flew through the saloon-style doors from the kitchen with three platter-sized breakfasts balanced on one arm. She grabbed the coffee pot with her free hand and made eye contact with Ronny. "Back in a sec."

Ronny wandered toward a table off to the side. As the waitress returned to the counter with the coffee pot, she tipped her wrist to indicate one for her, too, so the rushed young woman picked up a mug before she made the return trip. "Hungry? I've blueberry muffins still warm out of the oven."

"Maybe a couple to go. Right now, only the coffee."

The waitress nodded and took off. Three more men lumbered in. They were dressed in rubber boots and plaid shirts—garb more appropriate for farmers than truckers. The truckers were all in blue jeans and western-style shirts, coupled with work boots and ball caps.

Ronny enjoyed her break from the road, the smell of the coffee, the pleasantness of the waitress, the honky tonk whining away on the jukebox, and the anticipation of blueberry muffins coming home with her to the little rented house—her sanctuary from the world. The property may belong to Gaby Ridgway on paper, but 15 Poplar Street is hers right now.

His gait was rolling and confident. She failed to recognize him at first. Once her brain accepted the fact it was him, she couldn't put her thoughts together, or figure out where to focus her eyes. She kept her face toward the table, and hoped he wouldn't recognize her with this short platinum hair style. His appearance could be a fluke, but this hope proved futile. He saw her right away and sauntered over to the table as if they had intended to meet there, in this place, all along.

Duncan Taylor had become a different man in the four years and four months since she last saw him. He was always tall and lean—not exceptionally attractive, with a face shaped like a garden trowel and slightly protruding teeth—and clean-cut. He used to have straight brown hair. His head was shaved now. He looked more muscular—bigger. Prison would give a guy motivation to work out.

Duncan swaggered over to the table and sat down across from her. The chair scraped on the old lino floor and made her skin crawl. "Long time no see, Janine. Aren't we like two different people from another world! You've changed your name and look a helluva lot different. Love the hair! Sexy! Thought I might not be able to find you."

Had her heart stopped? She felt like her heart had stopped. Her dry mouth made her lips stick together. With careful precision, she set her cup back down on the table, swallowed the mix of fear and hatred burning the back of her throat, and steeled herself to make eye contact with him. He wore a white T-shirt and black jeans. His sneakers appeared the worse for wear. His nails were chewed to the quick and his arms were liberally tattooed.

"So, what's with the new name, Janine? Tryin' to hide?" His expression oozed a sick sweetness. Her recollection of him was that this was what he was like when he was drinking, but it was early morning and he seemed sober.

"What do you want, Duncan? How did you find me?" Exhausted already, she attempted to keep the vibration out of her voice.

"Got out a couple of months ago. I wanted to find my wife. Is there a problem with a guy who wants to find his wife?"

"Yes!" Her voice hissed. "You are not to be anywhere near me. I have a restraining order and we are divorced—signed, sealed, and delivered. You are violating your parole! I could call the police right now!" She gritted her teeth and fought to hold her emotions in check as hysteria began to bubble up.

"Cool your jets, Janine. I tracked you down so I could apologize; you know, make the situation right between us. I've forgiven you. Can you forgive me?" Again, with the sweet, cat-that-ate-the-canary smile.

"I have to go. I'm on my way to a meeting."

"Yes, I know. You and the other counsellors are meeting in Carter River today."

She reacted. She knows her face flushed and her eyes popped. She couldn't stop herself. "How the hell do you know about my work?"

His face darkened. He controlled the conversation, like always. "I have my ways. Listen." He leaned over the table, big forearms spread out in front of her. "I aim to stay in the neighbourhood. I like the area. Lots nicer than Sudbury. I never liked Sudbury." He patted her hand. She pulled away so fast, he laughed. "I'm not poison. You worry for nothing. I won't hurt you." He then scraped his chair back, hoisted himself to his feet, and sashayed out of the restaurant. He acted for all the world like he owned the joint. She noticed a bar code tattooed on the back of his bald head. She absently wondered if it represented a particular grocery item.

Ronny watched the clock and waited five minutes before she approached the counter and paid for her coffee. She forgot about the muffins and made her way to the Buick, determined to believe he had left like he said he would.

A little voice reminded her that he never did what he said he would. As she bent over to insert her key in the door lock, his arm closed around her throat so she became wedged firmly in the crook of his elbow, so close his tattoos became a blur. She froze.

"Open the car door. Throw your keys and your purse inside." His breath in her ear felt like needles. She followed instructions. He pressed the lock down with the edge of the palm of his free hand and kicked the door shut.

Ronny scanned the parking lot, eyes frantic to see someone, anyone, who might help her. The gravel expanse was empty except for the five dogs watching intently. "Walk with me. Do not make one sound or, I swear to God, I will break your neck. You will fall dead on the ground right here and I will be gone. No one will ever know I came near you."

Again, she followed instructions.

They manoeuvred to his truck, a nondescript green Ford F-150 parked out of sight around the corner near the tire pressure hose. He opened the passenger door, reached for the handcuffs waiting on the bench seat, and snarled her arms behind her back. Then he blindfolded her with a scrap of dirty grey fabric, maybe a dish towel. Her mind raced. Someone had to see this. The truck stop is a busy place, but she knew no one would be able to observe her struggle behind the open truck door. She had no choice but to allow him to push her into the cab and down on to the floor.

Her long legs screamed for mercy as she became scrunched into the cramped space in front of the passenger seat. Blindfolded, she had no idea what hit her when a sharp prick invaded her upper arm. There was no more need to cover her eyes. She blacked out.

****

The weather is hot. August can be brutal and this summer has been no exception. The cabin is stifling, despite the three holes open to the outside. The temperature must be one hundred degrees. Sweat creeps down between her breasts and off her forehead. Her attire is for a meeting. Both her sandals or her scarf are missing. He must have taken them. The old floor is chipped and in need of a sweep but she assesses her bare feet will be in no danger. She unbuttons the top two buttons of her blouse.

Her watch is gone. She has no idea how long she was knocked out, so she'll have to wait until the sun starts to set to determine the time. She pours water into the paper cup and sits back down on the bed, scared to death but happy to be alive. He could have easily killed her and left her someplace. *Remember what happened to Roz Dover around this time of year back in '81?*

Roz Dover was a cleaner at the Hayworth Community Hospital. She left work one night and was never seen again. Her car was found in the yard of an abandoned farm way out in the middle of nowhere, but Roz has never been seen since. There was no sign of a struggle. The people of Hayworth have wondered and worried about the young woman ever since. Every yard was combed; every building was searched. The shadow of her disappearance has cast a pall on the community. This is the time of year when the local RCMP schedules a town meeting to talk about Roz. They continue to try and jog the memories of anybody who might have been out and about on the night she seemed to vaporize. Duncan was in jail then, but whatever happened to Roz could easily happen to her.

****

Darkness starts to settle in after what Ronny estimates is about two hours. There is no lantern, no flashlight, and not one candle. She begins to sense the cooler air drift across her sticky skin. Could she die from the heat before anybody notices her absence?

The throb of her headache starts to dissipate as fresh air continues to trickle into the cabin. She eats crackers and peanut butter before darkness envelopes the space. This was a favourite snack years ago. Both the box and the jar were sealed, so she is certain he hasn't poisoned them. He took the time to provide food he knew she liked. Why?

****

Janine and Duncan Taylor were married in 1966. He was twenty-six and she was twenty-five. She believed they would have a great life before her world changed. The first time he hit her, she chalked his behaviour up to rage and grief. They were married for about five years when she miscarried. He was overcome with anger and despair. The doctor said they could try again; these events sometimes happen. His over-the-top and alien reaction shocked her.

She had no way to comfort him. Maybe she tried too hard. He hit her. At the time, she labeled his violence a cuff; a slap, maybe. He couldn't control himself. She should have done a better job of preparing him for the possibility of a miscarriage. Who would think of such a thing? Now she knows she was hit hard, regardless of her rationalization at the time. Her tooth was chipped. She had to have dental work and told her dentist she had slipped and fallen. The dentist was suspicious. She ignored his concern.

The second time he hit her, he had lost his job with the Town of Sudbury. He drove a truck and did municipal maintenance chores. As a local boy, he always had the benefit of the doubt until he drank his lunch one day. Then all the late arrivals, the sick days, the belligerence to the supervisor, and the poor evaluations reached a climax. They let him go. He became unreasonably angry. Somehow, in his rage, he found a way to blame her. Ronny's job, back when she was Janine, was as a clerk for a mining company. Her paycheck kept them afloat. He drank almost all the time, then, and wouldn't even search for another job.

The next ten years of marriage turned into a blur of tension, hospital visits, and respite at work. She made sure she never became pregnant again. It wouldn't be fair to a child to expose them to this life. She hid her prevention strategies. It wasn't difficult. He seemed indifferent, anyway, after the miscarriage.

She never talked about her plight but she believed people knew. One time, when she went to the emergency room because Duncan had broken her wrist, she met Faith, from the local women's shelter. She happened to be there because another woman, a former client, was getting patched up after her husband had beaten her. The doctors, since they had seen Janine on many occasions, requested a consultation while Faith was in the hospital. Janine was cornered.

The two women talked for a long time. Eventually, Duncan appeared in the emergency department. He acted like the conquering hero, coming to rescue her from the jaws of some abyss. Faith whispered in her ear, to let her know she had options, but Janine went back home. She thought about Faith. For the first time since the start of the abuse, she came to understand she had a way out. She contacted Faith the night he tried to cut her throat.

Chapter 2

Ronny

Darkness is sudden and absolute, streaked with chill and hidden unknowns. Ronny curls up at the head of the cot with her back against the wall so she is able to face the outside door. Her bare feet are tucked under the rough wool blanket. She wraps her arms around her knees, sits still, and stares into inkiness. Her fears are contained within the force of her long thin arms. After a few minutes, she can make out the shadowy form of the counter, as well as the hint of the iron bars, on the opposite wall. The evening is clear but the moon must be less than half. It struggles to provide the sliver of light she is to be given. The wild roses scratch against the house as the evening wind nudges them. She is afraid to close her eyes; afraid of her defencelessness if he shows up. Eventually, she will have to surrender to sleep.

****

Duncan Taylor went to jail in December, 1980. With time served prior to his trial, he would not be out until April, 1984. Janine Taylor obtained her divorce and a restraining order which remains in effect into the future. She planned her disappearance with care. The task wasn't difficult.

Faith helped. Faith used her professional contacts to line up the job for Janine as a lay counsellor and support person at Segue House in Hayworth, Alberta. Once her divorce from Duncan became final, Janine left Sudbury behind forever. At least, that was her goal.

The day before her scheduled departure on the bus, she walked into a hair salon where she knew no one. She had her mane of naturally thick and curly dark hair shaved as short as the hairdresser would permit. Then they dyed it platinum blond. She hardly recognized the woman reflected in the mirror. The transformation proved remarkable.

She called her father and told him about her plan to leave, but not her destination. The conversation became stilted and weird. She wanted him to care, somehow, but he hadn't for a long time.

"I want you to know I will be leaving today, Dad."

"Well, tell me where, in case somebody calls and wants to know."

"Here's the issue, Dad. I want to disappear. If there's an emergency, like somebody dies, you can contact Faith at the shelter and she'll find me. I won't be back."

"You shouldn't have sent him to jail, Janine."

"He tried to kill me, Dad." She sighed with the effort to explain for the umpteenth time. Her father seemed to think she should have stayed with a man who went to jail for spousal battery and attempted murder. He said it shamed him when she aired all her dirty laundry in public. He said people gawked at him.

"He'll get out soon enough. You can't hide. He'll find you."

"I plan to be somebody else, Dad. I wanted to say goodbye."

She heard rustling noises, like he might be anxious to get back to his newspaper. He said no more.

"Bye, Dad."

"See ya', Janine."

From the time Janine boarded the Greyhound bus in Sudbury, with a one-way ticket to Hayworth, Alberta stashed in her wallet, she began the change process. Curled up on the blue vinyl coach seat, she focused her gaze out the blotchy window and recalled her mother's favourite movie star—Veronica Lake. The French word for pond is étang. She chose a new name with some familiarity. She hoped the name would help her stay in character. *I am Ronny Étang* became her mantra.

She would tell those who asked, about how she has a French last name but could never speak the language so she had to leave Québec to secure a good job. Her parents are dead and she has no siblings. The scar on her neck is from an old car accident. Once in Hayworth, she would see a lawyer and legally change her name. The date was May 10, 1981.

All the details fell into place after she arrived in Hayworth. Ava Burrway, who would be her supervisor at Segue House, had put her in touch with Amanda Wolski, the manager of a small apartment building called The Station. Ava knew Ronny's real identity, but no one else would. Amanda's husband, Chester, met her at the local diner where the bus let her off. She felt like she stepped into the 1950s as she got off the bus and surveyed her surroundings.

The Station proved to be a microcosm of personalities and interactions all on its own. She arrived in town a couple of days before the Victoria Day long weekend and received an immediate invitation to a private wedding to take place at The Station. The managers, Chester and Amanda Wolski, needed to renew their vows and only the residents and the Justice of the Peace would ever know about the event. Ronny learned the details later, how Amanda married Chester before she had a divorce from her first husband—some rich guy who was unfaithful.

Other residents were equally intriguing. All had managed to come to Hayworth to get away from their pasts, but the death of Benjamine Tullis, the former tenant in Ronny's apartment, had a profound impact on each of them. Ben lived and died in Number Three. She gave up her antique business when she became sick. All the residents took care of her so she could remain at home until she succumbed to pancreatic cancer. Ronny thought the history of the space would bother her, but instead, the knowledge proved a comfort, like the old lady was protecting her somehow.

Rose and Maggie Woodward lived together across the hall at the time Ronny moved in. Rose was the building busy body, but she appreciated their help and friendship from the beginning. Maggie turned out to be the bookkeeper at the shelter and had to know Ronny's real identity, but she has maintained strict confidentiality. Cheryl Nadler lived upstairs and still does. What a beautiful young woman; a social worker at the provincial government services offices, fondly known as the Hexagon. Joe Dodd lived across the hall from Cheryl, and is the carpenter who built the marble-topped peninsula left in Ben's apartment after she died. Patrick Hollinger was the first person she ever met in Hayworth—a young chap who lives in the attic at The Station. He works at the Hayworth Diner and seems to treat everyone at The Station as family. He has always been a little odd, but Ronny has been unable to quite figure out why. She has never heard any gossip about him.

Ava helped Ronny with all the details regarding her identity change. She met their lawyer, Murdock Blackney, who had the paperwork all drawn up. He is a round and balding wearer of brown suits with waistcoats to hide his expansive girth. Tufts of hair sprout out of his enormous ears. He proved efficient and precise. Once she signed the necessary documents, they secured a closed hearing in the local courthouse. The formality took a matter of minutes. Mr. Blackney took care of her driver's licence and her social insurance, so they would reflect her new name. He notified the tax people and vouched for her at the bank so she could open an account. She suspected the issue was complicated, but he handled all the details and she summarily sailed along as Ronny Étang with not another whisper or issue—like magic.

No one has ever questioned her story. She eased into this new identity with surprisingly little effort. Her transition from Janine to Ronny became as simple as the purchase of a new pair of comfortable shoes. Oftentimes, she startles herself when she catches a glimpse in the mirror. She misses her hair, but the change in her is so dramatic, she has made a silent pact never to relent and let her hair return to the long and dark unruly curls that once defined her.

Ava and Maggie were the only two employees at Segue House when she started to work there, but Ava soon hired Sheila Pasco as the overnight person. Sheila remains unaware of Ronny's secret.

Segue House is a nondescript six unit apartment building located in a residential neighbourhood at the edge of town. The structure has three floors plus the basement. The main floor houses their offices and meeting rooms in the two ground-level units. The upper two floors contain a total of four apartments designed to support single women or women and their children. The basement has a laundry room, utility room, and a bedsitter now occupied by Sheila. The place is in generally good condition, thanks to a bevy of volunteers who paint, mow, shovel, and scrounge for used items like appliances and bunk beds.

Security is tight. Embedded in the wall on the outside of the building is an intercom where any visitor or staff must first identify themselves. Each staff member has an employee number. There are no exceptions to the routine. Once entry is granted into the vestibule, a visual must take place before the person is buzzed into the building. There have been a couple of incidents where someone has gained access to the inside vestibule when they should not have been admitted—angry husbands. The police station is nearby, so help can arrive in no time. Ronny embraces the security surrounding her at work.

The living room of the apartment to the right of the entry is used as a reception area. Ava's office is in the former master bedroom. Maggie uses the second bedroom as her office. The living room of the apartment on the left is maintained as their conference room. Ronny's office occupies the one bedroom in that unit, although she more often talks to residents in their own space. Most prefer this approach, unless they're obliged to share shelter apartment space with someone else. Ronny uses her office as a sanctuary to complete paperwork and meet with colleagues—those inside Segue House and those from other agencies with whom she works.

On Thanksgiving of her first year in town, she hosted a potluck and invited all the residents of The Station. After the wedding get-together when she first arrived, she came to understand how the group seemed to need to socialize. Her party validated this assumption predicated on observations of mutual support and trust. Patrick revealed why a woman, known to many of them, had been implicated in a death back east. Gaby Ridgway, Joe's guest that day, was the family counsellor involved. Her knowledge of the affair seemed obvious from the look on her face, although Ronny never learned all the details. Gaby left her work at the Hexagon and went into business with Joe shortly afterward.

At Christmas, Gaby and Joe hosted dinner at Gaby's house on Poplar Street. The afternoon was festive and homey. As Patrick was always anxious to say, they were family. Ronny fell in love with Gaby's house. A couple of years later, Gaby and Joe built a new home, and Ronny has rented the little bungalow ever since.

****

Light still comes early even though the length of the days starts to change with increasing speed in the north this time of year. She must have slept. There is still no sign of Duncan, or anybody else for that matter. Where could they be? They are now aware that she missed her meeting and has not appeared at her desk this morning. Ava would have to know there's a problem. She would have to know! Ronny sits on the side of the cot and stares through the bars of the window to the right, out at the roses and sky beyond. It promises to be another hot day today. The farmers will be happy.

L. P. Suzanne Atkinson

****

Ava Burrway is the long-serving director of Segue House. Ronny has never managed to learn many details about her history. Ava avoids talk about her personal life and never socializes with the staff outside the shelter, except at the annual fundraiser ball they hold each year in October. Ronny assumes her boss is single, perhaps divorced, maybe widowed, and certainly not married now. She must be in her fifties. She has a wilted appearance about her— sagging skin, limp hair greying at the temples, a curved posture like she is too tired to sit up straight, and a penchant for sensible shoes. Her voice rolls somehow, like the sound is being pushed through gravel and water.

It is a rare event to experience Ava upset or angry. She seems to have nerves of steel. Ronny remembers the first time she saw an irate husband manage to get into the vestibule at the front of the shelter. He said he had a delivery, and Maggie bought his story so she buzzed him in past their first line of defence. When Ava realized his identity, and with a calm determination, she told him to leave and informed him the police were already called. He pounded on the tempered glass of the vestibule until they all thought the whole wall would shatter. By the time he left, they saw Constable Fiona Werbowski, a fixture in the community and a regular contributor to programming at the shelter, parked out front.

Ava, not rattled in the least by the experience, called Ronny, Sheila Pasco, and Maggie into her office to review the rules. Ronny was impressed by her calm, since her own heart beat out of her chest when she thought about the ramifications should this man have gained access. Maggie wrung her hands and hung her head, but Ava assured her mistakes happen and this is precisely the reason they have a double door security system. They reviewed the proper protocol—how any delivery has to be proceeded by a phone call so the shelter can call back the business and confirm the delivery and the name of the person who would represent the company. Most of the locals— truckers, shop keepers, repair people—already knew the drill.

Ava hired Sheila Pasco to work overnight a couple of months after she brought on Ronny. Up until then, coverage at night consisted of periodic checks by the RCMP. Anyone in residence at the shelter had to be entrusted not to answer the door, regardless. The situation carried its own set of risks, and the three of them were thrilled when Ava secured additional funds and

Sheila could be formally hired. They all worked together to make the little suite in the basement as comfortable as possible for her. She wouldn't be paid much, but she would have a safe place to live.

Ava is mysterious, as far as her life before Hayworth is concerned, but she possesses a sterling reputation in the community. She is no-nonsense. She meets with community members to obtain support for donations—from children's toys to diapers to food stuffs for stocking the kitchens. She torments local professionals to present workshops on subjects from money management to child care. Her life appears to be devoted to the shelter. She has even managed to get renovations done for free, with both materials and labour contributed by local businesses. She is a force of reckoning and Hayworth residents assist when Ava asks. She is remarkable in many ways.

Maggie Woodward, the bookkeeper and general administrative assistant, has worked her way from a position of three days a week into a full-time job. She used to be a neighbour of Ronny's, and lived across the hall with her sister, Rose. Maggie is very child-like in many ways. She always sees the bright side; always sees the best in people. She never complains about her lot in life. On the other hand, she often has a structured way of speaking, like she might be reading from a script or from cue-cards. She laughs if her formality is pointed out; saying years in an institution taught her to measure every word.

Ronny envies Maggie's hair. In addition to her general attractiveness, which is mysterious in a vacant way, she has beautiful long hair. Ronny's heart aches for her real hair, but forces herself to keep hers exceedingly short and dyed almost white. This is the price she pays to be Ronny Étang.

Maggie is very forthright about her past. She was institutionalized in Ontario, courtesy of her abusive parents, from the time she was eighteen until she turned thirty-one. Her sister brought her to Hayworth about four years ago. She seems to have no appreciation for the gravity of what happened to her. She very much lives in the moment. Ronny is fascinated with how she can be so open and so out of touch all at the same time.

It is also commendable how Maggie, for all her naivety, has never spilled the beans regarding Ronny's true identity. Months went by before Ronny felt assured this ethereal woman who is so open, could be relied upon to keep her confidence. Ronny is convinced she has never even revealed the secret to Rose.

Sheila Pasco is another story. She and Ava have a connection, but the details have never been shared with Ronny. She arrived in Hayworth and Ava took her in. She had nowhere to go. When the funds were approved for overnight staff, Sheila took the job. She has a fierce loyalty to Ava. She has never discussed her past or how she ended up back in the area. Ronny knows her parents are Ukrainian immigrants who farm further north. For some reason, Sheila left home at sixteen. Ronny estimates her age as probably not quite thirty.

Sheila is a big woman—big boned—hefty, some would say. Ronny has seen her hoist a stuffed chair into her arms and manhandle the awkward load up the stairs to one of the apartments. She would never be called pretty, or even striking. Her skin in marked. Her brown hair is long, often unwashed, and always pulled together into a pony tail with a rubber band. Ronny has only seen her in blue jeans, extra tight across her ample behind, and sweat shirts of one form or another. She always wears runners. She watches television in the staff lounge all night and sleeps most of the day. They often meet up near the end of the work day as Ronny prepares to go home. Sheila will appear in the apartment occupied by the lounge and Ronny's office, more than likely eating a sandwich and sporting a large bottle of cola tucked into her armpit. She will nod. Sometimes she makes a comment about the weather. Then she will drop into the recliner, situated beside the television especially for her, and put her feet up. She calls this particular spot her office.

Ronny has made attempts to engage her without success. Despite all this, Ronny trusts her and would not hesitate to call for her help if the need ever arose.

****

Ronny would love to see Sheila outside the little cabin window right now. The realization causes tears to spring to her eyes. She knows this is big trouble. This man went to jail for his attempt on her life. What has he got to lose? She paces the broken linoleum floor in her bare feet. What the hell did he do with her sandals?

Chapter 3

Ava

Ava Burrway uses an assured and weighty index finger to depress the outside buzzer at Segue House on Tuesday morning, August 7. Of course she has keys, but she sticks to their protocols with a passionate discipline. An intruder might overpower her and take advantage because of the keys. Someone could be lying in wait. By pushing the buzzer and following their entry system, an incident might be prevented—she hopes.

Sheila responds to the alert with a bark into the speaker. She listens for Ava to identify herself with her employee number, and the outside door becomes accessible. They nod to each other as Sheila unlocks the inside glass door.

"Any news from Ronny after I left yesterday?" Ava's movements are brisk. Her square-heeled pumps thump on the linoleum of the front hall as she makes her way through to her office. Sheila tags along behind, like a dog expecting to be fed. Ava figures her security person had been up all night, although her hair's in a tangle and she has soda stains on her sweatshirt. She might have nodded off a couple of times.

"Nuthin'." Sheila straddles one of Ava's straight-backed office chairs while Ava scrapes off her jacket and stows her purse. The day is warm already. "Want me to check her house? Only take ten minutes."

"No. Let's wait and see if she turns up. We can give her until half-past eight and then I'll call. I still can't believe she never showed for her meeting in Carter Creek. She might be sick and forgot to let us know." Ava is fully aware, as she says the words, of how stupid they sound. Ronny not informing them about being sick would never happen.

"I don't mind lookin', Ava."

"No. You go to bed, Sheila. You're exhausted. You'll hear me call if I need reinforcements. Maggie should be here any minute."

Sheila lifts her ample frame off the chair, salutes her boss, and without another word, lumbers back through the reception room and out into the hall. Ava hears the muffled thuds of her sneakers as Sheila makes her way down to the basement.

What might have happened? Ava forces herself to recognize the facts. Duncan Taylor is likely out of jail, and this could well be an incident of some sort, but how would he ever have found her here in Hayworth? Maybe she *is* sick; so sick she never canceled her meeting. *Not Ronny.* The woman is nothing if not reliable.

Ava shifts in her chair. She makes a mental note to wear her sandals and get rid of these one-size-doesn't-fit-anybody pantyhose she forces herself into every day. *Tummy control, my arse!* She stands up and readjusts herself again as the buzzer bleats. The ringer will be Maggie. She races to the intercom and soon her administrative assistant is inside with one question on her lips. "Is Ronny here?"

"No. I haven't heard from her and Sheila said it was quiet all night. I thought I'd go over to her house and see if everything is okay. I know she keeps a key in her desk in case she was ever to lock herself out by accident. I can take it with me. What do you think?" She needs confirmation, although not exactly sure why.

Maggie's eyes widen. Her hair flies around her face as she follows her boss to the back of the apartment and their offices. "You have to do something, Ava. I am so scared." Her voice is a whisper. "He might be out by now, but he would have no idea where she is…unless, of course, she told someone from back east but never told us she confided in anybody. Would she reveal her secret? Not Ronny! Oh, God! I hope she's okay." Maggie's face is flushed and her hands shake. She hops around her desk like a sparrow in a shoe box.

****

Ava parks her 1983 white Chrysler Le Baron at the curb in front of 15 Poplar Street. The house belongs to Gaby Ridgway who now runs a contracting business with Joe Dodd. Ronny's car is not in the driveway.

She walks up the steps to the covered porch. Each footfall echoes. The quiet unsettles her. Ava makes a conscious effort not to let her pounding heart and sweaty fingers overwhelm her as she utilizes the seldom-used spare key to unlock the front door. The house is sweet, in a cozy-little-bungalow kind of way. Ava has been there before and stands in the entry as her eyes scan the compact office to the left, and the comfortable furniture spread out over what could best be described as a living room and dining room combination to the right. The randomness of Ronny's decorating style clashes with how particular she is about her personal style. There are odd stuffed chairs, and a couple of wooden ones placed without obvious order around the room. A shag carpet, in a nasty yellow variegated shade, covers most of the floor. There is a framed photograph hung on the wall by the door. The picture is of a tiny island cabin, taken from a shore somewhere. Ava is quite sure she and, possibly, Maggie are the only people who understand the significance of the photograph.

She kicks off her pumps and pads out to the kitchen. The house is so quiet, she becomes aware of her own breathing. The kitchen renovation and modernization occurred when Gaby lived here. Ava suspects this is how Gaby first met Joe. He did the work. She notices the start of a grocery list on the table.

"Ronny! Ronny, are you here?" Her voice rattles inside the small space.

One foot forced in front of the other, she makes her way into the bedroom. The double bed is made, the white cotton curtains are pulled open, and the window is up about an inch allowing the scraps of an August morning breeze to filter in through the screen. Ava steels herself to have a peek in the bathroom, also renovated when Gaby lived here. Ava finds herself thinking it might be time to do some work on the old 1930s saltbox she inherited from her mother. Nothing appears amiss.

She returns to the front, wiggles her stocking feet back into her pumps, locks the door, and steps back across the damp grass to her car. She will call the RCMP. Ronny has been gone more than twenty-four hours.

****

Ava Burrway wasn't born in Hayworth. She was born in Edmonton in 1932, the singular offspring of a young couple whose life goal involved farm ownership. They bought a place a few miles east of Hayworth and Ava grew up on the property. She still lives on the land where her father died without warning while he repaired his tractor in the barn; where she nursed her mother through recurring bouts of pneumonia and a lengthy struggle with dementia, until she died fifteen years ago.

Ava, who is a registered nurse, started the Segue House project when she found herself alone at the ripe old age of thirty-seven. She took women into her own home at first. Then she used her parents' money to buy the apartment building. Government grants plus some fundraising and volunteer support manage to keep the place running. The whole project has been a labour of love. More of her own and her parents' money has been invested than the community would ever realize—part of the reason why her house has never even seen a lick of paint in almost twenty years. The place is sound, not too far from town, and serves her purpose. She leases the land and makes enough money to pay the utilities and the taxes. This way, she keeps her salary low at the shelter. Segue House has become her substitute family over the years.

****

Back in her office, she bellows at Maggie. "Get the police on the phone for me, Maggie. Ask for Fiona, first. I might have to break Ronny's confidence so the cops will take me seriously, but I think we have a situation."

Maggie pounces on the phone and instantly does as requested. "Line two, Ava. Constable Fiona Werbowski is on hold."

Ava snatches the phone from the cradle and punches the blinking light. "Fiona. Ava here. I think we have a problem. Can you come over?"

The response is calm and measured, as it always is with Fiona—one of the reasons Ava trusts and likes her. "What's going on, Ava?"

"Ronny's missing. She never made it to her meeting in Carter Creek for ten yesterday morning. Her driveway is empty. She leaves a key here so I went over and did a walk-though and her place appears normal." She hears Fiona catch her breath. "Everything is exactly as I found it. I kept my hands in my pockets. But there's other stuff I need to tell you."

"On my way, Ava. Be there in five minutes."

When Fiona arrives, Maggie buzzes her in and the three of them retreat to Ava's office. Maggie plants herself near the door so she can hear if any of the current residents come into reception. Most often, clients emerge around noon.

Ava observes Fiona as she tries, without much success, to make herself comfortable in the office chair. These poor people have to wear so much paraphernalia around their waist; Ava wonders how they can sit in a police car all day.

Fiona is olive skinned and has big brown eyes. Her long dark hair is always pulled into a tight knot at the nape of her neck. Ava knows she looks like a different person altogether when not on duty. "Tell me what you know, Ava."

Ava leans over the desk. "Fiona, I know she left to go to her meeting in Carter Creek."

"How do you know?"

"Well," Ava hesitates. "She wouldn't miss her meeting. She is as reliable as anyone I've ever met!"

Fiona repeats her instructions. "Tell me what you know, Ava."

"Okay. She did not make her morning meeting in Carter Creek. They called me yesterday afternoon and told me. She has not appeared here today, or overnight. Her house is empty, tidy, locked, and there is no sign of her car."

"What else?"

"I know her ex-husband, Duncan Taylor, was released from prison in April. He did time for attempted murder...of her."

Fiona stares at Ava and then glances over at Maggie.

"We're the only two who know, Fiona—other than the lawyer and judge, of course. Nobody else." Maggie's words sound like an apology. "Ronny changed her name when she came here in 1981. She was Janine Taylor. Unless she revealed her location to someone, there's no way he would know she lives here. She showed me a picture of what she used to look like and you wouldn't even recognize her!"

"She showed you a picture?" Ava is unable to hide her surprise as she turns back to Fiona. "I've never seen a picture of what she looked like before."

"Okay. Here's what we can do." Fiona is all business. "The office can dig up all the details they can on Duncan Taylor. We'll try and determine if there's any indication he traveled this way."

"Are you going to try and look for her car?" Ava is anxious. She feels compelled to butt in.

Fiona is patient. She nods. "Sean and I will drive toward Carter Creek and do a search for her vehicle. She owns a black Buick, right? Like a funeral car? I can get the plate number from Motor Vehicles Branch."

"Good." Ava sighs, but there is no relief in the sound of her voice.

"If you hear from her, which you probably will, call the office so they can radio me. Try not to worry; we'll get to the bottom of this."

Fiona hoists herself out of the chair and plods toward the foyer. As an afterthought, she turns back to the two women. "Call her friends, her landlord. See if anybody has any relevant information. We can get officers in Carter River to cruise around and hunt for her car." She pats Ava's arm. Ava realizes her reaction is akin to that of a stricken parent. "It'll be okay. Most of the time, there's a logical explanation for situations like this—even when circumstances seem illogical in the beginning, as they most often do. Talk to you soon."

The constable must have read Ava's mind, because she thinks this is the most illogical behaviour Ronny could exhibit, if for no other reason than she would know Maggie and Ava would be beside themselves with worry. She avoids saying any of this to Fiona.

"Yes. Yes. Call me when you know anything, Fiona."

✳✳✳✳

"Dodd's Contracting and Interiors. How can I help you?"

"Gaby? Ava Burrway calling."

"Hi, Ava! What can I do for you today?"

"Sorry to bother you, Gaby, but I need to know if you've heard from Ronny in the last couple of days."

"No." Gaby's voice holds an element of caution. "Is there an issue?"

"Hard to say just yet. Fiona Werbowski asked me to call her friends and her landlord. She was supposed to go to a meeting in Carter River yesterday, but she never arrived. I went by her house today—she keeps a key at the office—and there's no sign of her, or the car. I'm worried sick."

"Did you go through the whole house—basement and backyard?"

"No, I didn't, Gaby. I think Fiona might already be a little worried I could have disturbed a possible scene so I hesitate to go back, at least not until I've talked to her again. She and her partner are driving to Carter River to see if they can spot the car."

"Okay, we won't go over to the house either, Ava, but if you need Joe and me to help in any way, all you have to do is let us know, okay? I have a customer and have to go. Please call me after you talk to Fiona."

Ava places the receiver back in its cradle with more care than necessary, absorbed as she is in all the possibilities of what might have happened. Maggie's sudden presence in the doorway startles her.

"Sorry, Ava, but June wants a quick word before she and her kids walk down to the Hexagon for their appointment."

June Kendall and her two little girls, Kelly and Amber, aged six and eight, presented themselves at Segue House a couple of weeks ago. They are from a village north of Hayworth and are getting help from Family Counselling to relocate. She said her husband belted her once too often, so she threw both children in her car and left. She and Ronny have spent many hours talking, as she attempts to get her life in order before school starts in the fall.

"No problem. Send her in."

June appears alone. Kelly and Amber must be out in the living room. She looks a little frazzled. The twenty-seven year old mother's dyed blond hair hangs down over one eye, and her ratty handbag dangles from the fingers of her right hand. "Sorry, Ava, but have you seen Ronny? She planned to come with me to Family Counselling today, but her office is empty."

"When's your appointment, June?"

"Half an hour. Did Ronny say when she'd be back?" Her big brown eyes are puddled, like she could start to cry any minute—a common affliction for women under this kind of stress.

"Ronny is not around today, June. Sorry." She is unsure of how much to reveal. "She missed her meeting yesterday and failed to come in to work this morning. The details are being investigated. It will likely be fine, but you need to make it to your appointment on your own." She makes her voice sound soft and reassuring. The effort is exhausting.

"Do you think she might be in danger, Ava?"

Ava, fingers tormenting her lower lip, is conflicted. "In all seriousness, I simply do not know. Please keep this to yourself, June. The RCMP is involved now and we will have to wait the situation out. Can I depend on your confidence?"

The young woman attempts a smile. "Ronny is a wonderful person, Ava. She has been terribly kind to me and so good to my daughters. Of course, everyone has been great. Try not to misunderstand, but my closest relationship has been with Ronny. She has been my rock. I won't mention this to anybody, Ava." She gets up to leave and turns on her way out. "Can I check with you later?"

"Of course." Ava sighs. She hopes there will be information to check by the time June returns from her appointment.

She hollers out her office door to Maggie, after she hears June exit through the foyer. "Maggie, can you come in here for a minute?"

Maggie appears in an instant, almost like she was hidden behind the door casing. She has this uncanny ability to materialize out of thin air. This behaviour can be unnerving. "How can I help, Ava?"

"Do you know who Ronny's friends are, Maggie? You and your sister lived across the hall from her for a couple of years. Do you know who she spends time with?"

"Other than people at The Station, I don't know of anybody. She and Cheryl Nadler got on quite well right from the very start, but that could be it. She always comes to little Station affairs we have, even now. I know she likes Patrick Hollinger. She told me once about how she has no problem taking herself out to dinner because she goes to the Hayworth Diner and talks to Patrick. Do you want me to call them and see if they've heard from her?"

"Can we be discreet? I called Gaby Ridgway and had to tell her Ronny seems to have disappeared. And I told June the same thing. I imagine you'll have to tell the truth when you talk with Patrick and Cheryl. Pretty soon the whole town will know."

Maggie shakes her head and her hair flutters around her shoulders. "Maybe information is good. The more people who are aware of the situation, the more they start to notice what might have gone on around them." A pensive expression washes over her face as she stares at her boss. "Do you remember when Roz Dover disappeared a few years ago? I know Duncan Taylor was in jail then and whoever took Roz couldn't have been him, but boy, this whole situation reminds me of then. Everybody in town searched in their sheds and garages. People were on edge. They found her car after a few days, but they still haven't found her. I am afraid, Ava."

"I know, Maggie. I know. It is hard to believe Duncan managed to locate her here in Hayworth, but if he did, then I imagine he would be the one who grabbed her."

Chapter 4

Maggie

Maggie is bent over her desk, entering July's expenses into a ledger, when Ava appears at the door. "I think we should get everybody together before the end of the day—you, me, Sheila, June, and Marjorie. Once we hear back from Fiona, we will have to tell everyone. What do you think?" Maggie detects anxiety—an uncommon emotion that she finds unsettling—in her boss's words. Ava is their anchor.

Always pleased when asked for her opinion, Maggie wants to be supportive and quickly agrees. "I expect we'll hear from the police by noon. June will be back and Sheila will be awake. We can all meet then. Okay?"

Ava nods. Maggie notices how Ava's whole demeanour droops more than usual. From her limp hair to the sag of her breasts, all of her person has settled under the weight of the circumstances. Her heart goes out to her boss. Maggie feels like Ava looks.

She continues to scratch out her accounts. Long hair trails across the paper, even though she makes frequent attempts to flip wayward strands out of her way. She dislikes her hair tied or pinned. It reminds her of her years at Forest Hills Institute. She was forced to stay there from the age of eighteen, because she wouldn't stop running away from home. Her parents found a way to keep her tangled in the system with no opportunity for discharge. Almost four years ago, when Maggie was thirty-one, Rose brought her to Hayworth so they could live together. Since then, the changes in her life have been miraculous.

The jangle of the telephone startles her out of her reverie, which is, in essence, desirable. She tries to avoid thoughts about her past institutionalization, her abusive and now estranged parents, or even how she has progressed to where she is today. She has learned to live in the moment and appreciate small steps. She has survived.

"Segue House. Maggie speaking. How can I help you?"

"Maggie, Fiona Werbowski calling for Ava. Can you put her on the phone?"

"Sure, Fiona. Hold on a second." Maggie punches the hold key, satisfies herself the line is blinking as expected, and calls to Ava. "Fiona's on Line One. Can you pick up?" Ava doesn't respond, but Maggie sees the light stop flashing.

She listens as well as she is able, since Ava's office is next to hers and the door is ajar.

"What?"

"Where was the car?"

"Did you see her?"

"Did anybody see what happened?"

"Fiona, what are we to do?"

The half of the conversation Maggie hears gives her enough information to know they found her car, but not Ronny. She sits down at her desk and patiently waits for the light on the phone to go out.

Ava stands in the doorway. Her face is ashen. "They found the Buick in the Four Corners Petro-Can lot, Maggie. Her purse and keys were locked inside. They interviewed staff there and tried to ascertain who else was present in the restaurant. Perhaps some local farmers were having coffee, because it would be pretty hard to track down truckers. Fiona will call when they've finished."

Maggie's vision blurs as the tears well up in her eyes. Her throat is raw and she knows her face is flushed. "Just like Roz Dover, Ava." Her voice is barely a whisper. "I'll call Patrick and Cheryl, now, and try to be discreet, but I need to calm down first."

She makes a pot of coffee, and stands in front of the little apartment kitchen window to gaze out at the side yard and the street beyond. Maybe Ronny is fine. Maybe she parked her car and went with someone of her own free will. Maybe she felt sick and one of the restaurant workers took her home with them. She realizes she is starting to think in patterns like when she resided at Forest Hills Institute. Maybe her parents would come and get her. Maybe she wasn't sick at all. Maybe Rose would take her home to live with her…well now, sometimes fantasies actually come true, so maybe Ronny will be okay. The smell of the fresh coffee drags her back to reality once more.

****

"Hayworth Diner. Nancy speaking."

"Hi, Nancy. It's Maggie Woodward. Is Patrick on shift this morning? I need to talk to him for a minute."

"He won't be here for another half hour or so, Maggie. Can I get him to call you when he gets here? He always arrives early, so he'll have time."

"Okay. Thanks, Nancy. I'm at the shelter." She provides the waitress with her number and presses the disconnect button so she can make another call.

"Hi, Cheryl. It's Maggie."

"Hi, Maggie! You caught me between appointments. What can I do for you?"

Maggie notices a forced cheeriness in Cheryl Nadler's voice and knows, full well, how the social worker frowns on personal calls at work. She is very professional and keeps her home life and her private life decidedly separate. "Sorry to bother you. I know you're busy, but we have a situation, Cheryl."

She interrupts. "A new client? Do you guys want me to come over later today? Usually, Ronny calls with a referral, Maggie. Has she asked you to help out?"

Maggie sighs—a feeble attempt to maintain what little composure she is holding together. "So here's the problem, Cheryl." She measures her words and places each one into the conversation with care. "Ronny appears, at this point, to be missing." She hears Cheryl gasp, but soldiers on. "She was a no-show to her meeting in Carter River yesterday. When she failed to come to work this morning, we called the police. They found her car at the Four Corners service station with her purse and keys inside. Ava asked me to call and find out if you have talked to her in the last few days or if you might have any relevant information. Cheryl, we're all pretty worried."

"My God, Maggie! I haven't seen Ronny in about a week! We visited after I came over and met June Kendall and her children. There was no real need for my involvement, but I made the referral to Family Counselling." Her voice sounds like panting. Maggie has never heard Cheryl lose her cool. She finds the prospect a little scary. "My daughter is here visiting so I've been busy. I hate this! I keep thinking about Roz Dover. If her case had ever been solved, maybe I wouldn't be so skittish."

Maggie immediately assesses, from the social worker's response, that Cheryl is not privy to Ronny's secret identity. If she knew, the conversation would be quite different. "Listen, Cheryl. None of this is public yet. The RCMP, Fiona Werbowski, will fill us in later. I'll keep you posted. I have to go. The other line is ringing."

She flips from one light to the other. "Segue House. Maggie speaking."

"Hi, Maggie. It's Patrick. What's up?"

"Hi, Patrick. Thanks for the callback. Have you talked to, or seen, Ronny in the last few days?"

"Yeah, sure. She ate supper here a couple of nights ago. I had a break and we had a chin wag. I like her a lot. Nice lady."

"Did she mention a problem or a trip?"

"What? Trip? No. We talked about how happy she is here is Hayworth. What's up, Maggie?"

"We may have a problem." Maggie tells him the story. "You and Cheryl seem closest to her outside the office, so Ava asked me to call you both and see if you might have noticed any differences about her."

"If Ronny missed a meeting and didn't show up for work, she must be in trouble…or worse. You know her as well as I do, Maggie. She is not a thoughtless person, no matter what. Can I help?"

"Please keep our conversation to yourself for right now, Patrick. Fiona may want to talk to you, but other than that, we will have to wait and see what happens."

"Okay. I work a split today. Want me to call this afternoon?"

"No. I think maybe Rose and I will come to the diner for supper, so we'll see you later, okay?"

She hangs up the phone again. The deathly quiet seems to insert itself into her little office, and ram into all the corners of the shelter apartment. She wanders through the kitchen in search of more coffee and finds Ava at the sink. Her stooped shoulders face the room. Maggie rests her hand gently on her boss's arm and sees the tears stream down her face.

"All we can do is wait for Fiona to call, Ava. I can make sandwiches for everyone for lunch and arrange a building meeting for half-past twelve. The clock on the stove says almost eleven, so we should hear any time."

****

The shelter kitchen is stocked with basic food stuffs. Even though residents are expected to buy groceries if they can, Ava ensures a well-stocked pantry, regardless. Maggie methodically removes bread from the freezer. Tuna salad and peanut butter are the two most popular options. She has a stack of each made in no time. When finished, she runs upstairs to the second floor apartment on the other side of the hall, and knocks on the door. Marjorie Westerman answers almost immediately, like she was waiting on the other side.

"Good morning, Marjorie. We plan to have a luncheon meeting downstairs around twelve-thirty and we would like you to be there. Okay?"

"Yes, of course. I expected to meet with Ronny this afternoon to finalize my plans. I wanted to start my trip to my sister's in Ontario by Friday. Today's Tuesday, so we have a little time. What's the meeting about?"

"No need to worry, Marjorie. We have some concerns about Ronny, and Ava wants to talk to everyone over lunch. I made some sandwiches."

"I can contribute a bag of cookies. Is Ronny okay?"

Maggie endeavours, without much success, to sound calm. "We hope so, Marjorie. Come to the meeting. Cookies will be great. We'll sort it out then." She turns on her heel and races back down the steps, without permitting the older woman an opportunity to ask more questions.

Marjorie has been at the shelter for a couple of weeks. She assembled the nerve to leave her drunkard husband after thirty years of marriage. She has some money, inherited from a maiden aunt a number of years ago and protected from any divorce proceedings, so is not in as dire straits as most who appear at the door. She and Ronny have worked out a plan whereby she will go to live with her sister somewhere in Ontario. Marjorie has no children and is retired from her job as a clerk with the Department of Agriculture. She has a nice car. She has investments. Her husband has never seemed to give a rat's ass. The transition will be relatively straightforward.

Maggie continues down to the basement level and knocks on the institutional green door to Sheila's living quarters. She has to rap a couple of times before a dishevelled and somewhat grumpy Sheila finally opens the door a crack. "What the hell? God, Maggie, it's not even noon! What do you want?"

"We've called a meeting upstairs for twelve-thirty with staff and residents, to talk about Ronny. I made sandwiches. Ava wants you to be there. Sorry if I woke you."

In an instant, Sheila's attitude makes a one hundred and eighty degree turn. She rubs her eyes, drags her fingers through her hair, and pushes wayward bits behind her ears in a useless gesture designed to flatten her bed-head. "Is she okay? What do you know, Maggie?"

Maggie is abrupt. "They found her car. They haven't found her. Everybody's worried. I talked to a couple of her friends and they have no information whatsoever. Do you need me to come back down before the meeting, so you can go to sleep again for a while?"

"Nope. I'd rather come up and grab some coffee. I have to shower and change my clothes. Have a hot date this afternoon. He said he would take me out for supper." Her smirk is lecherous. Maggie cannot even imagine Sheila in any sort of relationship.

"Does your man have a name? Anybody I know?"

"Don't think so. He hasn't been up north here very long. Name is Devon Thompson. First saw him over at the ball field. He comes to watch women's slow pitch." She rolls her eyes. "He gave me a lift home from the paint store a while back, and we started goin' out."

"Does this Devon have a job?"

"Not yet, but he's lookin'. He drove a delivery truck or somethin' in Calgary, so he wants to do that here. I hope he won't have to go to Carter River, but it ain't easy to find a job in Hayworth."

Maggie nods and turns in the direction of the stairs. "The coffee's already made. See you upstairs." Sheila with a boyfriend. Will wonders never cease?

Maggie assumed, when she originally moved out of her sister's apartment at The Station and into the one across the hall, it would give her a better chance for some independence; an opportunity to meet someone. She continues to spend the majority of her spare time with her sister, though. Unless you count periodic interactions with Sean Knox, she hasn't met anyone. Since Sean is with the RCMP, he oftentimes turns up, with or without Fiona Werbowski, to do interviews or fact-check. She knows she has no skills for socializing with men, and is a little afraid of men, if the truth be told. Sean is different. Maybe because he happens to be a cop. He is nice to her. He always smiles and sometimes has a coffee, if she offers. She knows he's single.

The move out of her sister's place proved to be a good idea, in the end. Ronny rented Gaby's little house and Maggie moved into Ronny's apartment. Number Three used to be Ben Tullis' place. Ben was a great friend to everyone at The Station. She died there and her death influenced all of them in different ways. When at her apartment, Maggie senses Ben's spirit around her.

June, anxious and sweaty in the midday heat, arrives back at Segue House near noon, daughters in tow. Maggie explains about the meeting. She hustles her children upstairs to the apartment on the next floor above the offices, to get them sorted out and washed up before they join the group downstairs.

Maggie lets Ava know everyone will be there. The phone bleats. The caller is Fiona.

****

Everyone arrives at the meeting on time. Maggie plays hostess and hands out napkins, sandwiches, and juice. She is determined to keep busy. June's two little girls play together in the corner. They are always quiet. You can tell the kids who've learned over the years when to stay out of the way. Maggie sees a lot of herself in June's children. Marjorie acts like an employee instead of a client. Perhaps she copes this way. She has said a couple of times how she could go to a hotel, but since the shelter is rarely full in the summer, she appreciates the added security until she leaves town. She said Segue House could expect a sizable donation from her when she leaves. Sheila grabs a straight chair from the kitchen, flips it around back to front with an uncommon dexterity, and plunks herself down. She rests her arms and shoulders on the back, blue-jean-clad legs spread across the seat. She appears to have cleaned herself up a bit, which is unusual. This Devon character must be quite the guy.

Ava enters the reception room and nods around at the attentive little group. She takes a deep breath and begins. "I have spoken to Constable Fiona Werbowski. They have found Ronny's car with her purse and keys locked inside. It was in the lot at the Four Corners Petro-Can. They have interviewed staff at the service station restaurant and are in the process of trying to locate a couple of the patrons who were there when Ronny stopped yesterday morning. They will contact Gaby Ridgway, who owns Ronny's house, to allow them access to do a more thorough search. I went over earlier to see if she might be home sick, or perhaps hurt, and found the place in perfect order. Please be aware the situation is in the hands of the police now, and all we can do is wait." With eyes facing straight ahead, she says, "Maggie, would you join me? Sheila, perhaps you could clean up when lunch is finished." Before anybody can formulate a question, Ava returns to her office.

Maggie ignores Sheila's expression of utter surprise, and trots after her boss.

"Close the door."

Maggie does as instructed and sits down. She figures she is better off in a seated position. "What else did Fiona say, Ava?"

"People at the restaurant saw her with a man they described as tall, shaved head, tattoos. Nobody saw his vehicle."

"Did she leave with him?" Maggie's head pounds with anxiety.

"They said he left and she waited at least another five minutes before she left. No one on staff noticed her car. The stop is a busy place with lots of trucks and steady comings and goings. Fiona told me I couldn't tell this to anybody but you."

Maggie is finding it hard to breathe.

"Did Ronny ever describe her ex-husband to you, Maggie?"

"No, but I imagine the police will have a picture of him by now." Maggie's insides quake in abject terror for Ronny. Reverting to old habits she learned at the institute, she forces her fears out of sight.

****

By the time Maggie gets to The Station, she sees her sister's 1979 silver Malibu already parked in the front lot. Perhaps Rose had a good day. Oftentimes, she arrives home late from the doctor's office where she works. As Maggie unlocks her door, Rose pops her head out of her apartment. Their two cats, Caesar and Caramel, trot across the hall into Maggie's place without as much as a backward glance. Caramel gives a little mew of acknowledgment as he follows the older and wiser tabby. Caesar has been a roommate of Rose's for many years. He owns Rose. Caramel is an orange cat and Maggie adopted him in the days after Ben died; after the sisters returned from their last fateful trip to visit their parents. The trip proved to be their pivot point. It was when they decided to let Ruth and Abner Woodward go.

Maggie is unable to prevent a grief-stricken look from clouding her face.

"What's the matter, Maggie? Bad day?" Rose is always worried Maggie will slip into some shroud of mental instability. She can fuss and be overprotective, but today, Maggie welcomes the attention.

"Can we eat at the diner tonight, Rose? I have to tell you some stuff, and I told Patrick I would stop by. You haven't started supper, have you?"

"No. No. Just arrived. My God, Maggie! Are you okay?" Maggie is immediately surrounded in a bear hug. She is enveloped in the fabric of Rose's tutu-inspired and over-gathered skirt, as the cotton crunches against her. Rose sews all her own clothes. Some creations turn out better than others.

"Let's feed the boys, Rose, and then go to the diner. I can tell you the whole story, now. I guess the time has come for you to know."

Chapter 5

Shelia

This sultry Tuesday in August has not started out to be like Sheila expected. She was happy to see Ava come through the door this morning so she could return downstairs, have a sleep, and get ready for her afternoon and supper with Devon. Now, after being at the meeting, she thinks she should drive around town in search of the counsellor they have all come to depend on in some way.

Ava is Sheila's rock. Sheila struggled in Edmonton. When she made her return home to Hayworth after all her trials and tribulations in the city, her parents slammed the door in her face. It was Ava who took her in.

With abruptness, she split for the city when she was barely sixteen. She put the farm and her violent father behind her, but her circumstances deteriorated at lightning speed after her departure. She found no job because she had no skills. Driving a tractor and a mower were not considered qualifications. She tried to find work in the oil patch, but a woman with no experience or formal training—even though she knew she could drive any piece of equipment given to her—had no leverage.

She drank too much. She lived on the street for most of the next two years. She was attacked twice. A big guy, all wired up on some chemical shit, slammed her head into the sidewalk the second time. Now her memory is unreliable and she often finds herself frustrated for no reason. They caught her up in "The Edmonton Sweep" of 1982. The cops arrested everybody living in tents in the river valley. Scary didn't begin to describe it. Social Services gave her a bus ticket home, so she returned to Hayworth.

Forced to make her way back to her parents' farm, with her tail between her legs, turned into the final insult. Her mother let her in but her father threw her out. She had nowhere to go but the shelter because she didn't really know anyone else any more. Friends she knew when she was in school had moved on. If not for Ava's kindness and understanding, Sheila thinks she would be back in Edmonton on the street, drunk or worse. It shocks her to remember what she contemplated doing when she was hungry and wanting to forget who she was.

Now she has a real job and a real place to live. She feels valuable. She knows the staff and clients are safe because she is up at night and alert to anything that might happen. She is a protector of little children. She confirms her self-assessment with a perfunctory nod, as she prepares to go upstairs and wait for Devon.

Her apartment is basic—two simple rooms with a bathroom. She has her own little fridge and a counter with a cupboard. She and Ava both thought she should cook her suppers upstairs in the office kitchen rather than down here. No need for a hot plate. Shelia knows Ava worries about her memory problems and how she might leave a hot plate turned on; about how she sometimes gets confused and forgets. She does okay most of the time, but would never argue with Ava. The rooms are on the back and the only two windows face out into the fenced yard, so natural light is minimal and there is no view except an old slide and teeter-totter for the kids. The space is enough. She feels safe here. Maggie and Rose gave her a log cabin patterned quilt for the bed when she first moved in. Each time she looks at the blended shades of red, brown, and orange she feels accepted. The quilt is her favourite possession.

She checks her watch. He said he would pick her up at about two, so they could go for a drive and then have an early supper. This way, she can be back at the shelter in good time. Most often, she is there anyway, but if she goes off somewhere, Ava wants her back by eight. Sheila is okay with the arrangement. This is how Ava likes the house to run, but Devon sometimes grumbles.

****

His truck sputters into view. The vehicle looks junky; an old Ford that's seen better days. When she catches a first glimpse of him behind the wheel, Sheila's heart gives a little flutter. She met Devon in the oddest way. She went out for a walk one afternoon. She told Ava she'd go to the hardware store and get the gallon of paint they needed for the front entry. Ava always has a project of one sort or another on the go. This guy pulls up beside her and asks for directions to the Creek Tavern. She'd seen him at the ball field a couple of times as he watched the women's slow pitch league. He was there again as she left the store. She was carrying the pale yellow paint Ava wanted, and he offered her a lift.

Under normal circumstances, she wouldn't accept a drive from a stranger, and the shelter was nearby, but he charmed her. She could take care of herself. If he tried to hurt her, she had a gallon of paint for a weapon, so she felt pretty safe. She climbed in the truck while he introduced himself.

"Thanks for the directions. My name is Devon Thompson, new in town."

"Hi. I'm Sheila Pasco. I've lived around here all my life. Why are you here in Hayworth?"

"Oh, I guess I might want a job…maybe driving a delivery truck. I used to drive trucks before. Do you know anybody hiring?"

Sheila settled herself on the threadbare bench seat and positioned the paint in the centre of her lap. "Jobs are scarce, but I can ask around. Thanks for the lift. The building where I live isn't far."

"Oh, I know. Up here a piece…the women's shelter, right? What's the name? Something House?"

Sheila felt a little weird that he knew where she worked. He even had an inkling of the name of the shelter and what they did there. "Segue House." As their destination came into view, she pointed through the cracked windshield. "You can let me out right there." She indicated the curb directly across from the building. "Thanks again for the lift. Nice meetin' you, Devon. Good luck findin' a job."

In a short couple of days, she saw him again when she wandered down to the diner. The air sweltered hot and humid for the first week of July and she had trouble sleeping, so she decided to take herself out for lunch. A burger and fries would serve to lift her spirits and add to the width of her thighs, but who cares anyway? Sheila is well aware that she is a big woman; husky, she says, but how she presents herself has never been a concern. As she prepared to bite into one of the diner's special burgers, in strolled Devon. He wore a ball cap and sun glasses, as well as a jean jacket, but she recognized him nonetheless.

"Care for some company, Sheila?" With one smooth motion, he slid into her booth as he spoke.

She grinned and nodded. He must like her. He could have simply waved and sat down at the counter. After a hasty swallow and a quick swipe at her lips with the paper napkin, she managed to speak. "Hi. Are you following me?"

"No." He seemed a little offended and she felt sorry for her remark. "I thought I'd sit across from a familiar, and I must say, pretty face."

Sheila felt her nose turn red. If there was one characteristic she knew she wasn't, and would never be, it was pretty. He tried to flatter her and it worked. She lapped up his line. "Nancy." She called the waitress over to the table. "Could you get my friend Devon a menu, please? He's havin' lunch with me today." Sheila made sure Nancy knew she and Devon would eat together.

"Coming right up. Something to drink?" She addressed Devon directly.

"Coffee, Nancy?" He stared straight at the name tag pinned over her left breast. Nancy blushed. She turned on her heel and darted into the kitchen.

Devon could pour on the charm—like sticky syrup on a stack of pancakes. He leaned across the table and reached for one of Sheila's fries—intimate, somehow. They barely knew one another, but he seemed to feel he could put a hand on her food. "Tell me how you've been. What's new at work?"

Sheila had no experience with people taking an interest in her outside of the confines of the shelter. "I'm not allowed to talk about what we do, Devon. Ava says to tell folks our work is confidential." She carefully pronounced each syllable.

His smile was full of understanding as he tilted his head ever so slightly to the side. "Of course not," he whispered. "I know all about confidentiality, but you can tell me who you work with and what the other staff at the shelter are like. Who works there is public knowledge, right?"

Nancy delivered his coffee and took his order for "whatever his friend Sheila was having," and they resumed their conversation. "Tell me about the place, Sheila. I'm all ears." Shelia is hypnotized by his interest in her and her life. No one has ever treated her like this before.

"Well, Ava Burrway is my boss. She started the shelter years ago. She would be called the manager, I guess. Then there's Maggie Woodward, the secretary and bookkeeper. She was the first person Ava hired to help her. They're tight. Ronny Étang has been the counsellor for a few years now. She just talks to the clients and they all love her. She helps Ava raise money, too.

Then there's me. I do night duty and have a couple of rooms in the basement to call my own." She frowned down at her plate. "Ava's been pretty good to me. She saved me from a bad life."

His expression exuded interest. He seemed so sincere and genuine. He asked Sheila if she ever took a night off. Maybe they could go out and she could show him the sights. She told him she could have a night off if she wanted. Ava would stay, but she never asks.

"You should ask."

They saw one another on a regular basis all month. He would cruise by the shelter and she would jump in the truck and off they'd go. She hadn't told anybody about him until Maggie, today. She is not sure why, except the relationship seems unreal for some reason. Sheila tries to identify her uneasiness, but oftentimes she doesn't trust her instincts anymore. It all stems from the fact that not once has he ever put the moves on her; never kissed her, or even hugged her. He always seems interested in what goes on at the shelter, though. Sheila sometimes wonders if he thinks he might get a job there, but she has difficulty imagining what he would do. There's no real call for a handyman. The place is relatively small. She and Ava manage most of the odd jobs.

****

She opens the truck door and hops up into the cab.

"How's it goin'?" He grins at her from under the brim of his ball cap.

She feels conflicted about whether she should tell him the news. She is uncertain if details have been made public, but what harm could there be? "Ronny's been gone since yesterday morning and they found her car at the Four Corners." She heaves a sigh as she blurts the story out. She wishes she could remember if she said she would keep the situation quiet.

"Have the cops been by?"

"Oh, yeah. They found her big old Buick. Nobody knows if she went willingly or not, but her keys and purse were locked in the vehicle. Seems bad to me. Maybe we should drive around; try and find her." She knows the idea is ridiculous as the words leave her mouth. Ronny will not be wandering the streets of Hayworth waiting for somebody to come upon her.

"We can drive around all you want, Sheila, but would it matter? Sounds serious, though."

"Well, I want to be gettin' back soon, in case Fiona comes to the shelter with some news. Let's have supper early, okay? I need to be back before six. Sorry." She feels overcome with the need to apologize, and isn't sure why.

"Who's Fiona?"

She explains about the RCMP constable who has taken the lead in the investigation. Everybody likes her.

They cruise the streets of Hayworth and then follow an old road down to a spot where the creek spreads out and residents sometimes congregate to swim; to bask in an unusually warm summer sun. The water level is too low for swimming, but there are people there picnicking and lounging. For a Tuesday afternoon, there are lots of folks who appear to have little to do. Devon and Sheila sit in the truck with the windows rolled down. Kids are splashing at the water's edge. Parents seem to either holler or laugh. The resulting atmosphere seems weird. How can people be so contented when Sheila is convinced a catastrophic event may be happening in her life? She is overcome with restlessness. All she can think about is Ronny. Where is she? What has happened to her?

She glances across at Devon, slumped in the seat with his ball cap pulled down over his eyes. He could be napping. "Well, nobody I know here. We might as well get back to town, Devon. Sorry for not being very good company. I'm worried about Ronny and I want to go home soon."

****

By the time they pull up at the Hayworth Diner, her watch says twenty past five. Under normal circumstances, Sheila would feel quite important, going out to eat with a big, tall guy who nobody in town knows. Instead, she feels consumed by anxiety. She wants to get some supper and return to the shelter. She did not anticipate the inner conflict she felt when she left Ava and Maggie today. She should have stayed with them.

The Hayworth Diner is the favourite spot for locals in town. The old building serves as the coffee shop, take-out restaurant, and destination for good, old-fashioned home-cooked meals at a decent price. There's a dining room at the hotel, but the location has never caught on and seems to be used only by the guests actually booked into the hotel. The diner is the obvious option. No fast food franchises have ever seen fit to establish themselves in the prairie town going nowhere. As a result, the Hayworth Diner does quite well, despite its 1950s decor comprised of leatherette booths, and plywood accents. The interior consists of a row of booths across the front windows and the side wall at the far end, with a long counter and stools opposite the booths. Swinging doors lead to the kitchen. Nancy and Patrick seem to run the place although the business is owned by a local accountant named Margo. She appears on the rare occasion when they are short-staffed. The main cook is Danny. There are a couple of transient-types who fill in to man the dishwasher.

Tonight, Patrick works the counter and the tables. The smell of French fries greets the couple when they push open the plate-glass entry door and opt for a booth in the back. Devon is wearing his standard ball cap, sun glasses, and jean jacket. Sheila thinks the late afternoon is warm for such a get-up. She chose her clothes with care earlier today and is proud of her blue short-sleeved blouse and navy cotton pants; her usual garb of sweat shirts, T-shirts, and blue jeans left behind. She is wearing sandals. She wanted to look nice.

When Patrick approaches their table with menus and glasses of water, Sheila calls him by name. Everybody knows Patrick.

"Hi, folks." He nods at Sheila and she beams up at him.

"Hi, Patrick. This is my friend, Devon. He just moved to town."

Devon stares up at Patrick, like he can see through him, somehow. "I've been in before. What's the special tonight?" His tone is sullen; disinterested.

Patrick turns to look toward the chalk board behind the counter. "Tuesday is meat loaf. Here are the menus. Be back in a minute."

Sheila sputters her thanks, embarrassed by Devon's abrupt, if not rude, attitude toward Patrick. She leans over the table. "Patrick's a really nice guy, Devon. He knows a lot of people. He might know somebody who has a job opening."

"He seems a little freaky. Did you see his hand shaking? What's wrong with him?"

Before Sheila has a chance to respond that she has never noticed Patrick's hand trembling, there's a commotion at the door as Rose and Maggie Woodward come tumbling through. As they gaze around to locate a seat, Maggie spies Sheila and makes a beeline straight for their booth. On her way past Patrick, she tells him she and her sister are there for the special and tea.

"Hi, there! So this must be Devon!" She extends her hand and Devon, who appears more than a little uncomfortable, has no option but to respond.

"Yes, I'm Devon. And who might you be?"

"I'm Maggie Woodward. I work with Sheila. And this is my sister, Rose."

Maggie's older sister, standing slightly removed from the gathering, in a sun dress with a puffy skirt, along with a white sweater over her shoulders—the whole ensemble serving to make her come across as more dumpy than she actually is—turns up the corners of her mouth with polite distraction. "Look. There's a booth up front. Nice to meet you."

Sheila gives Rose a little wave and then makes a valiant, although amateurish, attempt at small talk. She hopes Devon will appreciate her position in the community, and want be a part of their group, too. "Do you and Rose come out for dinner here often?" Maggie seemed quite comfortable rolling in and placing her order before even sitting down.

"Oh, no. We've known Patrick for a long time. He lives in our building, so is a friend. We watch our pennies, especially since we have our own apartments now, but neither of us felt like cooking tonight. I'm exhausted with worry and I want to explain the situation to Rose."

She glances over at her sister and then back toward Devon. "Sorry, Devon, but today has been very strained. Right, Shelia?"

Shelia nods but struggles to get a word in.

"We are hoping for good news any time now. I imagine you're waiting for orders, so back I go to sit with Rose. Nice to meet you, Devon. See you tomorrow, Sheila. By the way, Ava stayed at the shelter when I left, so I expect she'll wait until you get back, before she goes home."

"I figured she would stay. I wanted to eat early so I could get back and help out. Devon understands." She shoots a quick conspiratorial look across the table, but Devon isn't paying any attention. Instead, he fiddles with his napkin and runs his finger up and down the condensation on the outside of his water glass.

Once they're by themselves again, he speaks up. "Everybody seems awfully cozy."

The remark sounds like a criticism; a slur of some sort. Defensiveness suddenly bubbles up inside her. "Hayworth's a small town. We all work together in one way or another. Ronny used to live in the building where Rose, Maggie, and Patrick live. She rents a house from Gaby Ridgway who used to be a family counsellor at the Hexagon. Cheryl Nadler, another worker at the Hexagon, lives at The Station and does a lot of work with us at the shelter. We're a tight group." Hearing her own words, she wonders if she is as much a part of this group as she likes to think she is.

Chapter 6

Ava

Segue House simmers in the late Tuesday afternoon August heat. Ava, with a silent resignation, wishes for air conditioning. The building is quiet except for the muffled footfalls of a family preparing for supper on the floor above. *Where could she be? Is she hurt? Is she even alive?* She tries to think of happier times; afraid to contemplate possibilities, however remote.

Ronny arrived in Hayworth on the May long weekend of 1981. She started to work for Ava on Tuesday, May 19. She finds it difficult to believe three years have passed since she first appeared with Maggie at the security door of Segue House. Ava arranged for her to meet Murdock Blackney, the shelter lawyer, to get her name legally changed and her documents sorted out. She secured an apartment at The Station and Maggie Woodward turned out to be a neighbour. She seemed to fit in right away. Ava overheard them when they discussed the Victoria Day party, and how much fun they had together.

Ava is not socially inclined, but she makes an appearance at the annual fundraiser held for the shelter society. Once Ronny became involved, the affair progressed from a simple dinner and dance attracting local supporters, to a dining experience and silent auction coupled with a "ball". The RCMP held their annual gala in October. Ronny navigated the cooperation between Segue House and the police. Attendees dress to the nines. The presentation of all those police officers in their red serge is always spectacular. The evening has become the most anticipated social event of the year. The amount of money raised doubled in 1982 and then again last October. They expect to do even better this year.

One of the first tasks Ronny, Gaby, and Fiona accomplished was to assemble a committee of the biggest local donors. They asked each one of them to find five more like-minded groups and businesses from Hayworth as well as surrounding communities. They gather silent auction items months in advance—a trip to Vegas, luggage, contributions from local artists, antique dealers, and other merchants. The Aboriginal art is second to none—pieces the public would not be able to obtain from a store. They never hesitate to go outside Hayworth to take advantage of the generosity of businesses in Carter River. After all, many Hayworth residents support that community, too. Donations come in from as far away as Edmonton and Yellowknife. One of the most popular auction items has become the barge trip from Hay River to Tuktoyaktuk, NWT. People get crazy—they will pay an exorbitant price for the opportunity to take a trip not available otherwise!

Ava's shoulders heave with her sigh. The money they've raised since Ronny came on board has been used to update both the wiring and the heating system in the building. All the windows have been replaced and the security system is the best they could find. The roof is new. Sure, they could use some updated furniture and perhaps a paint job and some nicer flooring, but all in due time. Right now, she would easily put the building maintenance needs of Segue House aside to hear Ronny's voice through the familiar crackle of the intercom.

She pulls out the bottom drawer of her desk and fishes for the Mars bars tucked away in the back. Yes. Yes. She knows this will ruin whatever supper she might plan to concoct when she finally gets home. Yes. Yes. She knows how the God-only-knows-how-many calories will go straight to her widening hips and her increasingly droopy breasts. She decidedly does not give a damn. Right now, she cares little about what she eats or the state of her figure. They have no bearing on the rising tide of dread lapping away at her psyche. Ava knows she is fast becoming panic-stricken. *If the phone doesn't ring soon; if Fiona doesn't call....*

****

The intercom sounds. She leaps from her chair, and hastily wipes possible chocolate drool from her lips with the back of her hand, as she runs to turn on the speaker.

"Yes?"

"Hi, Ava. It's Gaby and Joe. Can we come in and visit for a minute?"

"Of course!" Ava pushes the buzzer so the couple can gain access to the glassed-in foyer. Once she has a visual, she buzzes again and they open the plate-glass interior door. Gaby reaches for Ava and wraps her in a bear hug. Joe, silent and stoic, rests his hand on Ava's shoulder. Words aren't necessary. The gravity of their situation is clear. Ronny has been gone for well over twenty-four hours now.

"Come into the office, you two. Coffee? Tea? This is my post until Sheila gets back from supper with someone. Trying not to stray too far from the phone."

"Fiona will no doubt call to give you an update, Ava, but I thought you might want to hear about our trip over to the house." Gaby chooses a chair in Ava's office and shakes her head in response to the refreshment offer.

Joe sits down with a thud in an armchair nearer the window. "There's not much to tell you, Ava, but we wanted to stop by and let you know we went over the house and the yard with a fine toothed comb. I even convinced the neighbours to let us search the run down garage next door." His deep voice vibrates in the small room.

Gaby's tenor is more anxious. "All this reminds me of when Roz Dover disappeared. I lived at 15 Poplar back then. I went down into the basement and peeked in every corner. I walked the perimeter of the fenced yard." She turns to Joe. "Remember when I told you the garage next door gave me the creeps until the owners went through the place?" She turns back to Ava and adds, "Poor Joe, he figured we had better take the bull by the horns when the cops were at the house. The bottom line is we found nothing out of the ordinary. The house could belong to anybody, except for that framed photo on the wall by the door—the one of a little cabin on an island in a lake somewhere. It doesn't strike me as relevant to Ronny, but the whole house seems to lack her signature, if you know what I mean. We think Fiona is convinced Ronny has been abducted, but we have no idea why. I assume there's information we lack. Anything you can talk about?"

While Gaby's stream of consciousness fills her office, Ava is reminded of a bird that was trapped in her kitchen once. It flew in all directions, and in order to gain trust, she had to stay calm. Ava tries the same approach now. She knows Gaby's background in social work makes her sensitive to the potential confidentiality issues involved. Since Gaby trusts Joe, she could reveal Ronny's background without repercussions, but she abruptly decides to keep Ronny's secrets to herself.

"There are a lot of moving targets, Gaby. The police have some additional details, but I think I had better respect Ronny's privacy until we know more. Suffice to say, I am worried sick. There has not been any more information after they found her car earlier today. I know Fiona has tried to locate a couple of the locals who had coffee at the same time as Ronny did yesterday morning. I expect her to call or show up any time now."

Gaby Ridgway and Joe Dodd have been a fixture in the community for a while. After Gaby left Family Counselling Division at the Hexagon, she went into business with Joe. She runs the storefront of Dodd's Contracting and Interiors. People say the house they built is beautiful. Ava has never been in.

They are a very private yet well-known couple. No one knows, for sure, if they're married or not. Some people say yes. Others say no. Maggie swears they aren't, because she and Rose would have been invited to a wedding. They host a Christmas dinner every year for old friends from The Station.

Joe is a big, barrel-chested man with a receding hairline and an ordinary face; not someone you would ever pick out in a crowd. He has built a reputation in the community for both meticulousness and fairness in the contracting business. Ava estimates him to be about fifty, but one never knows.

Gaby is terribly thin and almost angular. Her naturally curly, yet wispy light brown hair never seems to be contained. She often tries, without much success, to use combs or clips but then she'll pull them out and stick the offending strands behind her ears. She had a bad time in her job as a family counsellor. She was stalked by a client who ended up charged with a murder down east. In addition, some kind of investigation into Gaby, personally, happened. Ava knows she was vindicated, but she must have lost her taste for the profession, or her confidence somehow, because once circumstances were back to normal, she quit and went into business with Joe.

Dodd's Contracting and Interiors appears successful, considering the slow growth in Hayworth. They employ people, and are big donors to Segue House.

"Well, she won't have much to report after her time with us, Ava. I hope they've discovered more details at the Four Corners Petro-Can." She sighs as she gets up and prepares to leave.

Joe nods to Ava. "We'll keep in touch, and let you know if we hear any news."

****

As Ava busies herself making a toasted tomato sandwich in the office kitchen, since the Mars bar seemed to do nothing for her appetite that thrives on anxiety, the phone rings. It's Fiona Werbowski.

"Ava, I wanted to give you a couple of bits of information. First off, there's nothing out of the ordinary at Ronny's house. I imagine you already know this. I saw Gaby's vehicle parked in front of the shelter when I went by. We ran down a couple of farmers who had coffee at the Petro-Can the same time as Ronny yesterday morning. They both remember the guy who sat down with her. The descriptions were pretty detailed. We're sure the man is Duncan Taylor, although both witnesses said the person had a shaved head and lots of tattoos. Before his incarceration, he had hair and no tattoos. Keep this information to yourself, Ava, but tell Maggie, since she is already in the loop. We're certain Ronny's been grabbed by her ex-husband."

"What about the vehicle? Did your witnesses see a vehicle?"

"Nope." Fiona sighs long and hard into the phone. "He might have stolen a car or truck before he made his way out here. The search for a vehicle will be like a needle in a haystack. I'll call again tomorrow, but keep a close eye on your security over there. The situation is extremely fluid."

Ava sits down in the main reception room to eat her sandwich and nurse her tea. Duncan Taylor did time in prison because he threatened to murder Ronny. She has the scar on her neck to prove it. Ava tries to come to grips with the fact that he could actually kill her this time. What else besides his freedom has he got to lose?

She checks her watch and sees it's after five-thirty. She hopes Sheila returns soon. Although it would be no trouble to stay the night, Ava yearns to be home for some reason. She has serious ruminating to do about her current personal circumstances. Maybe she needs to get rid of the farm; buy a little bungalow out in the new sub-division; be closer to people. She shakes her head. This is a fine time to focus on herself, she admonishes in silence, although self-analysis seems to be the only alternative to horrible thoughts about Ronny's current predicament.

****

"Knock, knock! Anybody home…or still at work?" Marjorie Westerman pushes open the apartment door left ajar since Gaby and Joe departed earlier.

"Hi, Marjorie. Come on in. Have a seat. I am about to finish a supper sandwich while I wait for Sheila to get back, so I can go home. Wanted to avoid leaving the place unmanned tonight." Weariness and anxiety seep between her words, despite her best efforts. "Make yourself a cup of tea if you like. The kettle should still be hot."

"Thanks. I imagine there is no news, or you wouldn't be sitting here. All I can do is worry."

Ava, mindful of her conversation with Fiona, focuses on the information Marjorie already knows. "Her keys and her purse were locked in her car. Her house seems normal—no signs of a problem—like she vaporized. Do you remember when Roz Dover disappeared, Marjorie?"

"Oh yes. Rumours are the police know who took her but they need evidence. They must need the body. What a sad state of affairs. Her parents had their picture in the paper when they came here to try and find information. The world is full of broken hearts, Ava."

Ava nods as she kicks off her shoes and wiggles her toes inside her pantyhose. Definitely bare feet and sandals tomorrow, if the weather stays like this.

"What can I do to help out? I thought I might cook dinner for everyone tomorrow. Wednesday, right? I've lost track of my days since I moved in here. Out of my routine." She brushes a stray lock of professionally highlighted hair off her forehead. Her gold bangles clink together on her wrist as she lowers her arm.

Marjorie is well off because of an inheritance. You can tell she has money by the quality of her clothes and jewellery; by the new Lincoln sedan in the back parking lot. She is also educated. Why she stayed with her idiot husband for thirty years is beyond Ava's comprehension. She must have wanted to keep up appearances.

"What would you like to do, Marjorie?"

"I saw the barbecue on the back deck and thought hamburgers—and hot dogs for June's children. I can prepare everything and we can invite both the staff and residents—even Maggie's sister, Rose, if she is so inclined. What do you think? I would like to make a contribution. Under the circumstances, I think it might be a good idea to gather everyone together. Feeding people has always been my best option in a crisis." She tilts her head toward Ava, who is still slumped in the arm chair.

"Sounds very thoughtful, Marjorie. We will put a note on the bulletin board, but also tell everyone as we see them. We can plan for supper at six and hope the weather stays fine."

The intercom buzzer blasts. The sudden noise startles Ava. "Sheila Pasco, 1982-55."

"Hi, Sheila." Ava buzzes her into the foyer, waits until the outside door self-closes and locks, and then buzzes her into the main floor hall.

"You're still here. No news?"

"None to speak of. Fiona called and they're working on all the angles. Marjorie will barbecue for all of us tomorrow night. Will you be out gallivanting, or can you come?"

"Oh, I can come. I guess Devon won't want to eat out two nights in a row."

Ava stares down at Sheila's sandaled feet. She is more than a bit curious about the boyfriend. The outfit, including her footwear, has not escaped the older woman's keen eye.

"Sorry you can't invite him, Sheila. Only approved guests. You know the rules."

"I know." She follows Ava back into the office waiting room.

Sheila looks nice. Ava thinks this fellow must have made an impression. She wouldn't abandon her blue jeans and wear cotton pants for just anybody. "You're all dressed up. Out to the hotel for supper, were you?"

"Nah. Devon is pretty laid back. We went to the diner. Ran into Maggie and Rose. They seemed to be having quite the talk. I introduced Devon to them, though." She grins at her boss, exposing even but yellowed teeth "Ask Maggie what she thought. Know anybody who needs a delivery truck driver or a helper? Devon wants work. He will probably move to Carter River if he doesn't find a job soon."

Marjorie has been sitting quietly, sipping her tea, and watching the two women. "I could give you my husband's phone number. He often hires reliable labourers out at the farm. You'd have to say the information came from someplace else and not from me, though."

Ava can tell Sheila has no enthusiasm for this option. Maybe the guy would want to drive equipment, not do farm labour. "Give it a try, Sheila. Nothing ventured, nothing gained. Now, are you all set for tonight? No place else to go? If not, I think I want to go home. I can worry there as well as here, and it seems all we can do tonight is worry."

"I'm in to stay, Ava."

She returns to her office, grabs her purse, and navigates the exit to her car.

****

Ava gazes at her family home with a critical eye as she manoeuvres her white Chrysler into the barn-like garage. If she had the place painted and the roof replaced, she might make a tidy sum by selling. A new owner would probably gut the inside to modernize, but the house is comfortable and livable, now. Her current land renter has expressed an interest. Once Ronny is found safe and sound, she'll start to focus on personal issues.

She unlocks the door and steps inside, straight into the kitchen—or the kitchen-parlour as they called it during her childhood. The room is huge and contains the kitchen, a large dining area with seating for eight, and a sofa set in the corner. The original wood cook stove is long gone, but her father had a big fireplace and hearth installed in its stead, before she ever went away to nursing school. If inclined to sleep on the sofa, a person could almost live in this one room. The previous owners converted the walk-in pantry to a basic bathroom in the year before her folks bought the place. It became quite convenient when she returned after her father's death; when her mother started to require care. Ava was thirty. Her life hadn't even had a chance to take shape. She left a lot behind.

She shrugs her shoulders. No regrets. Segue House wouldn't have happened without the other. A lot of people have been helped over the intervening years.

So…Duncan Taylor is in the vicinity. His appearance has changed, but the cops know about him. Maybe he's been to the diner. Perhaps she should talk to Patrick, Nancy, and Danny. Better yet, she should call Fiona and make the suggestion. They see everybody at the diner. She whips off her hose in the middle of the kitchen floor, takes a moment to ponder the idea of tossing them into the empty fireplace, and then wanders upstairs to get out of her bra and into a cotton nightie. Not time for bed, but always time for a cotton nightie on an August night. If only the phone would ring and Fiona would tell her Ronny is okay.

Chapter 7

Ronny

I will not allow fear to paralyze my brain.
I will not go crazy.
I will not allow fear to paralyze my brain.
I will not go crazy.

Despite constant repetition of her mantra, Ronny's anxiety bubbles inside her like water in an over-filled kettle. Tuesday draws to a close. Her skin crawls. Grit and sweat torment her. Damp settles into her corners—under her arms, between her breasts, behind her ears. Her hair sticks to her forehead and the nape of her neck. The three holes for ventilation allow as much dust from surrounding fields into the room as they permit breeze to blow through. Flies have found their way in and she has no weapon. *Even a sandal would be better than the palm of your hand.* Her head aches with the heat and the indoor outhouse stinks. Her gag reflex is letting her down. She has never experienced such mind-numbing thirst, but her fear of drinking too much in the event he won't return with more water forces her to ration what little there is. The crackers and peanut butter make her throat dry. Maybe all this is part of his plan.

Which is worse—if he comes back, or if he stays away?

If he returns, he could have food and water, but he could come back to torture or kill her, or both. If he disappears, how long will it take them to find her?

Assume they've found my car. With my keys and purse inside, the obvious conclusion is I didn't go willingly. There were people in the restaurant. Surely someone could describe the guy who sat with me. Would Ava and Maggie reveal my secret to the RCMP? They would have to, wouldn't they? Assume the police have already determined Duncan is the one who grabbed me. Did someone at the Petro-Canada, besides the dogs in the semis, see his truck? He must have a place to stay in the area. Would they have a picture to show around to people? Would a search take this long? Do they think I'm already dead?

The kettle of her anxiety bubbles over.

Despite her attempts to calm down, Ronny's mind races back to the time he tried to kill her; when she left him for good. The summer night hung heavy with hot and muggy air—much like now. She sat on the back step of their shabby little rental house nursing a glass of lemonade. He was at the bar, or so she assumed. He spent most of his time there after he was fired. She thought, perhaps, she'd get lucky that night and he wouldn't come home at all.

Then she heard his truck as he turned into their driveway. He stumbled out and came around the corner toward the steps. His level of drunkenness surprised her. How could he have driven?

"Get your ass inside right now," he hissed, in a failed attempt to prevent alerting the neighbours.

She knew an argument would be useless, even with a sober Duncan, and a drunken version would be worse. She walked into the kitchen. He followed her. When she turned around, he had a knife in his hand. He had never used a weapon or threatened her with a weapon before. There were no guns in the house. Ronny checked regularly for guns. The Buck knife was familiar to her—a gift from Duncan's father—a classic with a brass and wood handle. The most impressive feature, to Duncan, appeared to be the nail-nick in the blade, designed to permit two-handed operation. Duncan's hands were so big he could open the blade with the thumbnail of his right hand alone, and not have to use his left hand at all. He often sat on the sofa, opening and closing the knife with one hand, practising.

She remained still, like a statue. He stood there. The knife clicked— *open, click, close, click, open, click, close, click.* Despite his inebriated unsteadiness, he could put the Buck knife into business position in no time. He never looked down.

He started to walk toward her.

"Duncan, put the knife away. What's the problem? We can talk about this."

"The guys at the bar said you probably could have more kids, but you're making sure you never get pregnant again. They said all women are sneaky. They get knocked-up when you don't want them to and then they won't get pregnant when all you want is to have a kid." He took another step and she backed up. She would soon run out of floor space. "Is that what you're doing, Janine? Secret birth control?" His eyes burned black and his voice had an embedded sneer—more threatening than she'd ever heard before.

She chose to try and double back; to escape through the front door, but he had his left arm around her neck and the thin point of the Buck knife up against her throat the moment she moved. The pressure felt like the jab of a needle over and over again in the same place. Warm blood trickled down her neck. He cut her.

"This is not what you really want, Duncan. You always tell me you love me; you say you don't know what you'd do without me. You can't want to hurt me, Duncan." She tried to keep her voice calm; to not focus on her neck and the pain, or her back and his twisting grip on her shoulder.

He let her go. He came to his senses for a split second and let her go. When he sat down on the couch with another beer and fell asleep after what seemed like hours, she grabbed her car keys and her wallet, left, and went to the shelter. Blood from the cut had oozed everywhere by then. They took her to the hospital and called Faith. They stitched her up, but the raggedy injury took weeks to heal and looked like hell. Duncan was arrested. He was not granted bail. No one, not even his father, would help him. The trial started a few months later and he went to the penitentiary in December, 1980. After her divorce was finalized in 1981, she changed her identity and moved to Hayworth.

****

I will not allow fear to paralyze my brain.
I will not go crazy.
Ronny starts to scour the cabin for potential weapons, of which there are none, of course. The floors are bare. She rattles the cot. It won't come apart without tools. All the utensils at her disposal are plastic. The water jug is plastic, too, and half empty—able to be swung, certainly, but without the benefit of weight, not much help. She runs shaking fingers along the walls and door inside the lean-to outhouse as she searches desperately for a piece of

wood able to be disengaged and hidden near the cot. She rattles and pushes, but with her limited strength and no tool, she is unable to dislodge a makeshift weapon. He could turn up at any minute.

Maybe I'll be able to talk my way out of this like I did before.

Maybe he just wants to scare me.

If I keep my cool, I can survive this. He won't want to go back to jail.

On the other hand, he will most certainly go back to jail. This is abduction and forcible confinement, right?

Maybe he has nothing to lose.

What about the toilet seat? The toilet seat covers the rough hole cut in the wooden bench of the outhouse. It moves around on the bolts. It has been loose all along. One of the wood screws is stripped. The seat must have been installed in a hurry to be crooked and wobbly. *Will the seat come off? Can I use a toilet seat as a weapon?*

For the next hour, hot and holding her breath most of the time in the windowless outhouse, Ronny uses all her power to wrench and wiggle the whole seat back and forth by grasping the closed front with both hands. She lets out a whoop for joy when she manages to loosen the screw on one side to the point where she can remove it. The second screw happens to be installed correctly and proves to be considerably more challenging.

Sweat rolls down her forehead and into her eyes. She forces herself to focus despite the stench. She is oblivious to the dirt and the smell. This toilet seat could save her life. The screw begins to rock. She yelps when the skin rips from her knuckles as she repeatedly grasps and tests for movement. She gasps for breath; she has a drink. The edge of the blanket on the cot is scratchy when she scrapes the fabric across her face to absorb the sweat. She cocks her head and listens for the sound of a vehicle. The rustle of the wind in the bushes is all she hears.

Another try, with renewed vigour. She is a woman on a mission. Despite a bloody knuckle on the index finger of her right hand, the wood finally gives way and she is able to remove the two-piece cover from the bench. The rough-cut hole is exposed. She is the conqueror; the victor. Ronny stands in the middle of the cabin and clasps the seat and top together with both hands, one on either side. She practises her swing, underhand and to the side, like a baseball bat. She can wield a significant force and is sure there would be enough power to knock him down. With a level of satisfaction she finds hard to describe, she tucks her weapon under the blanket at the end of the cot.

I will not allow fear to paralyze my brain.

I will not go crazy.

She sits down, exhausted, and pats the blanket beside her. *If I have to fight, I can fight. He made a mistake with the toilet seat. Either he did a piss-poor job when he did the installation himself, or he didn't do a thorough inspection when he set up my jail cell. Whichever, I don't care. If he dares to open the bars and enter the cabin, I will do more than defend myself. I will kill him if I have to.*

****

Gaby Ridgway was working as a family counsellor at the Hexagon when Ronny first met her. They often referred clients to one another back then. When Ronny hosted the Thanksgiving potluck at The Station back in the fall of 1981, Gaby came as Joe Dodd's guest. Gaby is her landlady now. Ronny has rented 15 Poplar Street since late 1983—almost a year! Gaby and Ronny continue to be connected through fundraising at Segue House, as well.

Gaby has a big dog named Martha. She has odd eyes. One's blue and the other is brown. Her coat is mottled grey, white, and black; a weird combination. The dog is inordinately well-behaved. Joe has a big old white cat named Blanche. Blanche existed in Joe's life long before Gaby and Martha. Joe jokes about how he lives in a house full of women.

As her mind wanders to her landlords, Ronny longs for her little house. She sits on the cot, pats the toilet seat hidden under the blanket, and thinks about the comforts of home. She imagines herself on the veranda right now, drinking wine, and anticipating supper. Her tastes are simple. Her furnishings are minimal—mismatched chairs, a big footstool, a coffee table, and a couple of lamps. She dislikes television, but enjoys the radio.

She thinks about her current clients, happy there were only two residents at Segue House as of yesterday. Marjorie Westerman will be fine. She expects to drive to her sister's place in Ontario. There are no money issues, but she has been taking her own sweet time making the arrangements. Ronny, with a sudden insight born from solitude, suspects there might be some other issue. Marjorie could have left days ago. Why is she still there, with no obvious obstacles to prevent her departure? Her sister in Ontario is a widow. Marjorie will stay with her while she finds her own place. Up until now, they have been focused on her commitment and determination to not return to her husband. Ronny has not focused on Marjorie's decided lack of commitment and determination to leave the shelter.

June Kendall is anxious to move and get her children settled. She needs the assistance of government services and all those details invariably take time. Her two daughters are the cutest little things. They're reserved. They play together and only speak when spoken to. Although six and eight, they've seen a lot of violence. Ronny remembers she and June had an appointment to go together to the Hexagon today—Tuesday. June would have had to go alone. Perhaps, in the end, her absence will be for the best. June has to learn to be independent. She can cling and be needy—unlike her children.

****

How long have I been sitting here, waiting? Is that thunder in the distance? Ronny hears a low rumble—the familiar introduction to a prairie storm. She continues to perch on the side of the bed, and stare through the bars of the window at an ever-darkening sky.

What if this is my last day? Have I made a contribution? Have I repaid the universe for the help I was given in Sudbury?

Ava Burrway was only hosting one family at the time Ronny first joined the staff. They were at capacity before long, though, with three apartments housing mothers and their total of ten children, plus two women without children in the fourth unit. Ronny hit the ground running. They set up her office in the bedroom of the unit across the hall from the main office. She saw clients there or in their particular unit. Mothers watched each other's children so they could each manage some private time with their counsellor. She fell in love with the work almost immediately.

One of the biggest issues seems to be alcohol. Couples drink, fight, get violent, scare their children, and spiral into a cycle of abuse. Ronny can relate. She heaves a sigh of regret, as she peruses her surroundings and realizes her personal circumstances have not improved, despite the efforts to change her life and put her own particular past behind her.

A sudden flash of sheet lightening propels her back to reality. She is parched and conflicted. If she drinks all the remaining water and he fails to return, she'll become dehydrated within hours. If he does show up, she will have to deal with the consequences. She relents and has a sip of water but avoids eating. Food will make her thirsty.

She returns to the cot. Hot and salty tears begin to roll down flushed and dirt smudged cheeks. This creates a welcome relief of sorts, like steam escaping from a pressure cooker. At least her tears can get away. She swipes at them with the back of her hand. Lightning flashes again and the thunder rolls. The storm is close.

I will not allow my fear to paralyze my brain.

I will not go crazy.

Chapter 8

~

Maggie

Maggie perches on the edge of her seat in the second booth down from the door. She and Rose have been huddled with their heads together, although Maggie hasn't shared much. She felt anxious with Sheila and her boyfriend on the premises. Rose is patient; appreciates her state of mind. Rose always knows.

By the time Patrick delivers tea and lemon meringue pie, Maggie finally organizes her thoughts enough to launch into her story. Just then, Sean Knox swaggers into the diner. His hips are loaded down with all the familiar paraphernalia. This added burden causes him to walk like some sort of cross between a penguin and a wrestler. The beige and black uniform serves to enhance his ruddy complexion, angular jaw, and broad chest—at least Maggie thinks so. She tries hard not to bat her eyes at him as he saunters over to the counter and asks Patrick for a couple of coffees to go. Maggie glances out the window in time to see Fiona hang up the radio speaker and yank her notebook out of her pocket.

Sean approaches their booth. "Hi, Maggie. Too hot to eat at home tonight, eh? Happy to leave those chores to the professionals?" He cocks his head toward the kitchen as Danny bangs the bell, alerting Patrick to another couple of specials in the window.

"Hi, Sean. Yes. The place is busy for a Tuesday night. This is my sister, Rose. Rose, this is Constable Sean Knox. I met him at work." Maggie finds it difficult to control her expression. She knows Rose can read her like a cheap paperback and she feels a little sweaty all of a sudden.

"Nice to meet you, Constable." Rose extends her hand. "Busy times right now all around. I hope we hear some news about our friend, Ronny, soon."

"Coffee's ready, Sean." Patrick hollers across the space from the counter to the booths.

"Yeah, me too. See you tomorrow, Maggie. Lots of work, double shifts, and extra members in from Carter River. See you tomorrow," he repeats. With a couple of turns, he bolts out the door and into the squad car. Maggie watches him hand over a coffee to Fiona as she pulls the vehicle out of the lot. By the time she returns her attention to her sister, her heart is back to its normal steady thump.

Maggie sighs as she senses more than sees the heavy sky start to move in. She can hear the thunder in the distance. Maggie is a weather fanatic. She loves the big sky. You can see clouds of rain as they approach. You can see a blizzard develop ten miles away, while the sun still shines on your face. There will be a storm tonight, and soon big rain drops will start to splash down on Rose's Malibu. Her sister snaps her back to attention.

"Maggie, I know you want to talk to me. The place has started to clear out. We've been here over an hour. Do you want to finish up and talk once we get home?" Her voice has the distinct ring of frustration.

"No, Rose. We can talk here. Once we go home, I want to watch the storm. I want to tell you Ronny's secret. I swore I would never tell, but circumstances have changed and I think you should know what I know."

"Secret? What kind of secret? My God, Maggie! What is your trouble? Tell me what's on your mind."

Maggie takes the last bite of her pie and washes it down with a sip of tea. She slides the plate to the side and leans further in toward her sister. "When Ronny moved here back in the spring of 1981, her real name was Janine Taylor. She is divorced from Duncan Taylor who served time in jail for attempted murder—of her. The scar on her neck is not because of a car accident. He tried to cut her throat!" Maggie's voice is raspy. Her eyes dart about every so often to ensure there's no one within ear shot.

"How long have you known about this, Maggie? I find it hard to believe you never told me."

"Confidentiality, Rose—the same as your job. I've known since her first day at work. Murdock Blackney handled all the paperwork to get her name changed, and her new driver's licence. In reality, her home town is Sudbury,

Ontario. She was not born in Québec. Her father's still alive but I guess she has no contact with him. She has created a self-imposed witness protection program." She leans in still closer. "I've seen pictures of her before she cut all her hair off and dyed it platinum. Her hair was as long as mine but really thick and curly. She told me her biggest sacrifice was when she cut her crazy dark hair." Maggie frowns with the recollection and then becomes more focused on the topic at hand.

"Duncan Taylor's release from jail happened a couple of months ago. We all think he grabbed her. Some farmers at the Petro-Can described the guy. They said he appeared big, with a shaved head, tattoos, and protruding teeth. His description is not one I would picture as Ronny's type, but there you go. Nobody saw his vehicle. The police said they would try and trace back to his release date, to see if they can get an angle on what he might be driving."

She drops her voice to a mere whisper. "He tried to kill her once, Rose. This is like Roz Dover all over again. We are still in the dark about what happened to her." Maggie's eyes fill with tears. She has wanted to cry for almost two days now.

Rose appears stunned. Rain has started to pelt the windows of the diner— big drops plop into the glass, one after the other. You can hear each one hit. Rose gathers her sweater closer around her shoulders. "I am at a loss for words, Maggie. This might be very bad. Can I help in some way?"

"I don't think so. Fiona will brief Ava tomorrow. One of the current residents wants to cook supper for everyone, so we can all be together. I think Ava will invite Gaby and Joe. They went through Ronny's house today with Fiona and Sean. You can come, too. Fiona has been put in charge of the whole investigation. She and Sean might be there. I have no idea."

The door opens and in waltzes Devon Thompson for the second time this evening. He approaches Patrick with his head down. He avoids acknowledging Rose and Maggie who are still there. He might not even be aware, as he shakes raindrops off his sleeves. He still has on a Maple Leafs ball cap and Maggie hears him order the special. Maggie is pretty darn sure he already ordered the special when he ate with Sheila barely an hour ago.

She decides to try and get his attention. "Hey, Devon. Can't get enough of Danny's meat loaf, eh? Just had to come back for a second helping?" She tosses the words out and lifts her eyebrows at Patrick.

Devon growls a response to the tease. "You two still here?" He seems surprised. "Thought I'd get another one and save it for later. Too hot to cook for myself…you know." His voice peters out like he has no words to justify the behaviour.

"You should stop in tomorrow, Devon. Wednesday is pork roast!" She turns back to Rose and tilts her head a fraction. "Let's go home before the rain starts to pour, Rose. We can have another cup of tea at my place."

****

By the time the two women navigate their way from Rose's car to the granite step of The Station entrance, the rain has begun to pummel in earnest. Rose holds her purse over her head while she fumbles with her keys. The big old front door has remained locked ever since Roz Dover disappeared. Maggie grimaces as the rain beats down and leaves her as wet as if she had been swimming. They fall over each other to get inside. Maggie locks the door behind them as she rustles up her keys for Number Three.

"Give me a few minutes to drop my purse and dry off a bit. Leave the doors open so Caesar and Caramel can wander over if they want to. Be right back." Rose barks her instructions. Sometimes she sounds too motherly or bossy but Maggie would never, ever, say so. If not for Rose, she would no doubt still be at Forest Hills Institute living in fear of her parents coming to visit, or worse yet, coming to get her. Rose can adopt whatever tone of voice suits her purpose. Maggie does not criticize her sister.

She enters her apartment and leaves the door ajar. Caesar, the tortoiseshell lord of the manor, and Caramel, the orange sidekick and juvenile delinquent, make their way across the hall almost immediately. Rose belongs to Caesar and Maggie belongs to Caramel, but the two women decided circumstances would be better for everyone if the boys were together most of the time. In the end, they spend their days at Rose's but most of their nights with Maggie. Maggie lets them both sleep on the bed, so this is probably the rationale behind the arrangement the felines, themselves, have created.

She fills the kettle and plugs it in. Back when she and Rose helped care for Ben Tullis before she died, Maggie developed a taste for herbal teas. Tonight she will serve a black currant favourite and one she knows Rose likes as well. Her thoughts return to Ronny…and Sean…and Devon. Her emotions are troubled; conflicted, but she unable to quite figure out the source of her concern. Sheila has a boyfriend. That, in itself, is odd enough, but this particular guy doesn't seem like he would be attracted to a woman like Sheila. He would be the kind of guy who would go for someone who looks like Ronny, or Gaby Ridgway. Devon wore a jean jacket and a ball cap at supper even though it was horribly hot and sticky before the storm. This observation eats away at Maggie, too.

"There! Dried off and dressed a little warmer! Wow! The air sure cooled down in a hurry!" Rose breezes into Maggie's apartment. She has changed into cream-coloured baggy cotton trousers and a navy sweat shirt with colourful appliquéd flowers across the bust. "The tea smells wonderful! Is it the black currant?" She reaches for the cups.

"I am so afraid for Ronny, Rose. This may not end well."

"Who else knows about her changed identity, Maggie? Does Cheryl know?" Rose casts her eyes skyward as if Cheryl Nadler, the Adoption Services Social Worker who lives upstairs, might be able to overhear them.

"I doubt it. I know she and Ronny are friends, but Ronny was very clear from the beginning. Ava, Murdock Blackney, the judge, and me are the four people who would know. She has never even told her father where she is. She told me that. I wish I could help her. She could be cold and wet, or hungry." Maggie's big eyes fill with unshed tears, again. She starts to shake—an old habit from years ago at the institute. Whenever she wanted to avoid a situation, like a visit from her parents, she would start to shake uncontrollably.

"Maggie, you're shaking!" Rose's strong masculine hands grip Maggie's thin upper arms. "Settle down! All we can do is wait. You and I both know this. Maybe he just wants to scare her. Maybe he'll drop her off down some dirt road someplace and she'll make her way back to town."

"We know Roz didn't get dropped off out in the country, even though at first everybody said she ran off. They've never found her body, but we all know she did not run off." Big tears, like the first rain drops from the storm, roll down her ivory cheeks.

"Drink your tea. Come over to my apartment and we'll watch some television together. I prefer you not be alone until you calm down." Television is Rose's answer to everything.

They make their way across the hall, balancing their cups of tea, with the cats trailing behind them. Maggie is content to listen to her sister's instructions. She still has a challenge with focus when she feels overwhelmed.

She recalls one day at work, not long after she started. The shelter was full and extraordinarily busy. Since no other staff existed yet, counsellors from the Hexagon visited the shelter to see clients, and the police appeared to conduct interviews. On this particular day, children seemed to cry from all directions, and the phone wouldn't quit ringing. Maggie started to go to pieces. She lost her focus. She began to shake. Through all the chaos, Ava must have seen the expression on her face, and approached her. Without a word, the two of them went into Ava's office and shut the door. "You stay here until you settle down, Maggie. No problem. We can switch desks for now." Other than when Rose removed her from the institute and moved her to Hayworth, Maggie feels this action is one of the kindest gestures ever directed toward her.

She knows she needs to calm down or she will risk slipping into an unreasonable spiral where she will be out of control. "Sit in the rocker, Maggie. Relax. I think we might be able to find an interesting program, a movie maybe, on TV tonight. Let me get the guide." Rose bustles around. She turns on the television, locates the guide, and flips through the channels. She settles on a rerun of *Magnum, P.I.* Maggie is distracted. She would rather be home. She wants to sit on her stool at the kitchen window and watch the rain, the sky, and the vehicles on the street.

"Fiona Werbowski said she would call Ava tomorrow morning." She attempts to refocus by talking about dinner again. "One of the clients said she wanted to cook dinner for everyone so we could be together. You can come if you want. Gaby and Joe will be invited, too. They're pretty shaken up like the rest of us. If Sean and Fiona came, then all of us who know about the situation would be there." She is painfully aware of her behaviour—like sharing personal thoughts out loud and repeating herself, as well. She risks drifting; losing touch with Rose and her surroundings. "Of course the clients, Sheila, as well as Gaby and Joe, are not privy to the details." She curls her feet up under her and sips on the fragrant tea. She holds the cup under her nose, the way she saw Joe do when he would come and visit Ben Tullis. He said he liked to absorb the rich and fruity aroma.

"Do you want to spend the night here, Maggie? Do you need some company?"

Rose leans over her knees to get closer to Maggie. The concern in her sister's eyes is obvious. "I'll be fine, Rose, just a bundle of nerves, that's all."

"You might need a session with Rachel."

Rachel Wilkerson has been Maggie's psychiatrist since she first came to Hayworth. Appointments have been sporadic over the last year or so because she hasn't needed the extra support. "Perhaps you're right, Rose" Maggie sighs, deciding not to argue with her sister. "I can call her office in Edmonton tomorrow; see when she will be in town next, and if she has any time. I think I need to go to bed now. Tomorrow will be another stressful day. Think about the barbecue and I will call you at work to confirm."

She gets up as she calls her pets. "Caesar! Caramel! Are you two with me tonight?" The soft thuds of eight cat paws as they land on the floor let both Rose and Maggie know they have been asleep on Rose's bed the entire time Maggie has been in the apartment. Maggie accepts her sister's hug. The boys follow her, like ducklings behind their mother, across the hall and into her apartment.

She shuts the door. The space is simple and uncluttered, not like Rose's apartment where the corners are stuffed with yarn and paper bags full of baby blankets and fabric. She has the standard couch and chair, the big old picnic table that Ben made so many years ago and then Ronny used, and the spare bed they dragged to the big bedroom when she first moved in. Along with the peninsula made for Ben by Joe, these are mostly all Ben's possessions and Maggie considers them to simply be in her care. She never owned a stick of furniture or a kitchen utensil to call her own until she moved into this apartment.

She stands in the entry to the master bedroom and contemplates turning down the bed. She avoids this action and meanders out to the kitchen. Without conscious thought, and while big tears once again start to roll down her cheeks, she fills the kettle and searches out another black currant tea bag. She stands at the counter and listens to the only sounds—boiling water and falling rain—and then makes her tea. Caesar and Caramel sit on the marble top of the kitchen peninsula. They are not supposed to sit there. She drags her stool over to the window and perches. This is her quiet spot. Maggie stares out the window and watches the weather like others might watch a movie. This is the method she has always employed to cope with her life. She disappears into the distance and becomes swallowed up by the landscape.

The sky is dark and light at the same time. The storm clouds start to move off, leaving a line of yellow and blue in the distance. The air will be warm and sticky again before morning. She concentrates on Ronny. She thinks about her so hard she is sure Ronny will feel herself to be in the thoughts of someone who cares. She thinks about Ronny for a long time, until her tea is cold and her back is sore. The cats have gone to bed.

The light begins to fade as she remains on the stool by the window. Anyone who might pull into the front parking lot, or go by on the sidewalk or road, would never notice the sad, long-haired creature in the shadows, as she nods or shakes her head back and forth. No one would understand her fear of losing control; the sheer terror of facing another loss; the challenges this woman encounters as she tries to channel all her energy toward her missing friend and colleague.

Chapter 9

~

Ronny

Ronny had been employed at the shelter for two weeks when she first met Fiona Werbowski in May of 1981. Fiona appeared to be a fixture of sorts in the small town. She served for six years in the Northwest Territories and then earned her pick of assignments further south. Small town Northern Alberta became her preferred location. She wanted to do basic community police work. She told Ronny her goal was to retire in Hayworth.

In late August of that first year, Ronny took a call from Lily Kettell. At first, Ronny thought the caller was someone's child on the phone. Lily's soft, hesitant voice sounded shaky. Her sentences were punctuated with bouts of sniffling and a baby cried in the background. She had no phone so used the one at her neighbour's place. She had been abandoned by her husband or boyfriend. Ronny couldn't determine which. They had no more food. Her daughters were two months and one year old. The well water smelled funny. Could someone at the shelter come and get her? He had been gone more than a week and she was afraid he would come back and hurt her, or take her children.

Ronny talked to pragmatic Ava. "Call the cops and get someone to go with you. Take my car. Tell her to stay at the neighbour's house until you get there."

Lily stayed at her neighbour's house until Ronny secured a police escort and called her back. She said the people at the house were afraid of him, so they asked her to leave. She never used his name. She always referred to him with a pronoun.

Fiona Werbowski arrived at the shelter. A small woman, not more than five foot, four inches tall, Fiona wore her long, dark hair in a bun at the nape of her neck and seemed weighted down by all the gear around her waist. Sean Knox, her patrol partner, waited in the car.

They introduced themselves. At the time, Ronny found it hard to believe this diminutive woman, at least six inches shorter than her, could possibly protect anyone from a husband in a rage. "You follow us. What are the directions?"

"She said we go about ten miles down the highway toward Edmonton and then turn left on to a cut road. There's no sign, but the property is right after a big wheat farming operation and they have about a dozen bins in the yard. The road is gravel and we'll have to drive about twelve miles until we come to the very end. There's a clump of bushes on the right, and no driveway. With all the leaves on the trees, she says it will be difficult to see the trailer, but it is there. The road stops. She said the last place before the end is three miles away. They have a phone and so she walked there with the kids to call, but she has to walk back because the neighbours are afraid of 'him'. There are no details, yet, about 'him'. She won't use a name."

"Children? What do we have?"

"A baby, two months old, and a one year old. Both female. They've run out of food and the well water smells funny. Constable Werbowski, I think we have many reasons to be concerned."

Fiona nodded toward Ronny. "Let's go…and I hope this will be the last time you call me Constable Werbowski. Just Fiona, plain and simple. I can brief Sean as we drive. I think we'll go first. I know the area, although I have to admit, I've never been all the way to the end of that particular road."

Ronny had driven very little since she left Sudbury earlier in the month. Ava drove a big old Impala at the time. The vehicle seemed to take up the whole highway. They drove down the cut road for a long time; like they would drive to the horizon and fall off the edge. The patrol car kicked up dust so thick she found it necessary to ease off the gas and close the vents. Fiona stopped at the end and Ronny pulled in beside her. Ronny had hoped they would find Lily and her babies on the side of the road, but they saw no sign of her on their trip in. Maybe the neighbour drove her back home.

When their dust settled, the quiet fell like a blanket—spooky, without a breath of wind. "You stay here, Ronny. Sean and I will have a look around."

Ronny nodded and remained by her car. The time seemed to drag, but was probably only a minute or two, when Fiona appeared from the bushes, waved an arm, and yelled for Ronny to come with her. The trailer, no more than an abandoned skid shack from the oil patch, was tucked behind a huge stand of thicket. Perhaps, if you made a focused attempt from the end of the road where the cars were, you could see the silver shimmer of the stove pipe.

"The wife is at the door. We went in and ensured no one else is there. I told her you would come in after we cleared the rooms." Fiona stared hard into Ronny's eyes. "The situation is pretty bad. I think we need to scoop them up and go; wait to give her what she needs at the shelter."

Despite the quick assessment, Fiona proved correct. Lily was using dirty rags that might have once been pillowcases, for diapers on both the children. The place stunk to high heaven. Both kids appeared emaciated and were filthy. The heat inside the trailer made the unseasonable eighty degree temperature outside seem cool.

At Ava's insistence—experienced with similar circumstances—Ronny packed diapers, formula, and some baby food in the car before she left. After she saw the place with her own eyes, she agreed with Fiona. No need to try and help her here. She wanted to come to the shelter. They would take her to Segue House and the sooner the better.

While Fiona and Ronny loaded Lily and her babies into the back seat of Ava's car, Sean wandered around both inside and outside the house. Ronny presumed he was scouring the place for weapons or drugs. She could not be sure until he rounded the corner of the trailer with a rifle of some sort in his hands. His face was grim and he said nothing. He nodded to Fiona and put the weapon in the trunk of the patrol car.

On the way back to the shelter, Lily and her babies quietly cried. All three of them, in the back seat, seemed to whimper. They sounded like kittens mewing for their mother. Ronny attempted to try and tell Lily how they would provide whatever she and her children would need, but she finally gave up and let them cry their way to Segue House.

****

So what jogged her memory of Lily and her babies tonight? Ronny thinks about the smell in the hot cabin; the spooky quiet; the bushes almost covering the window. She listens as the storm starts to move off and senses the stickiness return to settle like sandpaper on her gritty skin. It is one of the rare times she appreciates her short haircut. She knows Fiona is searching for her.

And then she hears a vehicle approach. The engine sputters to a stop. As much as she would like to believe Fiona is nearby, she knows the sound is not that of a police cruiser. The outside door must be padlocked. She hears keys rattle and metal against metal. The fresh air rolls in with a burst as he pulls the slatted wooden door open.

"How ya' holdin' up, Janine? I thought I'd deliver some grub." He slides a paper plate covered with tinfoil through the rectangular space under the lock in the barred interior door. He makes no move to enter the cabin.

She takes a step forward and reaches for the plate. He holds on for a second or two before he relinquishes his grip. "What's your grand plan, Duncan? You'll never get away with this. There'll be an army searching for me. Hayworth is a little sensitive about the sudden disappearance of women." She has trouble controlling the sarcasm in her voice, but her tone serves to disguise her abject fear of this man.

"God, I've heard about her a dozen times already! Some broad went missing in 1981 and people in town still look for her. Nobody knows for sure what happened. Is there some serial killer on the loose? Might as well keep them guessing."

"How did you find me, Duncan?" She tries to engage him. *Be calm. Maybe he'll let his guard down.* Maybe she can persuade him to let her go—no harm done.

He sits on the broken wooden stoop with his back toward the bars, about a foot beyond her reach. "So, tell me about the gals you work with. Where does Ava live? How old is Maggie? Fat Sheila's a piece a' work, eh?"

All of a sudden, cold overwhelms her. The humidity is no match for the chill that courses through her limbs when she comes to understand how much he already knows "How did you learn about the people I work with, Duncan?"

"Are you out of water, yet? I brought some more and a funnel. Go get your jug so I can fill it up. Aren't I a nice guy? Back in jail, nobody treated me nice like this. I hope you appreciate how I treat a prisoner." He lowers his gaze down and past Ronny to the lean-to outhouse. "Sorry, the stink is your problem now. All I can do is pour a little lye in from the back. Remind me to do that before I leave."

He lopes over to the truck and grabs a plastic container—it could be an old antifreeze jug—along with a funnel and a long tube. "Hold your bottle up here and so I can fill it."

Ronny hesitates. If the jug contained antifreeze, he could be in the process of killing her from the other side of the bars.

"No need to fret. I haven't poisoned your water, although I saw a story on TV about a bunch of kids at a camp who all died because they drank the antifreeze. Thought they lucked into some kind of Kool-Aid. The jugs look a lot alike." Then he leans over so his face is close to the bars. "Besides, Janine, if I decide to kill you, I will go straight for your pretty neck like I did the last time, only you won't talk your way out of it again. Now hold up the damned jug!"

Ronny does as she's told. After the task is complete, he sits back down on the step.

The sky has turned purple and azure. The sun will set very soon. It must be after ten. "We should be parents by now, Janine. You know, we would have been able to make our marriage work if you hadn't lost our kid. And you wouldn't have any more. I talked to the doctor. He said we could have a baby. What did you do?" His voice begins to shake. His shoulders, bursting out of the black T-shirt, are slumped.

She assesses his tattoos. "Are those a souvenir from prison, Duncan?"

"If you can't beat 'em, join 'em. This is the one I wanted." He points to the word "Janine" written in flowery script on his left bicep. "The rest are because there wasn't much else to do, I guess." He sounds like he did back when they were married, after the miscarriage, when they fought all the time—depressed, teary, and angry—all those emotions mixed together. The one positive element—she is quite certain he is sober.

"How did you ever meet Ava Burrway and get a job way out here?" He turns toward the inside of the cabin and sneers. "And you turned out to be quite the little fundraiser, too. Ava lucked out when she pulled you in off the street."

Ronny struggles to maintain calm; to keep quiet. She has resolved not to reveal any information. She will listen.

"Now, Sheila Pasco—what a brute. God, she has a face like a brick wall! She thinks I'm hot for her." He sneers again. "Well, I do have a 'thing' for her. I *'thing'* she is so stupid, she'll tell me whatever I want to know. What a dog!" His guffaw is more of a bark.

Ronny starts to put some of the puzzle pieces together. She still questions how Duncan found out her location in Hayworth, but he did. Once he learned Sheila worked where she worked, he gained an inside track. Poor Sheila. She probably thinks Duncan is smitten with her.

Duncan continues. "I gave her a phony name—Devon Thompson. Like it? I took her to the diner tonight and she introduced me to Maggie Woodward and the older sister—Rose, is it? Talk about your old maids! Maggie seems to have a few loose wires. She must be thirty-five if she's a day and she acts like a teenager! What's with her? Do any of them know you're Janine Taylor?"

Ronny's reluctant to tell him the truth, so she lies. "RCMP Constable Fiona Werbowski has become one of my closest friends. She knows. She'll figure out what's happened. They'll think of you right away."

"Well, they can't track me. I stole a truck from the back lot of some small town used car dealer outside Sudbury. They probably haven't even noticed a vehicle missing yet. They won't be able to find me."

His confidence and bravado have risen above his pathos again—the two sides of Duncan. There has always been the confident man who can do any job and handle any situation. Then there's the pathetic creature who thinks the whole world is against him and everyone is out to get him. He has never been able to face his own limitations and failures. He is compelled to blame them on somebody else. Like when he lost his job. He could be a good worker, but when his boss caught him drunk at work, he tried to use his wife's miscarriage as his excuse. Never take responsibility for behaviour you can blame on somebody else.

"Constable Werbowski is exceptional at her job, Duncan. Let me go and then you can disappear. If you're right, they'll never find you and I can go back to my life. What do you hope to accomplish?"

"Janine, I want to make you suffer like I suffered all those years in jail. Listen. What the food is like—doesn't matter. What there is to do to pass the time— doesn't matter. Who's with you—doesn't matter. All that matters is you're stuck, locked in a box. Day after day. I want you to know what confinement is like. You sent me into a box for forty months. You've been here for not even forty hours, so far! Now…I won't be back for a couple of days. Old Shelia might get suspicious. There's some kind of special dinner for everyone at the shelter tomorrow night. I expect to get some juicy information from her afterward. By the way, you might as well have these. They won't help you bust lose."

Before she has a chance to argue or encourage more details, he tosses her sandals in between the bars, and closes the outside door. Darkness is instant, with only the back light behind low-lying clouds to guide her to the cot. She hears the truck motor roar. He did not add lye.

Cold meatloaf in the dark. Ronny, oddly comforted as the dusk drifts away and blackness fills the voids, tries to put together what she knows. He found out she lives in Hayworth somehow. He knows about the fundraisers and the publicity might be a clue. He has convinced Sheila Pasco of his affection for her. Sheila has no idea of his true identity. He knows who Ava and Maggie are. She has suggested Fiona knows her history, which is a lie, but maybe Ava has told Fiona by now. She is confident they will review all stolen vehicles in the Sudbury area. He thinks he's in the clear. Ronny hopes he remains over-confident.

The meatloaf is good. The temperature in the cabin is too hot to leave the food for tomorrow, so she eats cold mashed potatoes with congealed gravy, hard little peas, and meatloaf with a spicy tomato sauce she could have done without. It could be days before she has options besides crackers and peanut butter.

She drinks the water he brought her. There is a reluctance born from awareness of the possibilities, but she has a need to defy caution and simply believe she will be okay. He could have poisoned the first batch of water, she rationalizes. It proved to be safe, so why would this water kill her? It feels cool and tastes good. She has had nothing but small sips for so long. A big gulp of water is a novelty. She rolls the liquid around in her mouth to wash her teeth and rinse away the flavours of the cold dinner. Refreshed would be too strong a word. She is satisfied.

Surely to God, Ava won't permit Sheila's new beau—Devon—to come to a shelter get-together. She is certain this dinner is an attempt to find a way to keep spirits up, given the circumstances. Everyone will be re-traumatized as this brings back memories of Roz. Ava and Maggie will know the difference. Fiona and Sean will know by now. Maybe they have even told her landlord. Gaby Ridgway wouldn't know her real identity unless someone told her. A staff and clients dinner at the shelter. Ronny fantasizes being there. She wonders if Marjorie Westerman is still a resident. If she is, she would be the one to do the planning. She wants to give back. She knows she has no need to be at Segue House anymore.

She stretches out on the cot and relishes her current lack of anxiety as her feet rest on the toilet seat safely tucked under the blanket at the end of the bed. He won't be back. She will sleep and hope Fiona finds her tomorrow.

Chapter 10

Ava

The local grocery store, an IGA with a smattering of most essentials, is busier than Ava anticipated for first thing in the morning. She makes a valiant attempt to pick up the items Marjorie said she would need for the barbecue tonight. With the money provided by Marjorie Westerman, Ava methodically chooses hamburger, buns, salad ingredients, ice cream, and a couple of sauces along with some sprinkles to make sundaes. Marjorie said she would take care of preparation but wanted to avoid being seen downtown in case her husband appeared. Her rationale is odd. She will go to the bank or to the lawyer's office, but currently refuses to go anywhere else. Despite her obvious concern about potential confrontation, the woman needs to make a move. The thought prompts a reminder to have a talk with her reluctant resident once Ronny is found.

Once Ronny is found…will there be a time when Ronny is found? Ava's face starts to crumble as she pushes her cart down the frozen food aisle. No one else in the store seems to have any idea the gravity of her circumstances. Nobody peers at her with unasked questions in their eyes. No one has even stopped her to say hello, even though she is well-known in the community. Maybe that's the problem! Maybe no one has the courage to even say a good morning. She makes an attempt at composure before she turns the corner and begins to roll toward the cashier.

"Hi, Ava. You're here early." Sadie, the most seasoned employee at the IGA, mans the register.

Ava suddenly realizes the woman would have no idea about the crisis at the shelter. Of course, there has been no public declaration. How would anybody know? How does anybody ever really know the pain of another? She forces a warm expression but senses the aura of a wince enveloping her face regardless. "Good morning, Sadie. I have a little staff dinner planned for this afternoon. Thought I'd get a head start and beat the rush." She explains her unusual behaviour with a semblance of the truth. As she hears her own words, she almost believes them.

Sadie, with a rhythm honed from experience, punches the numbers into the cash register and hands Ava her slip. They load the paper bags together. Ava always tries to help. After all, she must be ten years younger than Sadie.

When she pulls up in front of Segue House in her Chrysler, the place seems deserted, like an empty building one might understandably be afraid to enter. Maybe Fiona called. Maybe there's bad news. She takes a deep breath and unlocks the trunk as Sheila breaks all their security protocols and bursts through the steel door to come and help.

"I saw you through the window in the lounge. I can help you carry 'em. I know they're heavy."

Ava wants to yell at her; give the woman shit for not waiting until she was buzzed in through the security door into the space where she could be identified. To hell with security. Let her help. What difference will her behaviour make? "Sheila, you should have waited until I was inside," is all she manages to say as admonishment.

"Maggie's waitin' to buzz us in. No problem. See! I even have my ID in my pocket. I remembered." She smirks at Ava. Her lips stretch across her neglected teeth. She seems to receive Ava's unspoken thoughts telepathically. "I wanted to help you, Ava. Marjorie's already downstairs and chompin' at the bit to get busy in the kitchen. Maggie's been tryin' to slow her down until you came back."

Ava shakes her head and throws the handles of her purse across her shoulder. "Come on then. We should be able to manage five bags. Careful. This one has ice cream and needs to go straight to the freezer."

"Did you get vanilla? I only like vanilla, Ava."

She sounds like a child sometimes. "Yes, I bought vanilla as well as chocolate. I found butterscotch and chocolate sauces, too. I also gathered up all the essentials for a salad. Salads are good for you. Your diet could do with improvement, Sheila." Sheila has her eyes down, intent on the bags, but Ava knows she is paying attention.

They manoeuvre up to the front door where Sheila leans on the buzzer. When the intercom cracks and Maggie answers, Sheila jams her face against the box and yells out their identification. Ava's sure the neighbours two streets over probably heard her. Once in the foyer, with the outside door secure, Maggie buzzes them in and reaches for a bag to help. Marjorie rushes out and whisks the ice cream off to the freezer which is tucked into an empty corner of the kitchen.

"Okay, Marjorie. I will leave you to your chores. If I missed an item, let me know and I will try to go back to the store at lunchtime. We decided we are nine adults and two children, right? Gaby and Joe will be here and we can assume Sean and Fiona will at least have a burger when they turn up. You and June plus the three of us and June's children. Are we set?"

"Does your count include me, Ava?" Sheila turns to ask as she puts the bag with the meat on the counter.

"Of course you're included, Sheila. Why? Do you prefer not to have dinner with us tonight? Fiona said she and Sean would brief us all on what's happened with the case so far. Ronny's been gone forty-eight hours!"

"Can Devon come?" She presents doe eyes and a twisted pout to her boss, but all Ava sees is a poor, plain girl in all likelihood sucked in by some smooth operator.

"You know the cops have to do a check on him, first, Sheila. Take him to the police station so they can get his information and run a background. Then we'll see. Don't push, Sheila. I have no patience today. Will you come to supper or not?"

"Nope."

"Then we will be eight adults and two children, Marjorie. If we're settled, I need to spend some time in my office." She no sooner gets her purse stashed into her file cabinet and her ass stuffed into her chair when Maggie's soft tap breaks the momentary solitude she so craves.

"Did you hear any news overnight? I need to talk to you."

"Now, Maggie? Is it important? I expect Fiona to call any minute."

"Two topics, Ava." Maggie sits in the chair across from Ava's desk.

Ava knows there is no way to stop her assistant once she starts. "I'm all ears, Maggie. What's on your mind?" Ava leans back in her chair.

"First, may I invite Rose tonight? I know the police will be here. I told Rose last night, Ava. I wanted you to know I told her Ronny's secret."

Ava isn't surprised, except maybe that Maggie hadn't spilled the beans earlier. Maggie is exceedingly close to her sister, but fiercely loyal to Segue House. Rose is cleared as a friend of the shelter and Ronny wouldn't mind, given the circumstances. "Yes, Rose is more than welcome. Tell Marjorie we're back up to nine adults, okay?"

Maggie nods, then checks to ensure the door is closed completely, and ploughs on. "Rose and I met Sheila's boyfriend at the diner last night. His name is Devon Thompson. He seems odd to me, somehow. I'm puzzled about him."

"Odd how, Maggie?"

"Well, first of all, the air was so hot and humid last night before the storm and he sat in the diner dressed in a jean jacket and a ball cap. The ball cap logo was for the Maple Leafs."

"Maybe he has moved from down east, Maggie. Maybe he was cold."

She frowns. "He and Sheila left and then he came back by himself and bought another special to go. He had already eaten one. Why would he buy another one?"

"He might have wanted the same dinner for tonight. Maggie, there is little we can do for Sheila. I know you worry, like me, that some guy will take advantage of her, but Sheila is a grown woman. You go call Rose and speak to Marjorie. If the other line lights up, I want to answer because the caller will no doubt be Fiona."

"Okay." Maggie sounds resigned but Ava knows the topic will come up again.

The second line rings right away, and Ava is relieved to hear the sound of Fiona's brisk voice at the other end.

"I have some news, Ava. We have a lead on a stolen truck, taken from a community a few miles north of Sudbury in May. Although pretty nondescript, it should be easy to find in a town this size. Who do we have for the briefing later today?"

"The 'briefing' has turned into a barbecue sponsored by one of our residents. You and Sean are invited. Maggie will be here, along with her sister Rose. Gaby Ridgway and Joe Dodd said they would come. We have another client, a young woman and her two children, who will be here. Sheila won't be around."

"Okay. Sounds fine. My C.O. wants to come, too. Have you ever met him? Staff Sergeant Wendell Murphy? He wants to do the briefing. He wants to emphasize that we keep this out of the news as long as we can. Maybe not the best option, but he happens to be the boss."

"Yes. I agree—especially if you have a lead on the vehicle. In any event, you'll be able to tell him the people here are trustworthy. Everyone is anxious, supportive of you folks, and can keep information quiet. See you later today." After she hangs up, she goes out to the kitchen to let Marjorie know there will be one more.

****

Marjorie is busy in the office unit kitchen and out on the back deck all afternoon. Ava watches her and thinks it would be nice if they could have someone like Marjorie around all the time—like a house mother of sorts. Ava is decidedly not domestic. She has never seen Marjorie as contented as she appears to be this afternoon.

Maggie has asked three times if Sean Knox will be there for sure. Ava is surprised Maggie would express an interest in anyone, in particular, a policeman as reticent as Sean. He always seems to give Fiona the lead—a very quiet guy.

It is a blessing there are no new referrals. Segue House is often full to the rafters during the winter months. In the summer, women have more options. Travel to the home of a relative, or the city, is easier. School is out. Moving is less risky. In the winter, choices are limited. One never knows what will happen on any given day, but right now she can breathe easy and focus her attention on Ronny.

Having the opportunity to focus on her missing counsellor may not be a good thing. Although she tries to maintain control, ruminations about the possibilities reduce her to tears. In her fifty-two years on this earth, she has never felt so overwhelmed with fear. The closest was when her mother wandered off and she couldn't find her for almost four hours. At the time, Edna Burrway's dementia was advanced. Ava had rigged up bells over the doors so she could hear from almost any place in the house, if her mother tried to leave.

Mrs. Burrway continually searched for Ava's father who died a dozen years earlier. On this particular evening, the wind howled. Rain lashed the windows.

Ava was in the bathroom upstairs. The sound of bells on the back door must have been drowned out by the wind. She searched for an hour before she called neighbours as well as the police. Patrol cars went up and down the road. A farmer lit up his tractor and started to cruise through the fields. Thank God for the warm weather although they were all wet to the skin.

By midnight, the wind began to calm and Ava heard cries from the barn. She found her mother inside the locked building, under the tractor, crouched in almost the exact spot where Ava's father had collapsed so many years before. She had crawled in through broken slats at the back. Ava hadn't even known they were there.

The difference between her mother's disappearance and Ronny's current circumstance is no one meant to do Edna any harm. Regardless of the outcome, even though the result could have been tragic, there was no fear of intentional violence. Ava shivers, despite the warm day, as she thinks about Duncan Taylor and what he might do or has already done. She tries to calm down. Sheila appears at her door.

"I'm goin' for a few hours. Back in good time, though. Out for a drive with Devon, and then someplace for supper."

"I wish you would stay, Sheila, but the decision is up to you. I expect your Devon can manage one evening on his own." She tries to appear supportive but knows her irritation has percolated to the surface. Sheila does not need to go on a date in the middle of all this. If he were a decent guy, he would understand.

"He seemed pissed because he couldn't come here for supper. I don't want him to be mad at me. We just started to go out."

Ava's mind reacts to all the inappropriate elements contained in Sheila's excuse, but this afternoon will not turn into a teaching moment for the woman. To permit men to rule your life is the first step down a troublesome path, but Ava gives her the merest of nods and tells her to have a good time; to try to be back early. She prefers not to stay at the shelter past eight in the evening but does not want the residents to be there alone.

****

Not long after Sheila leaves, Marjorie peeks in the office door to report that a squad car and an unmarked police car have pulled into the back lot which is separated from access to the building by a locked gate. Anyone who parks in the back has to walk around to the front. The buzzer sounds.

Ava's knowledge of Staff Sergeant Wendell Murphy is limited. They met through the fundraiser ball they do each year in cooperation with the force. He's been in Hayworth for a couple of years. He has a wife and two teenagers. Ava can't recall their genders. Sean and Fiona are off duty and in street clothes. Despite their familiarity with the shelter, they remain a respectable distance behind their boss.

Ava starts to bark orders. "Maggie, run upstairs and get June. When did Gaby and Joe say they would be here?"

Maggie, her hand on the stair rail, leans back down into the foyer. "They close their shop at five, so anytime, I would think. Gaby said she would bring Martha, her dog, so June's kids will be occupied in the backyard during the time of the briefing." She nods to the three police personnel as they move toward the living room of the main office.

As predicted, just as Ava makes introductions to Marjorie, the buzzer jangles again to mark the arrival of Gaby and Joe, as well as Rose who has parked out front. Gaby hustles Martha inside, chats to the children, and introduces them to her dog. A friendly dog is oftentimes the great equalizer.

Marjorie comes in from the deck where she has heaped charcoal on the grill. She is obviously all organized in her role as chef. With a questioning lift of her perfectly groomed brows, she regards Ava from across the room.

"Okay. I think everybody's here." Ava glances over at Fiona and nods. "Sheila is out for supper tonight. I can fill her in later. For everybody's benefit, but especially Staff Sergeant Murphy, I will make introductions." She nods at each person as she goes around the room. "Gaby Ridgway and Joe Dodd are Ronny's landlords." She again meets Fiona's eye. "They are not yet aware of Ronny's history. June and Marjorie are current residents of the shelter, and they, too, are not aware. You all know Maggie. This is her sister Rose, a friend of the shelter and of Ronny. They, like me, know about Ronny's past. There. That's everyone." She continues to focus on Fiona, but the staff sergeant stands up to face the group.

Wendell Murphy is a big man. He fills the room. He makes the furniture appear miniature. His hands are like platters. Ava imagines him gripping a hamburger, and how the whole meal would disappear like magic inside his fist. His voice resembles a low rumbling muffler on a souped-up hot rod. He clears his throat.

"First, I want you all to know we are doing everything we can to locate Miss Étang. To brief those of you who do not know, Miss Étang was formerly known as Janine Taylor and was married to Duncan Taylor. He was imprisoned because he attempted to kill her. He was released from incarceration in April of this year."

Ava surveys the room. Gaby sits in an overstuffed chair while Joe is propped on the arm. Her left hand rests on his leg. The gesture is casual but Ava is overwhelmed by its intimacy. She yearns to be touched. She can't remember how many years it has been since anybody loved her. Maggie stands behind Rose, who seems to be quite uncomfortable in a straight-backed chair dragged in from the dining area. Both Maggie's hands are on the back of the chair and the act serves to make them appear as one unit. Again, Ava's heart lurches at the sight. An only child never connects in quite the same way.

Murphy continues. "Miss Étang is from Sudbury, Ontario. We believe Mr. Taylor stole a green Ford F-150 pickup truck from a small town north of Sudbury and made his way here sometime in late May or early June. Details are sketchy and we have no idea how he discovered Miss Étang's whereabouts. This is part of the ongoing investigation. We are certain he grabbed her at the Four Corners Petro-Canada on Monday when she stopped there for coffee on her way to Carter River to a meeting. Her car was located there with her purse and keys inside. There was no sign of a struggle. Witnesses at the restaurant describe a bald man with tattoos. The description provided consistently included a bar code tattoo on the back of his head. We know this man is Duncan Taylor. He may well go by an alias. We also assume Taylor had her under surveillance for some time and may even know where she lives.

"We need everyone to be alert but to keep this information confidential for another day or two. Constable Werbowski and Constable Knox will provide details of any updates. We are reluctant to involve the media for now."

Ava knows the importance of not spooking Taylor. If Ronny is still alive, they don't want to push him to hurt her. Murphy avoids pointing this out.

"Are there any questions?"

The group is silent.

Marjorie stands up. "Supper will be ready in the length of time it takes me to cook the burgers."

Chapter 11

Shelia

She is crammed into the passenger seat of an old grey Datsun pickup unfamiliar to her when he stopped in front of the shelter to fetch her. She hoped they'd go to the hotel for supper, but instead she watches empty fields and the Four Corners Petro-Can speed by as she assumes they're on their way to Carter River. The drive is long, but she refuses to complain. Devon is already cross with her for some reason. He seems mad. He neither makes eye contact nor speaks. She sees the service station where they found Ronny's car on Monday. The thought gives her the creeps as they whiz past.

"What's with the different truck, Devon?" She attempts conversation. He hasn't said much since they left Hayworth. He picked her up right on time. She was anxious to see him although hesitant when the Datsun stopped. She needed a split second before she recognized him in the cab. He honked the horn and then she was sure. They sped off. The cab is small and smells like cigarettes and stale sweat. The bucket seats are frayed and her window won't roll down.

"I thought I needed a change. The Ford had some problems. So, you didn't hear what the cops said to everyone?"

Sheila thinks he might be fishing for information that's none of his business, and not getting details is the reason for his bad mood. She wants to trust him but has no information to share. "The cops weren't there when I left. Sean and Fiona were coming, along with their boss. Gaby and Joe, Maggie's sister Rose. They will tell me more tomorrow. You could be a shelter friend like Maggie's sister, and be included in the social stuff. All you have to do is get cleared by the cops. Easy." She gazes over at him and attempts to lighten his mood with a big-eyed and trusting expression.

His face never changes. He takes off the ever-present ball cap to scratch his smooth dome. A bizarre tattoo is partially visible from the side. It seems odd because it looks like one of those symbols you see on boxes at the grocery store. "I don't have the time to get a clearance check. All I want to know is the status of the damned search. The cops must be pretty slow on the draw, if they haven't found her yet."

Sheila tries to change the subject. Ava wasn't pleased she went out instead of remaining with everyone for the briefing. Sheila hates her life when Ava is annoyed with her. Ava is the one person in the world Sheila wants to please. She attempts to understand why she wanted to go out with Devon tonight. Since he is her first proper boyfriend, she didn't want him to feel neglected. So now, Devon's mad because she has no information and Ava's mad because she left. For her effort, everybody's pissed with her. "Are we on the way to Carter River for supper? Remember, I have to be back to the shelter early, Devon. Ava's already ticked that I came out with you instead of staying."

At the moment she asks the question, he takes the turn into Pimiskaw, a small community about ten miles past the Petro-Can and down a side road. The whole place consists of a Co-op store, a grain elevator, a few scattered houses along intersecting pot-holed gravel roads, and a tavern. All the structures seem to be settled a few feet in front of the tangled bush leading to a vast expanse of fields and more woods.

"Do you know where you are, yet? You think you're so smart."

Despite oftentimes not recognizing the innuendos present in a conversation, Sheila doesn't miss the smirk and the mocking tone in his voice. All of a sudden, she wants to go home. "There ain't much time, Devon. I wanna be back at the shelter by eight, so we only have an hour or so for supper."

He walks in front of her as they approach the tavern. She hesitates. He seems different. He has a swagger about him that becomes exaggerated the closer they get to the building. When they go out in Hayworth, he always wears the jean jacket and the ball cap. This might be the first time she has seen him without the hat. He makes a habit of keeping his head down and his eyes on the floor. Here, his chin is elevated, his shoulders are back, and the sleeves of his jacket are pushed up to reveal more tattoos.

He hauls open the black barn board door with the brass handle finished to look antique. Sheila quickly lunges to grab it when he lets go. Her eyes take a moment to adjust to the dark. The tavern is one big room with two pool tables in an L-shaped alcove, a bar running the length of the space, and maybe thirty tables scattered about with four chrome and red vinyl chairs at each. The floor is wood the colour of molasses, and the walls are paneled in a slightly lighter shade. There's a juke box in the corner at the end of the bar, alive with lights provided by ribbons of pulsing neon around the sides. Charley Pride belts out "Honky Tonk Blues" as they enter.

"Find a place to sit and order supper if you're in such a hurry. I need a piss and then I have to talk to a guy." He never makes eye contact when he says this, and then he struts his way toward a "Cowboys" sign.

Sheila tries to get her bearings as her eyes become accustomed to the dimness and the heavy influence of cigarette smoke draping the dusty air. Although they are smack in the middle of farm country, the bar appears filled with bikers or biker-wannabes. They must be like Devon and drive trucks, because all she saw were two motorcycles parked in the lot. She searches out other women, and sees the waitress who serves drinks and another gal behind the bar. They seem normal enough, so Sheila starts to relax a little. She wanders over toward what she senses might be the safety of the bar, and catches the bartender's eye. "Can I get a couple menus?"

"There are no menus. We do rib-eye steaks and baked beans—supper, take it or leave it." The woman is attractive. Sheila is a poor judge of ages, but maybe thirty. She has long dark and wavy hair tied in a knot on the top of her head. She's dressed like the waitress, in a black low-cut T-shirt and black jeans, with a canvas apron around her waist tied with a knot in the front.

Sheila is anxious to order, but wants to know how Devon would like his steak cooked, so she nods her thanks and returns to the table. He's been gone a long time.

After twenty minutes, he approaches Sheila with an unapologetic, "Did you order?"

"No. I didn't know how you want your steak!"

"Well, you're the one in the goddamned hurry. Hey Penny! Two dinners. Make the steaks medium, 'cause we're in a rush. And two drafts." He glares down at Sheila. "Are you satisfied?"

His tone is snide; almost sarcastic. She doesn't understand why. Her stomach is in knots. Although she lacks relationship experience of any consequence, Sheila is confident she has done nothing wrong. She folds her hands in her lap and nods. She likes her steak well-done but says nothing.

"You must come here a lot, eh? You know the waitress by name." Sheila tries to control her voice, so the words sound like a comment and not a criticism.

"Until I met you, I ate here every night. I stay upstairs most of the time. They have cheap rooms. The place is out of the way. I like the people." This is the most conversation they have had since he picked her up.

It seems early to bring out a karaoke machine. Some big guy, with a shaved head like Devon, lugs the contraption from the back at the same time as their suppers are plunked down unceremoniously in front of them. A short fellow with red hair, dressed in a white sequined suit just like what Elvis used to wear, appears out of a dark corner. The outfit wants to be leather. It has a cape and a big turned-up collar. The pants are bell-bottoms. The guy also sports a number of blue silk scarves around his neck. Although dead almost seven years, people still worship Presley. Sheila, never much of a fan, is quite unprepared for what happens next.

The little impersonator reaches for the microphone and takes it from the stand. He simpers at the patrons—all dozen or so of them—and lifts the side of his lip in an Elvis inspired sneer as the music begins the introduction for "Jailhouse Rock". When he opens his mouth, the crowd, a majority of whom seem to know him and are fans, start to cheer, whistle, and stomp their feet. Sheila thinks the singer is so good, if you close your eyes, you could almost believe Elvis is in the room. Before the song is over, the tavern has filled up. There are people at every table and some move spare chairs to expand the seating capacity at other tables. The good folks of Pimiskaw obviously know what time this guy sings. They all seemed to come in at once.

"Sing 'Blue Christmas'," somebody hollers from the far end of the bar, and Jonah, as Sheila has learned this is his real name, happily obliges. Everybody joins in on the chorus. A part of Sheila would like to hang around until later in the evening. If this is the commotion he causes before seven o'clock, she wonders what the place will be like in a few hours.

Devon appears oblivious to the music or the increased size of the crowd. He feverishly saws at his steak and wolfs down the beans. He hunches over the table and elevates his elbow, as he shovels in the food. Sheila's suddenly a wee bit disgusted, as she watches him chew with his mouth open and, for all intents and purposes, ignore her presence. She has nibbled around the corners of her steak and forced down a couple of spoons full of beans. She hopes maybe Marjorie put leftovers in the fridge and she'll eat when she gets back to Segue House, the sooner the better.

Jonah is on a roll, and now serenades the crowd with "Love Me Tender" as Devon scrapes back his chair, tosses a twenty on the table, and raises his eyebrows as he glares down at Sheila. She takes the hint and gets up. She peers around, hoping to catch the eye of the girl tending bar to nod her thanks, but the place is jumping and nobody seems to notice their departure.

The August evening sunshine blinds her as Devon opens the tavern door. She forgot it would still be daylight and squints like she has just emerged from another universe located deep in the earth.

"We should be back before your curfew. You wanted to go back, right?" Devon looks toward the truck and not at her as he speaks.

She sighs. "Right. Ava said it was important I get back by then, but it's not a curfew! Sorry if I ruined your evening somehow." She feels a little pouty and knows her voice contains an annoying whine.

"Find out what the cops reported about Ja…Ronny."

"They'll tell me about the briefing, Devon, but stuff might all be confidential. Don't expect me to repeat things I shouldn't. I could lose my job."

"Nobody would fault you if you told your boyfriend, now, would they?" His voice is soft. He reaches across the smelly cab and pats her knee.

The words "boyfriend" or "girlfriend" have never been said before. Sheila's confused. She thought he wouldn't call again after the way he acted tonight. He parks on the street, down a couple of spots from the front of the shelter. He leans across the cab again. This time he takes off his ball cap and kisses her right on the lips.

Sheila feels tingly and shaky all over. She reaches up to touch him but he pulls away and slaps the cap back on by the time Rose and Maggie drive by in Rose's Malibu.

"I'll call you tomorrow and take you for coffee later on."

"Okay, Devon. Talk to ya' tomorrow. Thanks for the trip to Pimiskaw so I could see some of your friends and where you stay." Still a little wobbly, she elbows the rusty door open and sticks out one ample leg. Slamming the door is harder than one might think. The hinges have begun to seize up and they creak with the effort. She leans over and waves a flat hand behind the frozen passenger window. The truck shutters and smoke rushes from the tail pipe as Devon jerks down the street.

Ava answers the intercom and they go through the mutual ritual of identification so Sheila can re-enter her home and workplace. Everybody is gone except Marjorie, in the kitchen tidying up, and Ava, packing her big purse as she prepares to leave for the night.

"So, what did the cops say?" Sheila's anxious to get back in the loop.

"Not a lot, really. Can I catch you up later tomorrow after you've finished your shift and had your sleep? I'm exhausted. The whole day has been a challenge. Suffice to say, they haven't found her yet. Everybody's pretty sick about the whole situation." She sidles past Sheila, who remains in the office doorway. "Thanks for all your efforts, Marjorie. Supper was great and I appreciate all you did. We'll talk tomorrow. See you, Sheila." She adds as an afterthought, "I assume you enjoyed a nice supper with, what's his name again?"

"Devon. Yeah. Fine. We went all the way out to the Pimiskaw Tavern. We can talk tomorrow." Sheila struggles to disguise her disappointment. She had imagined arriving, sitting down at the kitchen table, and listening to Ava tell her about the meeting while she ate leftovers. The front door bangs shut.

Sheila starts her evening routine. She ensures both dead bolts on the back door are secure. She will go around and check the gate before she tries to find a bite to eat.

"Can I get you a plate, Sheila?" Marjorie is still in the kitchen, wearing yellow rubber gloves and a flowered apron. She seems, for all the world, like Lucille Ball about to start her day. Instead, she has cleaned up after a barbecue where she prepared food for Sheila isn't sure exactly how many.

"What's left over? I'm starved."

"I thought you went out to dinner."

"The food wasn't very good, Marjorie."

"Well, I can get you whatever you like. If a couple of burgers reheated in the microwave is okay, I can make you up a plate. Sit down. You can double check the locks after I fix you some supper. Tell me all about this boyfriend of yours, and where you went."

Sheila is anxious to secure the premises. She has a routine and is focused on sticking to it. That way, she remembers every step. "You fix me a plate while I take a spin around the property. Then you can buzz me back in." Sheila's never spent much time with Marjorie before, but she seems nice enough; motherly, somehow.

She checks all access points. The back gate is secure. For a second, she thinks she sees Devon's old green Ford rumble along the street behind the shelter but even if it is the Ford, he said he got rid of it, so it would not be him anyway.

She returns to the intercom at the front so Marjorie can buzz her in. Security is fine. She sits down at the kitchen table in front of a fine meal of barbecue leftovers. "There's ice cream for dessert, too." Sheila loves the way Marjorie smiles at her from the other side of the table, and how she holds her tea mug with both her hands—interested; as if she cares.

"Were you at the briefing? Want to fill me in on the details?"

"My goodness, Sheila! I have no authority to report to you. I might get a piece of information wrong."

"Come on, Marjorie! I won't hold ya to it. What did the cops say?"

"They haven't found her. Ronny Étang is not her real name. They have a description of the guy and the truck they think he stole. They think her ex-husband took her but there are few details. I am not very good at names or places. My husband used to say I couldn't keep track of particulars, so you would be wise to wait for Ava to fill in the blanks. They did say any information shouldn't go outside the house. They don't want the media to know what's happened yet. I think they're afraid, if they alert him and he hasn't hurt her, he might feel cornered and…"

Sheila munches away on her second hamburger, satisfied to know something of what's happened. Whoever took Ronny is sure to be long gone by now. Ronny is no doubt dead. She swallows and then takes a swig of iced tea. She'll have patience and wait until tomorrow to find out the details, although she expects it won't make any difference. Nobody has ever located that other girl. The north is a big place—lots of spots to hide a body where it will never be found.

Chapter 12

Ronny

He forgot, perhaps on purpose, to leave her any lye. After two and a half days, the stench has settled like sour milk in the back of her throat. She takes little breaths through her mouth. The process has left her exhausted and the taste of the air is foul. If the weather would break, she might have some relief, but the dust and grit stick to her damp skin. Thank God her hair is short, but her scalp itches, nonetheless. She tries not to imagine an infestation of lice or fleas. She continues to be afraid to drink too much water in case she runs out.

Would a cry help? What about a scream? She hasn't heard the sound of machinery, so harvesting does not appear to be going on nearby, and Wednesday is almost over. She expected someone would be out combining. If they stopped for any reason, she would yell at the top of her lungs. This hope has been her abiding light, but now it has begun to fade.

She wipes the sweat from her forehead with filthy hands. She is panicked she'll lose her grip, so tries to rope her emotions together with memories in order to escape the desperate uneasiness of what might be in store for her.

****

One of the most positive happenstances, when she first moved to Hayworth, was her initial residency at The Station. She met Patrick first. The bus let her off at the local diner and he was occupied behind the counter when she stumbled in the door. He had trouble with the correct pronunciation of her last name. Everybody did. They wanted to know if they were saying it right. She can smile now, as she recalls her rationale for the name change from Janine Taylor to Veronica Étang. Étang is the French word for pond and her mother's favourite movie star from the 1940s was Veronica Lake. Lake. Pond. She thought the name symbolic. Murdock Blackney, the local lawyer who handled all the paperwork after she moved, thought she could have been less creative and more practical. In any event, people started to call her Ronny and figured out how to say her last name after a while. She is Ronny Étang now, body and soul. When Duncan calls her Janine, she experiences nausea, like he expects a dead person to answer.

Patrick Hollinger is a nice kid. She thinks "kid", but he must be near thirty. When she first arrived in Hayworth and was a guest at the Wolski's second and secret wedding ceremony, he was renewing the relationship with his father after years of separation. Before Thanksgiving, he was embroiled in a situation involving some woman who had murdered a guy down east. He transformed from an ordinary young guy who worked at the diner, to a very troubled fellow—paranoid, sullen, and uncommunicative. After Charlene Quinn was arrested, he snapped back to himself. He told her he sees a psychiatrist and takes medication for schizophrenia. Maggie has the same shrink, Dr. Rachel Wilkerson, and is quite forthright about her history in an institution.

She met Chester, Amanda, and their little boy, Mason soon after she arrived at the diner. The Wolskis manage the six unit apartment building, and were very good to her right from the day she arrived. Amanda, with her bright red hair, was always easy to find and generous with help, advice, and even her telephone until Ronny settled in. Chester, a Ford mechanic, is exceedingly attractive. His movie star handsomeness seems to improve with age. Amanda invited her to their secret "second" marriage. The small ceremony took place at The Station on Victoria Day of 1981, a few days after Ronny arrived. Later, Amanda revealed she was married years ago to some rich low-life guy. When she caught him with someone else, she jumped in her truck one day and drove west. After a couple of years, he divorced her, but not until after she had already married Chester. Her friend, Ben Tullis, helped her resolve the situation. Amanda and Chester have a little girl, Melanie, as well now.

Rose and Maggie Woodward both lived across the hall from Ronny's new apartment. They introduced themselves the afternoon she moved in, took her to the local grocery store, and invited her to supper. Rose is very motherly and works at Dr. Gunton's office. She has been employed there for years, and seems to know everybody in town. Maggie is a contradiction; a creature of mystery with no secrets. To describe this ethereal, yet down-to-earth, woman who is frank but secretive somehow, is always a challenge. She is so open, personally. She will tell you absolutely any detail you might want to know and sometimes you get more than you bargained for. As the bookkeeper at Segue House, it was necessary she be informed about Ronny's identity change. Ronny is quite certain she has never told anyone, not even Rose. The whole town probably knows by now.

Ava Burrway is the undisputed foundation of Segue House. Ronny permits herself the luxury of remembering her boss for a few minutes. Ava showed her the ropes but graced her with enough confidence to allow her to create her practice while she established a niche in the support community of Hayworth. As a lay counsellor, she needed a great deal of help. Ava provided whatever professional guidance she required; still does. Since May of 1981, Ronny has completed all the courses necessary to obtain her Social Work Certificate from the community college. Ava gave her the time and the encouragement. She firmly believed Ronny, a former mining company clerk from Sudbury, had the capability necessary. Ava took a chance on her, and Ronny will be forever beholden.

Ronny still knows very little about Ava, whose private life remains unreachable, even after more than three years. Ronny suspects Ava owns the former apartment building used for the shelter. It seems to be the logical option. There's no landlord and the amount of money they manage to raise, through the Segue House Annual Ball and government grants, would never be enough to pay a lease on a place like Segue House. The bills are always covered. Ava will magically secure another grant at the last minute. Maggie probably knows how much support Ava kicks in, but would never reveal any information.

Ronny, through her work, met Cheryl Nadler before Joe Dodd, the two other Station tenants. Although they managed a few joint cases from the very start, Ronny and Cheryl became fast friends when Ronny hosted Thanksgiving dinner and Cheryl asked if she could help out. The social worker is odd in many ways, but a nice odd. Ronny knows Cheryl is quite particular; almost obsessive. As she revealed parts of her history to Ronny over the years, she said she was once much worse. She experienced a terrible childhood. Ronny does not know every detail, but is quite sure Cheryl was a runaway or abandoned when she was a teenager. She has a daughter she gave up for adoption at birth. Her name is Amy and she's eighteen now, or almost eighteen. She has been to visit a couple of times and Cheryl is very proud of her. She oftentimes gives Ben Tullis full marks for convincing her to make contact. Cheryl still resides at The Station. She says she stays because of the abundance of hot water.

Joe Dodd lived at The Station until the fall of 1983 when he and Gaby Ridgway made their relationship official and moved into their new house together. Gaby is a great landlord. Ronny loves her little house on Poplar Street and wants to buy if Gaby ever decides to sell.

Tears trickle down her grimy face. What she wouldn't give to be home, curled up in her overstuffed lounger by the window, enjoying the coolness provided by the overhanging poplars. Ronny's thoughts move from her recent life and friends to her family. Could someone have figured out where she was and then told Duncan? The idea seems far-fetched, but she reviews the possibilities.

Ronny's mother, Eleanor but always called Ellie, died of cancer when Ronny was sixteen. She was sick for a long time. Ronny was pretty sure her father, Jake, started to see Sophia before her mother died. Sophia is fifteen years younger than her father and they were married within a year of her mother's death. They had two babies, both boys, in rapid succession. Ronny left home at eighteen and went to work for Sudbury Mining. She worked in the office. The job was a dead-end, but the generous salary paid her rent so she could get out of the house. She was a non-person in the family after her father remarried, and she was a non-person at work.

Her life was boring and uneventful. Circumstances changed when she met Duncan. He was popular. He liked to party. She became involved in a life far different from babysitting younger brothers and reading in her apartment. They were together all the time. She felt important, valuable. He told her she kept him on the straight and narrow. He gave her credit for keeping him from getting into fights or drinking too much. He said when he was around her, he wanted to be responsible. She happily took the credit and praise. Of course, after they were married and she lost the baby, her place in his life changed. She is still shocked that she stayed with him for so many years.

She has learned self-awareness over time. She knows she had no self-esteem after her mother died and she left home. She knows she depended on Duncan to provide her value and no matter how mean he was, or how threatened her life became, she found it cripplingly difficult to even think about leaving. The fear of becoming valueless, yet again, was paralyzing. It was Faith, from the shelter, who showed her another option. God, she was stupid!

So, her half-brothers are now twenty-six and twenty-five. She knows they were both working in Sudbury. One is an accountant and the other was in law school when she left to come out west. The fact of the matter is that she has very little information about Chad and Chet at all. Cutesy names. Part of the issue about her miscarriage was because Duncan was so close to her little brothers. He wanted boys of his own. She never bonded with them, but Duncan did.

Nobody from Sudbury knows her whereabouts except Faith. There is no way Faith could have told someone who then told her father, Sophia, or one of her brothers who in turn told Duncan. But, why would any of them betray her, even if they came upon the information? They all know he tried to kill her. Her father might be old-fashioned and wish his daughter's marriage had survived, but he couldn't have found out about Hayworth and contacted Duncan.

Maybe the circumstances were random. Maybe he just appeared in Hayworth out of nowhere like so many other people. Maybe he ran into Sheila and found out about her by accident. Maybe he saw her leaving work one day as he picked up Sheila—a simple coincidence. But he inferred he sought her out; planned this whole episode. Her head begins to ache. There's no escape from the heat, the smell, and the dirt. She lies down on top of the scratchy wool blanket and shuts her eyes.

When she wakes up, the room is almost dark and there's an actual cool breeze struggling through the three ventilation holes in the old window frame. She closes her eyes again and focuses her attention on the August night air as it floats across her exposed skin. She imagines the movement has cleansing properties. She can smell the canola fields in the distance. Ripening canola has a disgusting, rotten-eggs-mixed-with-sweaty-socks smell most people dislike, but tonight the scent reminds her of flowers.

Long ago, Ronny used babysitting money to buy her mother a bouquet of roses. Ellie was overcome with emotion when she saw her daughter take tentative steps toward her bed with the precious vase of flowers. They were all different colours—pink, red, yellow, and white. They took over the room and forced the smells of antiseptic and sick into the corners for a brief time. Ellie patted the side of the bed and Ronny crawled in beside her. They both closed their eyes and let the smell of the roses transport them away. Ellie told her daughter to imagine they were at the beach. Think about the sparkling green water. Imagine the sound of the waves breaking on the sand and feel the hot grains under her back and against her shoulders. Ronny remembers the brightness behind her eyelids and salty taste of her lips—as if she was taken from that palliative care room to a place where her life was perfect.

So, tonight, she shuts her eyes and imagines that afternoon with her mother, stretched out beside her on the bed in her room. She conjures up the pressure of Ellie's body against her; the warmth and the weave of the cotton blanket on her skin. She remembers the visions of the beach and the waves as they hit the shore. Her mind then wanders to ocean glass and sand dollars, mussel shells and periwinkles, smooth stones and sea weed. She floats on the waves with her mother by her side. She wonders if she might be losing her mind.

The night is long. Her fatigue threatens her composure. The moon casts a minimal shadowy light around the cabin as Ronny paces like a caged tiger at the zoo. She does her best not to let Duncan get to her. The truth is that she is terrified she will not get out of this alive. If they fail to find her soon, he will tire of his own cat and mouse routine and kill her. He will kill her. She knows he will, in time.

The mysterious disappearance of Roz Dover still haunts the community. Ronny moved to Hayworth three months before it happened. The whole town crumbled under the weight of the tragedy. Roz's parents even came and tried to search. The RCMP worked like dogs to find her. They only ever found her car with her keys and purse inside. They said there was no sign of a struggle and they will say the exact same phrase about her. This is a big area. Roz's body could be anywhere. The grasses and weeds take over in no time. They will never find her.

As she paces back and forth in her prison of desperate squalor, ribbons of moonlight fracture as she passes through them. She wonders if history is about to repeat itself. She will never be found. He will kill her and bury her someplace far from here. Then he will burn down the cabin so there is no trace of her; no hairs, no blood; not a scrap of her for Fiona to find. She will become another Hayworth mystery. The tears start again and she swipes at them with her fingers.

Where is Ava tonight? What about Maggie? Are they worried about me? Of course they are! Duncan said there would be a bunch getting together for supper. Perhaps they're trying to troubleshoot; to make a plan.

She paces back and forth over the chipped and broken linoleum, her arms wrapped around her chest and her chin tucked in to her neck. She tries to be rational. *Where are the weak links in Duncan's plan? The stolen truck is the first issue. The second issue is Sheila. He might make a mistake and act suspicious in some way. Sheila is not the sharpest knife in the drawer, but her loyalty to the shelter is beyond reproach. I wouldn't want to be on her bad side. If she starts to suspect her new boyfriend, Devon, is not who he says he is, then maybe there will be hope for me yet. When the day comes Sheila discovers Duncan Taylor has taken advantage of her, I suspect he will happily return to jail rather than deal with the fallout from one wild Sheila Pasco.*

She breaks her pacing pattern to stand at the window and stare into the moon bathed darkness. She gets a visual of the deep black void above the brambles outside, with the ebony star-studded sky above. The wind whispers through the leaves as they scrape against the shingled outside walls. The heavy foulness of the air is broken now and again when puffs of breeze propel the scent of canola into the cabin. Given time, a worker will be out in that field.

Someone once said we are given an average of twenty-five thousand mornings in our lifetime and a person should never squander a single one. She hears an owl hoot in the distance. He has sighted a mouse; fur shimmering in the moonlight as the creature dashes across the field. She silently roots for the mouse tonight and hopes it, too, will have another morning.

Chapter 13

~

Ava

She manoeuvres her Chrysler into the yard and stops on the grassy driveway close to the back door. She feels too lazy to settle it in the garage tonight. Darkness will fall quite soon but, after a check of the sky, she is convinced there will be no rain, just some wind. The days are shorter. She locks the house door behind her and starts to peel off clothes as she makes her way up the softwood stairs to the big bathroom at the front of the house.

When her parents bought the old place, there was already a toilet and sink installed near the kitchen. They managed to scrape together enough money to convert one of the four upstairs bedrooms into a huge bathroom. Ava's favourite element has always been the claw foot tub. There's never been a shower, although the idea has crossed her mind more than once.

She piles her clothes in a heap on her antique spool bed and walks into the bathroom naked. She turns on the water and adds some lavender bath salts. Without understanding why, she stands and stares at her reflection in the full-length mirror hung on the wall beside the cast iron sink mounted there. She could stand to lose a few pounds. She peers at her shape, sagged and flaccid, like it belongs to an old lady. She sees herself as a bit fleshy, but still curvy, at least; and reasonably comfortable in her own skin. She shrugs.

With the tub full, she eases her weary body into the hot water an inch at a time. She stretches out as far as she can and rests her head against the smooth white porcelain of the six foot bath. She reaches for the facecloth draped over the side, dips the scrap of terry cloth in the hot water, wrings it out, and places the pale pink square over her face. With a deep sigh and a slight readjustment of her legs, she begins to relax. The scent of lavender wraps around the room.

His name was Jim Brewster. Ava's lips bend upward ever so slightly beneath her facecloth veil. *No doubt he still is called Jim Brewster. He is certainly not dead.* Of course, twenty-two years have passed under the bridge of her life since she ended their affair and came home to help, and ultimately, care for her mother after her father died. Jim was quite a guy, her one true love. There has never been anybody since. At fifty-two, she feels pretty much dried up and blown away in that department.

Jim Brewster, an ambulance driver, was tall and skinny. Every time he appeared at the hospital, she felt this incredible urge to feed him; to take care of him. They started to spend time together. She lived in a small apartment in a converted 1920s mansion down the street from the hospital; it became their special place. He was married. Jim wasn't handsome in the traditional movie star way you'd imagine. His face was crooked like he'd been in a fight and not healed right. His hair was straight, brown, and hung down over one eye if not slicked back. He was her one boyfriend. They met when she was twenty-three and they were together, if you want to call their status "together", until her father died seven years later. He never asked her to come back. He never said he'd leave his wife. She knew the score.

God! Where did all these thoughts of Jim come from? She suspects they stem from her observation of the quiet ease and closeness displayed between Joe and Gaby today. As she watched them, they appeared fused together somehow; like the two of them completed a unit. Even their movements in and out of coats, chairs, or even rooms, seemed fluid and as one. They're like water merged into a wave. *What would life be like to have oneness with another person; to exist as one; to own oneness?* Would she and Jim have been that kind of couple?

She sinks down a little further into the hot water. Wet rolls over the parts of her breasts that have been exposed to the air until now. The house is talkative tonight. The wind makes the old place chatter to her—the scrape of branches on the roof; the rattle of the ancient window panes; a squeaky door in the foyer responds ever so slightly when a big gust forces its way through the aged weather-stripping. She knows all the noises. She understands her decrepit home. She has no doubt she is safe despite the isolation and the long driveway.

What if Ronny is gone? What if she is never found? How will the community cope? Roz disappeared in 1981 and Hayworth still mourns, still searches, and still wonders every day. Ava, in a sudden flash of self-awareness, realizes she is no longer sure she would continue with the shelter if Ronny is never found—or found dead. This comes as a shock, but she knows in her gut she will not want to continue.

Her original intent was to groom Ronny to take over the shelter within the next few years. Ava hoped she could withdraw in time, and focus on her personal life. She would sell the farm, including the homeplace, and get an apartment or a smaller house—maybe not here in Hayworth; maybe in Edmonton. She could lease the shelter back to the Segue House Foundation which handles the fundraising. She frowns. Maggie couldn't run the operation. Sheila couldn't manage. They wouldn't even be able to cope together.

Her mind wanders to Marjorie Westerman. She could handle the job. Ava suspects she wants to stay but there's no room in the pinched budget to hire someone else…unless, of course, Ronny is gone. Ava shuffles around in the water. The air has started to cool. Ronny will be back. She must not allow herself to think otherwise.

Tomorrow, she will have to tell Sheila about what the police said. As far as the so-called boyfriend is concerned, there is no doubt Sheila will get her heart broken. Hopefully, she will be careful in the interim between new love and the ultimate heartbreak. Sheila hasn't said much. Maggie seems concerned, but then again, every little issue concerns her. She sees complications in the minutest of details, regardless of her sunny disposition and her child-like behaviour. Maggie is an enigma.

Ava is still surprised Sheila avoided telling Devon to spend an evening on his own so she could stay for the barbecue and the briefing from the police. No matter. Tomorrow, she will fill Sheila in and remind her about how Devon needs to visit the RCMP to obtain a clearance before he can become a friend of the shelter.

Five more minutes and I'll drag myself out of here, get into my nightie, and have a cup of tea. She stretches her legs so her toes touch the far end of the tub, heaves a sigh, and settles down for a couple more minutes. She tries to focus her thoughts on the water and her body—away from the shelter and Ronny. The water is still warm enough, and wraps around her thighs; around her breasts. The back of her head is nestled into the towel hung over the end, draped there to serve as her pillow. She lifts her arms out of the water and focuses on the gurgle the movement makes as she rests underarm to fingers on the cool porcelain. She thinks this is what total vulnerability must be like.

The wind increases as darkness falls. She never turned a light on in her bedroom, so the hallway is almost black. She can barely see through the opening where the barn board door is ajar. She left no lights on downstairs, either. No matter. She will brighten the place up once she gets the energy to haul herself out of her bath.

The lights cast an eerie shadow on the bathroom wall. She can hear, above the sound of the wind, the rumble of an engine as a vehicle approaches the house. *For God's sake, who has decided to turn up this time of night? Maybe Fiona. Maybe they've found Ronny.*

The driver cuts the engine. Ava listens for the slam of a car door, while she hastily pats dry with a towel and wraps her now damp self in a housecoat. Her car is in the yard, so maybe they think she has gone to bed, since there are no lights on. She creeps over to the window and peeks out, careful not to disturb the curtain. She avoids turning on a light. An old grey pickup, a compact of some sort with the driver's door part way open, backs up, makes a U-turn, and rumbles out the lane. The licence plate is dirty and nothing looks familiar.

Ava hates to admit she might be a tiny bit rattled. Under normal circumstances, living out here and somewhat isolated has never been an issue. The doors are locked. She shouldn't be concerned a vehicle drove down her lane, shone their headlights on her house for five minutes, and then took off. But, she has no recollection of anybody ever doing this before.

She switches on the bathroom light as she leaves. She turns on the hall light and her bedroom light. After she ensures her faded floral curtains are tightly closed, she tosses her housecoat across the bed and reaches for a long blue cotton nightie. The fabric is soft after hundreds of washings and feels cool as it brushes against her skin. She leaves the lights on and pads down the wooden stairs in bare feet still soft and supple from her bath. After she turns on yet another light in the downstairs hall, she trots into the big old kitchen to make her tea.

She decides to call the shelter. She needs to hear the sound of a voice.

Sheila answers on the first ring. She must be perched at Maggie's or Ronny's desk. "Segue House. Sheila speaking. How may I help you?" Her voice sounds robotic, repeating the words she has been taught.

"Hi, Sheila. Ava here. All quiet over there tonight?"

"Hi, Ava. Fine. What's up?"

"No problem, exactly. I was in the tub and a strange vehicle came in the yard, stopped, and shone their headlights at my house. I hoped to see Fiona, but by the time I hauled myself out of the bath, they had turned around. The vehicle was some little grey truck I've never seen before."

Sheila is silent at the other end of the phone.

"Are you there, Sheila?"

"Yeah. Are you coming back in?"

"No, of course not! I guess I wanted to talk with someone for a minute. The episode made me a little jumpy."

"Oh, probably some drunk who drove down your road. Some idiot who got confused in the dark."

"You know, you're right. All the lights were out because I started my bath when it was still daylight. The driver must have thought my lane was a road, driven down as far as the house, and then when they saw the car and all the lights out they assumed the residents were in bed so they didn't knock and ask directions. Everything makes me jumpy right now."

"Tell me what the cops said yesterday."

"Tomorrow. We'll talk tomorrow, either early before you go to bed or after you get up in the afternoon. Whatever works for you."

"I want to wait for you in the morning and hear what I missed."

"I wish you had stayed, Sheila. The atmosphere was like a family meeting and you were not there. We missed you." Ava makes it a point to show Sheila she is very much a part of the group. She refuses to permit an opportunity to emerge where Sheila would sense she is isolated or on the peripheral.

"I know. Tonight wasn't fun, anyway, so I might as well have stayed with you guys."

"Next time, Sheila. You'll know better next time. My kettle's boiling, so I'm going to go and make some rosehip tea before bed. Have a good night. See you in the morning."

"Bye, Ava. See ya' tomorrow." The phone clicks in her ear before she has a chance to replace her own receiver in the cradle.

The smell of the tea calms Ava. She loses the jumpy sensation she experienced when she first came downstairs. She wanders over to the kitchen sofa and curls into a ball in the corner. She realizes she wants to be in a position where she can see her door and her driveway at the same time. Maybe calmness has eluded her after all.

****

Ava and Ronny sit together at the big kitchen table. Ronny appears different. Her hair is dark and a mass of curls. She has on a white nightie and is in her bare feet. Ava is confused. Why is Ronny at her house in a nightie and bare feet? Has she stayed over? Why does she seem so different?

Ronny asks her about her love life and Ava starts to tell her all about Gaby and Joe; what a lovely couple they are; how nice her life would be if she could find someone and have a relationship like that. Ronny smirks and says a happy marriage is an impossibility; that people act like they're happy but it's all for show. When she throws her head back and guffaws, her hair flies everywhere and seems to fill the kitchen.

Ava expects her mother. She watches the door and waits for her mother to approach. Ronny gets up from the table and locks the door.

"What are you doing?"

Ronny snarls at Ava. "I don't want her here. I don't like her. Keep her away from me." Her voice is shrill. Ava wants to cover her ears.

"But we have to let my mother in, Ronny. She is my mother. She used to live here all the time. This was her home!"

Ronny continues to shake her head, and spray dark curls around the room like a halo. The yard lights up as a vehicle comes down the drive.

Ava jumps toward the door. "Mom!" She is confused about how her mother is here, because she never learned to drive. Someone must have brought her; maybe her father. Great! Part of her thinks none of this makes sense. Her parents are dead. But they're in a car in the yard! She is positive.

Ronny's voice is deep and menacing. Ava is scared. "Do not open the door! Do not let them in!"

"But they're my parents. I haven't seen them in so long, Ronny! You have to let me see my own parents! This is my house. I need to let them in."

Ronny marches toward the locked door and stands there. She glares at Ava. "We will sit here together and wait for them to leave. We will not let them in. Do you understand? It would change the future if we let them in."

They begin to knock. It sounds like a high-pitched beeping sound, not like a normal knock at all. Ava tries to understand how this irritation could be knocking.

****

Her alarm rousts her at six-thirty, as usual. Ava requires a couple of minutes to orient out of her dream and into the throes of her morning. She stretches her legs under the tousled sheets for a couple of minutes before she faces the inevitable and starts her day. Life goes on.

Her agenda will include a meeting with Sheila. She has to try and focus on necessary paperwork which now includes all the fall grant applications. She wonders, absently, about ongoing plans for the fundraising ball scheduled for early October. Also, Cheryl Nadler mentioned the possibility of a new referral coming from Child Protection Services. The information indicated the government would intervene if the mother refused to remove the children from the common domicile. These cases are always hard, but there's lots of room right now. She also has to have a heart to heart with Marjorie Westerman. She has to go. The other option is for her to find a place to live in the area, and then volunteer with them. Ava knows Marjorie has put off the move to her sister's, and she will definitely not be returning home, so they need to explore other options.

She thinks about all this as she makes her coffee, washes up, gets dressed in a light-weight suit with capri pants, grabs her purse and keys, and makes her way to her big white Le Baron parked beside the back door. Ava always locks her car—a habit she developed when she lived in the city.

The note is on yellow craft paper and wedged under a wiper blade. She casts a quick glance around the yard and bends open the folds. "She won't be back."

****

The first move Ava makes when she gets to the office is to call Fiona.

"Someone was in my yard last night. I saw the truck leave. They left a note on the car. It says she won't be back, Fiona! The note says she won't be back!" Ava starts to shake. She slammed her door in Sheila's face when she ran into her office to make the call. The drive to the shelter was a blur.

"Try to calm down, Ava. Was the note handwritten or letters stuck on the paper?"

"It was printed in pencil." Ava silently admonishes herself for not providing that information in the first place.

"Sean and I will be there as soon as we can. Did you see the vehicle? Try to remember as much as possible about times and descriptions."

Ava replaces the phone receiver. Her hands continue to vibrate. She stares at the note again. She scribbles down her vague description of the truck she saw in her yard and a rough estimate of the time. She takes a moment to sit in her chair and stare out her office window before getting information from Sheila about a referral she took from the hospital overnight. This may well not be a good day for Ronny.

Chapter 14

~

Maggie

As she goes through her routine on this Thursday morning, three full days have passed since Ronny disappeared, and she hates to think about her friend's circumstances. Instead, she reflects on the previous evening.

Upon their return from Segue House, Maggie and Rose sat across from one another on Maggie's pink floral living room furniture, lost in their own thoughts. Each had a mug of chamomile tea on an end table beside them. Rose stared over Maggie's head and out the window behind the sofa. Maggie fixated on the kitchen peninsula. She stole a moment of slight reprieve from concerns about Ronny, as she thought about her old friend Ben and how much she loved her peninsula with the marble top.

Even the boys seemed preoccupied—each was stretched out on the bare pine floorboards. They feigned sleep as they watched their mistresses. Maggie knows cats often sense distress in the air.

Rose broke the silence. She has less stamina for personal reflection. If Rose were alone, Maggie knew the television would be blasting. Maggie has a radio although she seldom turns it on. "The police don't sound too optimistic, do they, Maggie?"

After the briefing and supper at the shelter, Maggie helped Marjorie and kept busy, although she managed to maintain one eye on Sean the whole time. He appeared frustrated, tired, and a little grumpy. She couldn't ascertain, merely by her observations, if his mood was as a result of his boss being there or if it was due to the situation in general. He stood at the back of the waiting room/living room for the duration, and then went outside on the deck to give Marjorie a hand with the grill.

Maggie wanted to talk to him but couldn't find a right time and place. Then, all of a sudden, he was standing right beside her. "When all of this is over, maybe we can go out for supper or whatever." He focused on the floor, but stood so close his words were no more than a whisper. She could smell him beside her and the momentary experience made her heart jump to her throat.

"Okay," was the only word she could manage to force out of her mouth. She turned her head a fraction and caught his eye. He nodded as he walked away.

She wanted to hold this exchange close to her and recall Sean's words over and over. At the same time, her personal hopes felt like a betrayal of her friend, Ronny. For her to have positive thoughts of her own right now is selfish. If they don't find Ronny safe and sound, she will never be able to have a supper with Sean. The idea of a new relationship discovered at the time of such a horrible circumstance must be wrong.

"Sean seemed annoyed the whole time he was there. I figure he must be frustrated because they can't find her." Then she changed the subject with no warning. Rose has admonished her for this abruptness on more than one occasion. "Did you see the truck Devon drove when he dropped Sheila off tonight?"

"Some grey contraption? The truck was small and ancient. Vehicle identification is a challenge for me." She muffled a snicker. "I often fail to recognize my own car and remember the model. What difference does it make what car Devon drives, anyway?"

Maggie remained silent. She felt puzzled. Annoyance nagged at the back of her mind because she couldn't quite retrieve all the information. "When we were at the diner and met him last night, wasn't the truck he drove green... and bigger?"

"I didn't pay any attention, Maggie. What difference does it make what Devon drives?" Rose started to sound impatient.

"He appeared here out of nowhere. Sheila said she met him at softball practice because he would go and watch. Did you think he seemed like the kind of guy who would go out with someone like Sheila?"

"People are attracted to all sorts, Maggie. You would realize this if you had ever met my ex." She snickered again. "Now, we were a couple not suited to one another! Maybe Sheila's found a guy who likes her despite her failings. We know Sheila has lots of those!"

"Try not to be mean, Rose. Everyone has positive qualities, even Sheila."

Maggie was distracted as thoughts and images started to gel in her mind. She believed she should speak to Sean about Devon, but if wrong, Sheila would be crazy mad. Ava, too. She struggled with deciding what to do.

"Should I talk to Sean or Fiona about the green truck?"

"Maggie," Rose emphasized her response with a sigh of patience mixed with perplexity. "There are hundreds of green trucks. You aren't even sure what the make of his truck was. You may be making something out of nothing."

"What if it is something? What if Devon is really Duncan and I didn't speak up? Is it better for me to be quiet, than to be wrong?" She clutched her hands in her lap and her hair hung like a curtain on either side of her face. Caramel sensed her anxiety and took up a position half on and half off her legs.

"My best advice is to review your observations with Ava in the morning. Don't be rash; don't make trouble." Her sister frowned, concern punctuating her words.

Maggie's voice became very soft. "Ben would say you need to do what you think is best for the other person. If your intentions are honourable, then you are not wrong."

Rose shook her head with a bit more force than necessary to emphasize her point. "Ben is gone, Maggie. I am here for you, and I think Sheila's new boyfriend had a green truck and then sold it in favour of some other piece of junk. This doesn't mean you have to suspect him of kidnapping or lying about his identity! You are too dramatic!" She stood up as she concluded her outburst, and trudged across the apartment to put her empty mug in the sink. "I am going home to bed. This whole situation has worn me out. You should do the same, Maggie. We both have to work tomorrow."

Maggie lifted her eyes to meet her sister's frown and planted a superficial smile on her naturally red lips. "It's only nine, Rose. I want to do a little clean-up before I turn in. I might have a shower. See you tomorrow."

"Yes, I'll come get the cats in the morning and scoot them over to my place. Get some rest, Maggie. Maybe there'll be some good news tomorrow."

Maggie heard Rose open and close her apartment door. In the quiet of her own space, she became aware of the soft rumble of Rose's television. She must have flipped it on the minute she walked in.

The luxury of the almost stillness was marred by a soft tap on her door. She approached with a measure of caution. Who could be calling on her at this hour? "Who is it?"

"Maggie, it's Cheryl. May I have a chat with you for a minute?"

Maggie opened her door and discovered the compact and pretty Cheryl Nadler standing at her threshold. "Come in, of course!"

Cheryl Nadler is a petite young woman with a stunning figure. She has short dark hair and every detail about her is perfection all the time. She always dresses in soft linen pants or little summer dresses. She is a runner and can often be seen when she trots through town after work. Maggie remembers when Ben was dying, how Cheryl helped the old woman an awful lot. At first she did Ben's laundry. In the end, Cheryl assisted with a lot of private care. She acted more like a nurse than a social worker, and her behaviour flabbergasted every resident at The Station. After Ben's death, she changed somehow. Cheryl has a daughter she gave up for adoption and tracked down the spring after Ben died. Amy is visiting with Cheryl for a couple of weeks before school starts.

"Thanks, Maggie. I've been worried sick since you called me Tuesday. There's no information in the media, which can be good or bad, but I couldn't bear obsessing any longer. I needed to stop in and see if there was any news."

Maggie felt very conflicted. The police were clear. None of the information from the briefing should be shared with others. She would have loved to tell Cheryl the whole story but was reluctant. "Cheryl, the RCMP gave a briefing today at the shelter but we were told not to repeat any information. I can tell you they've talked to some folks who were at the gas station restaurant when Ronny was there. They think they have a description of the man she talked to. Nobody saw his vehicle. They don't want him to get any ideas, so nothing has been made public yet. We are all very, very concerned."

Cheryl slowly shook her head. "This is like Roz Dover all over again, Maggie. The whole town still searches behind every pile of garbage and inside every vacant building in the hopes they'll find the poor thing; like picking a scab on a wound that won't heal." She patted Maggie on the arm. "I won't keep you. I imagine you and everyone at the shelter have had a long day. I won't repeat what you said, either." She peered straight into Maggie's eyes. "I will not say a word to anyone. You can trust me, Maggie."

For a brief moment, Maggie felt compelled to reveal the whole truth about Ronny's identity and the fact everyone thinks Duncan Taylor grabbed her. Cheryl has social worker eyes—the kind of eyes that make you want to spill your guts. She must be fantastic at her job. She resisted the urge to share. "I know, Cheryl. The minute I can tell you more, I will. You'll hear from me first."

Cheryl turned and reached for the door knob. "Call me anytime, even at work. I promise to take your call no matter what, okay?"

Maggie nodded. While she closed the door and turned the dead bolt, she heard the click of Cheryl's heels as she retreated up the stairs to her apartment above.

****

Maggie has decided she will discuss her observations about the truck with Ava, who probably hasn't talked to Sheila yet.

She hears Rose's distinctive rap on the door. Each cat runs, like a furry butler, as they scurry to get there first. "The door's unlocked already!" Maggie sings out the familiar response. She tries to remember to have the door open so Rose can pop in before she goes to Dr. Gunton's office.

The cats scamper around Rose's feet and across the hall as they anticipate dry kibble and a day stretched out in the August sunshine created by a corridor of perfection streaked over the hardwood floor. "Do you want a ride to work? I can wait. I still have lots of time."

"No, thanks anyway. The weather's so nice, and I will no doubt be cooped up all day, so I think the walk will do me good." Maggie wants to take the time to review how she will present her observations regarding Sheila's boyfriend and his previous truck, to Ava. She worries she might sound jealous because Sheila has a boyfriend and she does not. She wants to share the information in a responsible manner so Ava will take her seriously. Maggie often worries about this, although she has proved she is trustworthy and loyal, time and time again.

"Okay…I'll settle Caesar and Caramel, not that they need my help, and then be off." As an afterthought, she adds, "Supper together tonight? I can cook, if you like. Hamburger and macaroni casserole?"

Maggie responds with a nod. "Sounds great, Rose. I can make a salad when I get home. See you later." She hears the door close, as she makes her way to the bathroom to brush her teeth before she leaves.

The morning is, indeed, beautiful. Despite the musky smell of canola floating across the town, Maggie relishes the soft breeze of early August as it caresses her skin. Her thoughts return to Ronny. *Where is she? Is she hungry? Is she hurt? Could she be unconscious in a ditch somewhere in a field in the middle of nowhere? There have to be answers. Will this be like before?* She never knew Roz and she still thinks about her every day, even after all this time. Fiona's boss said they would leave no stone unturned. Maggie is determined to pass on her observations to Ava. Ava will not ridicule her, but she knows she'll have to suffer Sheila's wrath if her suspicions are revealed.

She arrives at the shelter around eight. Ava, not Sheila, answers the buzzer and provides her access. "I thought Sheila would buzz me in."

"Oh, she went down to bed already—busy night. All hell's broken loose. Fiona and Sean should be here mid-morning, but the hospital called last night. They have a young woman who came in with a broken arm and a black eye. They kept her, even though it was unnecessary. They wanted Ronny to come down to see her this morning, so I guess I have the job instead." She turns toward Maggie. Big tears puddle in her eyes. "I miss her, Maggie. I fail to see how we will carry on without her."

"When are you going to the hospital? Can I talk to you before you go? Something's bugging me and I want your opinion before I decide what to do."

"Okay, sure. I told them around ten. I need you to let the RCMP in if they arrive before I get back. And I have to talk to Sheila, too. Coffee's made. Get yourself a cup and come on in." She places a gentle hand on Maggie's shoulder, a motherly gesture Maggie has come to appreciate over her years of working with this woman. Under normal circumstances, Maggie's response to overt displays of affection is shortness of breath and a feeling of being closeted. She has improved.

With a mug of coffee clutched in her small hands bereft of any adornments, even nail polish—Maggie finds rings and polish smother her somehow—she peeks through Ava's doorway. "Come in. Come in. Sorry if I seem rattled. Someone drove in my driveway last night and parked with the headlights on. It gave me the creeps. I had trouble sleeping, if you could call it sleep the last few nights—nightmares and ruminations. What about you?"

"I never sleep much, but now I think about Ronny and don't even try. I wonder if she might be hurt. Ava, do you know what kind of truck Sheila's new boyfriend drives?"

"Haven't the faintest, Maggie. I must admit, I pay very little attention to makes and models. What's the problem?"

Now that she has Ava's attention, Maggie takes a sip of her coffee, tucks her long hair behind her ears, and somehow wiggles down into the chair across from Ava's desk. "Well, when we met Devon at the diner night before last, he drove a big green truck. By big, I mean a full size pickup. Not big like Joe Dodd's but regular. You know."

Ava nods, but the expression on her face is more indulgent than interested.

Maggie continues. "Yesterday, I saw him in a small Datsun truck—grey and old. The big one was a Ford or a Chev., I think."

Ava's face has clouded over like an impending storm. "Staff Sergeant Murphy said Duncan Taylor might have stolen a green Ford truck, Maggie." She leans further across the desk and whispers, "Do you think there's some kind of connection or just a coincidence?"

"I am simply not sure, Ava."

"Do you know what Devon looks like? You've seen him or met him?"

"Yes, but I can't describe him because whenever I've seen him, he's in the truck or covered up with a jean jacket and ball cap, even in the diner. I would not be able to confirm whether or not he is bald and has tattoos, but maybe Sheila can. Should I tell Sean and Fiona?"

"Yes. By all means! Once I get back from the hospital and we can wake up Sheila to confirm some details. I sure as hell hope you're wrong. Someone drove a small grey truck down my lane last night and left a note on my windshield. It was scary. I must leave for the hospital now, so I can get back by the time Fiona and Sean arrive. Good work, Maggie. You are very observant." She rushes toward the exit.

Maggie basks in the glow of garnered favour, but is more concerned about the note. She wonders what it said and why Ava avoided telling her. She understands Ava must go see the poor client with the broken arm, but she wishes the hospital visit could wait. You'd never know Marjorie or June and her family were even in the building right now. They are busy with their plans to move on, and Maggie is sure they want to remain distant from current developments, so the staff can focus on Ronny. A new resident will complicate matters. She frowns with self-admonishment. *Clients are the reason you have a job. The woman will need a place to stay. Do not begrudge her!* She decides to call Sean, even though she knows they will be over soon.

"Constable Knox, please. This is Maggie Woodward from Segue House," she responds to the civilian who answers the phone at the local RCMP detachment.

"Please hold."

"Hi, Maggie. Sean here. What's up?"

"Hi, Sean. I have a concern about trucks." She tries to sound upbeat and conversational, but serious at the same time. "I told Ava and she said you would be over later, but I wanted to call. She went to the hospital about a new referral, and will be back in an hour or so. Will you be here soon?"

"We will. What's this about, Maggie?"

"Sheila's new boyfriend. He has shown up here in Hayworth out of the blue and calls himself Devon. His full name is Devon Thompson, I think. Hey! His initials would be the same as Duncan Taylor!"

"We need more than similar initials to provide us with a reason to talk to him, Maggie." Sean's voice is soft; almost affectionate in its indulgence.

"No, Sean! When I first saw him, he drove a green pickup! Now he has a grey beater of some sort—a small truck. Now, Ava says a truck like that came in her yard last night and left some kind of note. She never told me what it said."

"Can you describe Sheila's boyfriend, Maggie?"

"Here's the problem. He covers himself up. He wore a ball cap and a jacket at the diner Tuesday night, even though the weather was sweltering. His looks are plain. You wouldn't say he has buck teeth, but they stick out. He seems muscular, like he works out."

"Maggie, we'll be over by the time Ava gets back. Wake Sheila up, if she has gone off to bed already. We need to talk to her."

Chapter 15

Ava

Arriving at the entrance to the Hayworth Community Hospital reminds Ava of the old days. Until Ronny came along, Ava always did initial interviews referred to Segue House by the hospital. Little has changed even though she knows there have been renovations and staff turnover. The smell is the same. There's a certain flavour to hospital air. The light creates familiar streaks, like there are no shadows. The sounds are steady and fill all the empty spaces, like the drone of machinery, although in reality, the buzz is created by people who talk in subdued whispers while the intercom crackles to life every once in a while to tell a doctor they're wanted on Line Four.

Ava pokes her head in through the front office cubicle opening. The area seems quiet "Ava Burrway here to see Chrissie Hobson. What room is she in?"

"Visiting hours begin at one this afternoon." The chubby receptionist in the red blazer remains focused on her typewriter.

Ava leans in a little further. "I'm from Segue House. The unit expects me."

"From where? Hold on a minute." The girl sighs resulting in the emission of an annoyed growl as she hollers to her colleague at a desk in an alcove at the back of the office. "Can somebody from a place called Sedgeway, or whatever, go see a patient?"

"Oh, for God's sake, Millie!" A middle-aged and tidy little woman, supporting wire-rimmed glasses and a sweater over her shoulders, suddenly appears from behind a fabric wall. "Ava is from Segue House, the women's shelter! Hey, Ava? We expected Ronny. Go ahead in. Room 104."

"Nice to see you, Karen. Thanks for the help." Relieved Karen didn't ask about Ronny, Ava makes her way to Chrissie Hobson's room.

There she sits, in the chair beside the bed, with her left arm in a cast and a sling. She turns when Ava appears in the doorway. This action reveals her swollen left eye, shut and beginning to turn a nasty shade of purple.

"Hi. My name is Ava Burrway, from Segue House. The hospital called us last night and asked if I'd come over to see if we could provide you some assistance. They said you prefer not to go back to where you were living."

Her voice is so soft. Ava has to lean down to hear. "No, I want to go to Vancouver. Coming here with Aaron was a bad idea."

"May I sit down?" Ava's eyes dart around the room, only to discover she will have to settle for the foot of the bed.

"Sure." Chrissie is close to tears.

"How about you tell me what happened, and then we'll make a plan to get you home? Have you called your family?"

"No." She starts to cry—a soft child-like whimper. "They told me if I came up north with Aaron, to never call or come back. I hope they will change their minds, but they threatened to disown me. Besides, I have no money to call." She squints over at Ava as she wipes damp, wispy strands of long blond hair off the side of her face. "I left without my shoes!" She peers down at her feet, currently housed inside hospital-issue paper slippers.

"We'll take care of you, Chrissie. We'll get you some shoes." Ava quickly does a mental inventory of the second-hand clothes they keep in the closet of Ronny's office. There will be sneakers, at least. She is so tiny that kids' stuff should fit her. "Tell me what happened."

Chrissie starts to reveal her circumstances while she focuses her eyes downward and twists her fingers in her lap. "The company fired Aaron because he partied too much at the camp where we worked. He had to leave so I quit, too. We came south to Hayworth because he knows a guy with a house here. We've been in town a couple of weeks but his friend told us we had to get out because we hadn't paid our share. All my money was gone already. Aaron was really pissed. He punched me and threw me down the basement stairs. Somebody called the ambulance and they brought me here. I expect Aaron will show up this afternoon and want me to come back."

She establishes eye contact with Ava before she continues. "I will not go back,

Miss Burrway. The nurses told me somebody named Ronny would help me."

"Ronny works for me but is not available right now, Chrissie. By the way, everybody calls me Ava." She smiles at Chrissie, in an attempt to ease her obvious discomfort. "If you don't want to see Aaron and you want to make plans to go to Vancouver, we can work on all the details at the shelter. No one will tell him where you are."

Ava watches her glance at the door of her hospital room, like she might be contemplating an escape. "The nurses said I was discharged. They were waiting for Ronny, or you, I guess. I can go."

"Do you want to come with me?" Ava keeps her voice soft. She doesn't want to spook her new client, and she will not force her to choose the shelter if she has another option.

"Yes, Miss, eh Ava. I guess I am going to have to break down and call my mom."

"Okay. I'll go out to the nurses' station and see what we need to do for your shiner and when you need follow-up for your cast. Wait here until I get back." Ava, brisk and all business, gets the information she needs and returns to the room to find Chrissie standing with her jacket over one shoulder and a dilapidated cloth purse dangling from her good hand.

"You appear ready for the road, despite your footwear." She pats the young woman on the shoulder. "Come on. We'll go to Segue House and you can meet my assistant Maggie. She'll show you around and get you settled. I have some other business to attend to, but tomorrow we'll try to call your folks and see if we can make a plan. Sound okay?"

Chrissie's expression reminds Ava of when the sun starts to shine before the rain stops. Her smile is broad and genuine, as big tears continue to roll down her bruised cheeks.

****

When they arrive back at Segue House, Ava swings her Le Baron into the back lot. She directs Chrissie to come with her around to the front. Once through the identification procedure, Ava asks Chrissie to take a seat for a moment while she has a chat with Maggie.

"Yes, Sean and Fiona are on the way. They said they would be here about the same time you were expected back. I haven't gone down to wake Sheila. I thought I'd wait until you were here." Maggie is a bit breathless as she imparts her information.

"Good. I want you to get Chrissie settled in. Do all the paperwork—family contacts, birth date, last address—the whole nine yards. Take her upstairs and introduce her to Marjorie. She can have the pull-out sofa in that apartment. Marjorie will keep her occupied for the rest of the day, and tomorrow she can call her parents. We'll settle her in first, feed her lunch, and let her rest."

Maggie nods, but lacks enthusiasm. "I need to be part of the discussion with Sheila. May I please sit in?"

"We will all talk together at some point, Maggie, which is why I need you to process our new referral now." She knows she sounds abrupt. Her mind races. She feels almost frantic, but through the mess of her personal thoughts, she still needs Chrissie to feel safe.

Ava moves back toward the living room. "Chrissie, would you like a coffee or some tea? Let me introduce you to Maggie Woodward. She'll fill out our intake form—our routine bit of paperwork—and then introduce you to Marjorie, who is the only resident in an apartment on the next floor. You can get settled in with her today. Tomorrow, we'll contact your family and see what our options are. By the way, all the residents use first names here. It is not necessary to reveal your last name to anybody but staff. Marjorie will no doubt introduce you to June, who is staying in the unit across the hall, upstairs. She has two little girls."

Ava watches Maggie usher Chrissie into her office to do the intake and familiarize her with the rhythm of the shelter. She reluctantly enters the foyer on the way to the stairs and Sheila's apartment below. The clock says eleven. She knows Shelia has only slept a few hours but the situation is unavoidable. The RCMP will be here any minute. They have to find out if there is any possible connection between Devon and Duncan.

She knocks, not hard, but with determination. "Sheila, wake up, Sheila!"

"What? What's wrong?" Sheila's groggy voice is muffled as it seeps through the door.

"It's Ava. Let me in. I have to talk to you."

The door opens. "Ava?" Sheila stands there in sweat pants and a white T-shirt. Her sagging breasts are not well concealed by the thin cotton. Her nipples press against the fabric, acknowledging the sudden cooler air.

Ava is a bit taken aback—embarrassed, if the truth be told—but soldiers on. "Get dressed and come upstairs as soon as you can. Some information has surfaced about Ronny and we need to talk with you."

"Who's 'we'?"

"Sean and Fiona are on the way, Sheila."

"Have they found her?" All of a sudden, alertness spreads across Sheila's face.

"No, but there are questions and developments. You weren't here for the briefing. We want to go over some of the information and see if there are details you're able to add."

"What could I add?" She sounds surly all of a sudden.

Her voice has a tone Ava considers unacceptable, so she adopts a more direct approach. "Sheila, the police will be here any minute. Wash your face, get dressed, and come upstairs to Ronny's office. Coffee's made. Get yourself some toast and we'll meet you there in fifteen minutes."

"Okay! Okay! No need to get mad, Ava! I haven't committed some horrible sin, you know."

Ava hopes Sheila is right. "Come upstairs as fast as possible, okay?"

****

The buzzer sounds a few minutes later. Ava knows the police have arrived. Maggie has already taken Chrissie up to meet Marjorie. She sighs as she heaves her aching body out of the chair. *When did I start to lumber instead of walk? What's the matter with me? And where the hell is Sheila?*

Once she gets a visual on Sean and Fiona, she buzzes them in. "I am waiting for Sheila to come upstairs and Maggie to come downstairs. Good morning, you two. There's coffee in the kitchen. Here comes Maggie." All this is said as a means of introduction.

"Hi, Fiona. Hi, Sean. The new client is all settled, Ava. Marjorie should work here. She is a great mentor." Maggie peruses the group assembled in the foyer. "Where's Sheila?"

"You might have to go back downstairs and get her, Maggie."

"I shouldn't think so. I met her on the landing when I took Chrissie upstairs. She was on her way back down."

"Go get Sheila, Maggie. She must be around someplace." Ava is more abrupt than she intends to be, for about the third time. Maggie gives her a confused look and disappears.

****

Maggie returns to Ava's office and wedges into the confined space made even smaller by the presence of two police officers, to inform the group that Sheila is nowhere to be found and Marjorie's car is not in the back parking lot. "I went upstairs and Marjorie told me she loaned her car to Sheila. She said Sheila came upstairs and told her there was an emergency. She must have run up right after you woke her."

Fiona responds to Maggie's anxious look. "We'll find the car, Maggie. Now, can you repeat to me the information you told Sean over the phone? I want to make sure we have all the details. Sean, will you go upstairs and get a description of the car and a plate number?" Fiona is the epitome of efficiency.

Sean nods, and without a word leaves the office, but not before he gives Maggie a little pat on the shoulder. Ava does not miss her assistant's blush.

Maggie proceeds to sit down in one of Ava's straight-backed office chairs. She brushes her hair from her face and tucks the strands behind her ears. Ava notices this, too. Maggie has assumed control. She folds her hands in the lap of her pale blue cotton pants and begins. She is able, with considerable detail, to tell Fiona about when she first met this man Sheila introduced as Devon, at the Hayworth Diner. She describes the truck he drove, what he wore, the texture of his skin, and the condition of his teeth. She points out how he wore a ball cap and a jean jacket so she cannot make any determination about whether or not he has hair, or whether or not he has tattoos. She also relates how he came back to the diner a little later on, when she and Rose were having dessert. He bought another special after he had already eaten one. She wonders aloud if he bought the extra food to take to Ronny.

"That might be a bit of a stretch, Maggie. All we know for sure is Sheila's new boyfriend bought another special. He might have discovered he liked the dinner and wanted to have one for later." Her voice is kind and her look indulgent. Ava hopes Maggie's speculations don't colour the nature of her information.

"Then there's the little grey truck. He dropped Sheila off yesterday in an old, small grey truck—a truck like Ava saw in her yard last night, right?" She looks over at her boss for confirmation.

Ava nods to Fiona as she hands her the yellow piece of paper with the pencilled note, and another sheet with her description of the incident. "Last night, a small grey pickup truck came down my lane around ten o'clock and sat in the yard with the lights on for a few minutes. I was rattled, so I called Sheila to make sure the shelter was secure, and to be frank, I needed to hear another voice. She would have recorded my call in the log book. When I peeked out the window after I crawled out of the tub, I caught a glimpse of the back of the truck as it left. This morning, I found that note on my windshield."

While she completes her description, Sean returns to the office. "Marjorie's car is a dark blue late model Lincoln sedan. I have a plate number. I already called it in, Fiona." He continues to readjust his lapel microphone after his call to the office.

****

Ava and Maggie work side by side in the kitchen as they prepare ham and cheese sandwiches for everyone for lunch. "What did the note say, Ava?" Maggie has her back to her boss as she starts to set the table.

"The note said 'she won't be back', Maggie. There has to be a connection between Devon and Duncan. Sheila must be suspicious if she took off like this. I told her about the truck last night. She would remember if she had told her boyfriend where I live. There aren't too many Lincolns around this area. We are confident law enforcement will be able to find her." A tone of desperation creeps out between her words. "Sheila may know where Devon stays or where he hangs out. Maybe she took off to find him, so she can try and see if there's a link before she talks to the police. She doesn't have the descriptions we do. She doesn't know about the note, but she must be suspicious because I mentioned the grey truck to her last night."

Maggie starts to respond, but stops as Marjorie and Chrissie come around the corner and into the main living area. "Can we help? I brought chocolate cake I bought it at the bakery yesterday. I thought the children would like a treat. Making progress." She winks at Maggie. "Actually worked up the nerve to go to the store." She then turns to Ava and frowns. "I gather I committed a faux pas when I loaned my car to Sheila. What's happened?"

"Nobody knows for sure, yet, Marjorie. Did you explain our current crisis to Chrissie?" Ava takes the cake and starts to cut serving sizes.

"Of course not! The briefing was confidential and I would let you and the police determine what to tell new residents!" She turns her attention to Chrissie, who has taken a seat in a wingback chair in the corner of the living room. Her gaze is out the side window. "No offence, Chrissie, but this sort of thing is definitely not my place."

Chrissie nods but exhibits little overt interest.

"Would you like a cool drink, Chrissie?" Maggie attempts a subject change as Ava nods to Marjorie and they disappear into Ava's office.

"The police are investigating the possibility Sheila's new boyfriend, a guy who calls himself Devon Thompson, might actually be Duncan Taylor. Maggie thinks the truck she first saw him in matches the description of a truck stolen in Sudbury and therefore linked to Taylor. It is probably a long shot. Sheila never heard the briefing yesterday, but she has doubts—I think because he switched trucks and the one he's driving now matches the description of one parked in my yard late last night—and now she has taken off in your car without a word to me or to Maggie. Did she tell you why she needed the car?"

Marjorie adjusts the collar of her pink sleeveless blouse. She pats her hair. "No, not at all. She said she needed to find somebody in a hurry. Ava, I assumed the request was work related since you weren't back from your interview yet. Then Maggie showed up with Chrissie and I knew that wasn't the case, but it was too late. She was already gone. Have I made a serious blunder and complicated matters?"

"How could you have known, Marjorie? If this guy happens to be Ronny's ex-husband, I hope Sheila avoids a confrontation. She will be inordinately angry and I can't even imagine what she would do to the guy regardless of how big he is." Ava shakes her head. "Come on. All we can do is wait. Let's pay some attention to Chrissie and see if we can get her straightened out."

They return to the kitchen where June and her kids are munching on sandwiches and drinking juice. Chrissie is still sitting in the living room, but with a glass of iced tea in her hand and a sandwich on the side table.

"Has everyone been introduced, Maggie?" Once Maggie nods, Ava continues. "We will have an interview after lunch, Chrissie, and make a plan. Tomorrow will be a big day for you as we make a few phone calls and see if we can get you home." As she says this, she thinks tomorrow may be a big day for all of them, if her friend Fiona can untangle all the loose ends required to try and locate Ronny.

Chapter 16

Shelia

Sheila settles into the luxury of the soft navy leather interior. She rubs her left hand along the edge stitching of the driver's seat. *I could get used to this.* Marjorie was generous when Sheila knocked on the door. Of course she could borrow the Lincoln! She handed over her keys. She never asked any questions. Sheila departed the shelter parking lot before the police arrived.

She needs answers to the questions rattling around in her mind before she talks to anyone else. Ever since last night, when Ava said some little grey truck appeared in her yard, she started to get suspicious, or curious might be a better word. No harm in a drive out to the Pimiskaw Tavern to see if he might be there. She can talk to him and make sure there's no reason for her to worry.

The drive is uneventful. The road is quiet for a Thursday morning. There are combines in the fields. Big old farm trucks sputter past, but traffic is minimal. She whizzes by the Petro-Can, glancing at the graveled lot to see if the truck might be there. *No. Good. He could still be in Pimiskaw. It won't hurt to find out. After all, he said he'd call today. Maybe I can beat him to the punch. He kissed me last night. That must have meant something.* Despite a nagging nervousness in the pit of her stomach, she is convinced he will be glad to see her.

The tavern's neon open sign blinks on at the same time as she pulls the big car up near the entry. No truck in the vicinity. Maybe people who rent rooms upstairs park around back or someplace else out of sight. She starts to lose her nerve. *What if he is actually there, perched on a bar stool shooting the breeze with Penny? Can I wander in and sit down on the stool beside him like normal? Will he get mad?* She hesitates. Maybe she should stay in the car until he appears.

After five minutes of self-inflicted arguments both for and against her plan, she hauls her ass out of the car and walks, albeit slowly and with little determination, toward the imposing black door. As she tugs on the handle, she hears Patsy Cline straining out of the juke box. She fights to overcome her sudden loss of vision in the darkened space. The combined smells of stale smoke and fresh urinal disinfectant cakes assault both her nose and her eyes. *Thank God, Penny's at the bar.* The place is empty except for two guys in the back corner, drinking beer and cutting cards. *Bars must open before noon for a reason.*

Penny looks up as the door slams shut. Sheila waves. Penny recognizes her and waves back. Sheila's courage returns. "Have you seen Devon this morning, Penny?"

"Nope. He often pops in for a coffee when we open, but I haven't seen hide nor hair of him today. Can I get you a drink? Do you want me to give him a message?"

Sheila senses a message deposited with Penny would not be wise, although she is unable to put her finger on exactly why. Her instincts tell her to take off. She attempts another tactic first. "Maybe he's still upstairs?"

Penny shakes her head as she holds up another glass toward the neon light perched behind the bar. The sign says "Draft". She polishes the rim as she replies. "There was no truck like his in the lot when I drove in, so I figure he left already or never came home. If he were here, his truck would be parked in the front."

"Okay. Thanks, Penny. I thought I'd check. You don't have to bother telling him I was here. I'll catch up to him soon enough." She tries to sound casual, but is afraid she comes across as desperate. *Too late now.*

Snuggled back into the safety of the Lincoln—she feels invisible in this big, beautiful vehicle where one would never expect to see her behind the wheel—Sheila makes an attempt to think circumstances through. *If Devon turns out to be Ronny's ex, and if he knew Ronny worked at the shelter, then he used me to try and get information. If all this is true, then everything is my fault.* She cracks the window in an attempt to get more air on her sweaty neck and flushed face. Fear threatens to strangle her ability to think clearly;

to remember details. Her stupidity and gullibility might be the reasons Ronny has ended up in this mess.

Ten minutes pass before she turns on the car and starts back toward Hayworth. She'll stop at the Petro-Can and call Segue House, collect, from there. Maggie will be able to help her fill in the blanks. She feels confused; light headed. She'll get a bite to eat, too, before she goes home.

The trip to the highway takes less than fifteen minutes and then she makes her way down the road to the Petro-Can. The sun is high in the August sky and reflects off what is now a dusty windshield. The Lincoln has become yet another victim of Alberta's side roads.

She scans the area as she makes her way to the door of the diner. No grey truck. The pay phone is in the passageway between the service bays and the restaurant counter. She orders a roast beef sandwich to go and turns back to the phone.

All she needs is to get the operator and have her call the shelter. She is sure Maggie will accept the charges.

Shelia hears the operator's voice as she identifies how a Sheila Pasco wishes to reverse the charges. "Yes, yes. Thank you. Sheila? Where are you? You have Marjorie's car!"

"I borrowed her car, Maggie! I have permission! I will be home soon. I wanted to see if I could find Devon. Do you think he might be Ronny's ex? What did the cops say? Is this why they wanted to talk to me?" Words are falling out of her mouth. She never talks this much.

"Come back, Sheila. Ava and Fiona want you here, now. Everybody is worried sick. They thought you might have disappeared, too! And yes, there is a definite possibility your so-called Devon Thompson is Ronny's ex-husband, Duncan Taylor." Her voice sounds like June's when she corrects her children. "How long before you get here?"

"Do they know what Duncan Taylor looks like?"

"Hurry back, Sheila. I am going to tell Ava you're on your way. How long?"

Sheila sighs. She won't get a morsel of information out of Maggie over the phone. "About an hour. I'm at the Four Corners Petro-Can. I just have to pay for my sandwich. Tell Marjorie her beautiful Lincoln is fine."

Maggie's voice softens then. "You might be pleased to know Marjorie hasn't been the least bit worried about her car. She seems to think you're pretty responsible."

"Tell her thanks. See ya." Sheila hangs up the phone, pays for her lunch, and returns to the safety and anonymity of the car. The grey truck turns into the gas station lot before Sheila can even get her sandwich unwrapped.

She slumps down a little in the seat, although she knows he would never recognize the car or suspect she would be inside. He is wearing his standard jean jacket and ball cap. He goes in the restaurant for a few minutes and comes out with a bag and a cup of coffee.

Sheila fires up the Lincoln. She will attempt to follow him for as long as possible. He leaves the lot and drives across the highway. Sheila has never been down this road before. The traffic is light so she hangs back. The dust kicked up by the wide and graveled road obscures her from view. A red grain truck with a blue replacement passenger door approaches her from behind and she pulls over to let him go around. This action serves as a buffer between the Lincoln and Devon's truck. They drive for a long time. Sheila doesn't check the mileage, but fifteen minutes, at least. When the grain truck makes a left turn into a field, the grey truck is no longer up front.

She turns around and cruises at about twenty miles an hour back the way she came. She glances up and down side roads and cut lines into fields. After a couple of minutes, she sees the dust of a vehicle as it moves far down an overgrown track. She almost drives past. It looks to be a small truck. She backs up and parks so she gets a clear view down the road. She decides to stay put. She knows the truck has travelled too far into the distance to be able to see her parked there. The vehicle disappears somewhere on the horizon. The dust cloud has disappeared, now. She waits, then throws the big car into gear, and drives back to the highway.

Could Ronny be down that grassed-in road? Maybe Devon just wants to find a quiet spot to have his coffee. Once she gets out to the main highway, she is no longer exactly sure where the road was located. Those little side trails often go off to nowhere—they all start to look alike after a while.

****

She sees the lights on the roof of the police car. She steals a glance at the speedometer. She has not been speeding. Maybe the cop is after somebody else and she needs to pull over to get out of the way. As Sheila eases the Lincoln off on to the broad shoulder, the car pulls in behind her. The young female officer leans back into the vehicle to retrieve her hat, and closes the cruiser's door. Sheila watches all this in her side mirror as she pushes the button to roll down the driver's window.

"Turn off your vehicle, ma'am."

Sheila does as directed. The police officer approaches the window and leans down. "Are you Sheila Pasco?"

"Yes, officer." *How does she know my name?* Sheila is more than a little nervous someone might think the car is stolen, not borrowed.

"Does this vehicle belong to a person named Marjorie Westerman?"

"Yes. I have permission from her to borrow her car." Sheila feels compelled to explain; to defend her actions.

"I have been instructed to escort you back to Hayworth, to Segue House. Do you have any problem with this?"

"Not at all, officer. I was on my way back to Segue House anyway."

"Ms. Pasco, I will follow you. Please proceed." She turns on her heel and heads back to the cruiser.

Sheila re-engages the ignition key in the Lincoln and the motor roars to life. Her hands are clammy on the wheel, and shake as she checks her mirrors before she pulls back out on to the highway. The police car follows at a respectable distance. The lights no longer flash.

The drive takes a little longer than Sheila estimated. She now seems unable to force the big car to travel the speed limit. Her hands are sweaty. Her face is hot. Who sent a cop to find her? Did they follow her? Should she have told the officer about how she followed Devon? She tries to remember the exact location of the road he went down. She can't. *This is bad.*

When she reaches Hayworth and turns up the street where Segue House is located, the RCMP car stays behind her. In the back lot sits a second cop car. She suspects Fiona Werbowski already waits inside. She takes extra care as she parks Marjorie's sedan and trudges, without much enthusiasm, around to the front of the shelter. Sheila then follows the well-established protocols and hears Maggie's anxious voice crackle through the intercom.

"I have another RCMP officer with me, Maggie."

"I know. Ava will meet you both inside." The buzzer sounds and they enter the glassed-in entry. Ava trudges out of the office, shoulders slumped. She appears done in. All of a sudden, Sheila is overwhelmed with the gravity of the situation. *Ronny may be dead and I may have contributed to her death because I am an ignorant, affection-seeking bitch. I will have to leave Hayworth. Ava will hate me. Everyone will hate me.*

Ava pays more attention to the cop, who presses her identification against the glass. "Hi, Ms. Burrway. I'm Constable Megan Wiley from Carter River. I provided an escort for Ms. Pasco. I would like to speak with Constable Werbowski for a few minutes and then I'll be on my way."

Ava buzzes them both in. Sheila starts to go upstairs, but the dead weight of Ava's hand rests on her arm. "Fiona is in my office, Constable Wiley. Maggie, here, will show you the way."

Ava turns her attention to Sheila, who has been transfixed by the pressure of the older woman's touch. "When Fiona finishes with Constable Wiley, we will sit down and have a serious conversation." Ava's voice shakes. She sounds like she might start to cry.

"I have to take Marjorie's keys up to her and thank her for the loan of her car, Ava. I won't go anywhere." She stares down at Ava's hand, glued to her sleeve.

"I am going to come with you." The stairs seem especially steep all of a sudden. Sheila notices the laboured effort of Ava, who has one hand on the railing and her face down.

"Are you okay?"

Ava peers into her face. "Are you serious, Sheila? Ronny has been gone since Monday! Today's Thursday and there's still no sign of her! I haven't slept in days. You missed the briefing yesterday. Perhaps the police might have made some progress if you had been here."

By this time, they're at the top of the stairs and Sheila knocks on the door. Some stranger answers right away. Sheila turns to Ava for confirmation of some sort.

"Sheila, this is Chrissie. She will be with us for a couple of days. Chrissie, this is Sheila, our overnight person. She has rooms down on the basement level. Is Marjorie there?"

"Coming! Coming!" Marjorie rounds the corner from the kitchen, as she hurries to dry her hands on a dish towel. "I decided to make buns. I thought everyone might like a homemade treat." She squints at the two of them. She seems to require validation of some sort. "You know I need to keep busy. Chrissie is my able and trusty assistant." She pats the girl like one would pat a cat. "We all have to keep busy." Her eyes, as they scoot between the women in the hallway, are frantic and sad at the same time.

Chrissie stands expressionless.

"Here are your car keys, Marjorie. Thanks a bunch for loaning me the Lincoln. She is a beauty. I didn't have time to top up the gas tank. I suppose you know the police followed me home."

"No problem, dear. You can borrow the Lincoln any time you like, and I will take care of the gas." The expression on Ava's face—telepathically telling Marjorie there will be no more loans of the Lincoln—does not escape Sheila's notice.

Back downstairs, they wait in the reception room for Fiona. Maggie appears around the corner from her office. She points at Ava's office. "They're still in there with the door closed. Sheila, do you have any idea how upset we all were? Until Marjorie told us you borrowed her car, we all thought something bad might have happened to you!"

"Why would you think that? I've borrowed Ava's car before and you never thought there was a problem. Ava, Maggie, what in hell is going on?" She is hot and flushed again.

Ava ignores the question and asks one of her own. "Where were you? You were supposed to meet with me to learn about yesterday's update. You left the building."

"I went to find Devon. On the phone last night, when you called, you said the vehicle in your yard was a small grey truck. Devon drives an old grey beat-up Datsun. It bugged me all night. I couldn't get your words out of my mind, so I decided to go to the tavern where he stays in Pimiskaw, and ask him myself."

Ava's voice is quieter. "You know where he is?"

"Well, no. He isn't there right now, but yes—above the tavern in Pimiskaw. Do you know the place?"

"You have to tell Fiona this. You have to tell her whatever you know about this alleged Devon person."

"Did I do somethin' wrong? Am I in trouble?"

"No, Sheila. I suspect Ronny may well be the one in trouble."

Chapter 17

~

Ronny

Stretched out on the cot in the dark late Wednesday night, Ronny raked her brain as she tried to uncover her mistake. *Where did I go wrong? How did I blow my cover? The only possibility must have been the ball.*

Her involvement started when she and Fiona Werbowski tossed around ideas about how additional funds could be raised for the shelter. By this time, Gaby Ridgway was a part of Dodd's Contracting and Interiors, so she represented the business community on the committee responsible to plan the annual RCMP ball held every October. Fiona suggested the annual RCMP fundraiser could partner with Segue House. They met with Gaby and the idea was born.

Ronny and Gaby saw much less of one another after Gaby left Family Counselling Services. When you live in an apartment, you don't spend a lot of time at a business designed to cater to construction and renovation. Ronny was happy to reconnect with her. They had done good work together when Ronny first moved to Hayworth.

The women spent tireless hours planning what would be the biggest event ever held in the town. They decided to designate it a formal affair. All the RCMP members would be in red serge. The women would wear evening gowns and men would wear tuxes (or reasonable facsimiles considering they were in Hayworth, after all). The tickets would be more expensive but the evening would include a full-course dinner and the officer responsible for photography from the investigation division would do portraits and group pictures for a fee. They would have a silent auction and Gaby would browbeat every business in town to donate an item for bids. The police force and the shelter would each be responsible for fifty percent of the costs and would get fifty percent of the profit.

They plotted and schemed for weeks. The town was abuzz with discussions about ball gowns and the trip to Las Vegas put up for auction by the local travel agent. Tickets disappeared like hot cakes and the event was sold out before the end of September. They could breathe a sigh of relief. One hundred and twenty-five percent of the costs were recouped in ticket sales, so all other monies gained would be additional profit. The event was huge. People had a fabulous time. The band played long after the expected end of the evening.

Ava couldn't get over the amount of money they raised—equivalent to two full government grants.

The October, 1983 ball was bigger than the year before. They moved to a larger venue so they could sell more tickets. They sold out again. Prices for the auction items went higher. People drank more and posed for more pictures. The RCMP/Segue House Ball and Fundraiser became the place to be. They raised half of their operating budget at this last event, which was good, since governments had begun to cut back on social services in all kinds of different ways due to the downturn in the economy.

During the planning for last fall's gala, Ronny moved from Ben Tullis' old apartment at The Station into Gaby's house on Poplar Street.

The fundraiser made the local paper again, but this time the story was picked up by the Edmonton Journal. There were pictures. I was reluctant to have my picture taken, but I figured it would do no harm. I barely resemble Janine Taylor anymore, and no one I know would ever have access to a western newspaper. I had few worries about the photo afterward. It was a group picture with Ava, Gaby, Fiona, a couple of other business-types, and a few officers. No big deal.

Was the picture my downfall?

She was suddenly jolted out of her discussions with herself when she saw the flash of lights as a vehicle pulled up to the front of the cabin. It was late; really late, and he had said he'd be a couple of days, but she was sure it was him. She was sure it could not be Fiona. She realized she had lost all hope of rescue. She stood still in the dark and listened. The moonlight reflected her blond head cocked slightly to the side. She gave a quick glance at the blanket with the toilet seat cover hidden beneath—reassurance, as the latch on the door gave way and the hinges creaked when they moved on the frame.

"Anybody home? Are you awake?" A snarly guffaw accompanied his so-called joke. He stood on the stoop. The bars from the door made him appear dissected on the vertical, like their roles were reversed and he was peering through the grills instead of her.

"Duncan." She worked hard to keep her voice even and calm; a skill she learned in courses taken to deal with crisis intervention over the phone.

"I dropped Sheila off but the party was already over. Maybe, by tomorrow, there'll be more information about whether or not they've made any headway in the search for you. Pretty pathetic, eh? You've been gone more than two whole days already."

"They've made progress, Duncan, but I doubt you will know about it until they find you. They never tell the public all the details in their briefings. They say enough to make people think they're in the loop. Don't kid yourself. There's progress."

"I stopped at the diner on my way outa' town and bought you some fish 'n chips." He shoved the cardboard box through the bars. "And, hold on a minute, I brought some water, too." He turned and loped back to the truck.

"Different truck?" Although difficult to make out, she was sure this vehicle was smaller.

He turned and stared, like he'd just noticed it parked there. "Yeah. I though the other one might be hot by now."

She hated to admit, even to herself, how hungry she was and how good the greasy and cold fish smelled. She held her empty water jug so he could funnel water into it from beyond the bars. She mumbled her thanks, and then became annoyed. "What do you hope to accomplish, Duncan? By now they know you're the one who took me. You will go back to jail for a very long time. What the hell is the point?"

He ignored her questions and asked one of his own. "Have you ever wondered how I located you? You were deep undercover. Aren't you curious about who found you?"

"I figure you saw my picture in the Edmonton Journal. I am not sure how, but it's the single plausible explanation." She opened the cardboard box, picked up a limp French fry and nibbled on it from one end to the other. This behaviour reminded her of when she was a child and they would give her friend's hamster raw spaghetti noodles. She feigned disinterest in the information she knew Duncan was about to reveal.

"Ah, but how did I see the picture? And how did I know it was you?"

She sighed, tired of the game. "How should I know, Duncan? I'm not sure I care. How about you let me out of here, now. You've had your fun. I can make my own way home and no one will be the wiser." Faint hope, like a potential parolee.

"Chet sent me the picture! Your own brother! He visited me in prison all the time until he came out here to work. He lives in the city. He ratted you out! Do you believe it? Your brother thinks more of me than he does of you!"

Ronny's heart pounded in her chest. Chet must have recognized her, even with her hair all shaved off. "Chet's an idiot."

"Try not to be mean, darlin'. He is your brother after all—or half-brother, anyway. He told me he thought we should get back together and he could never understand what all the fuss was about and why you sent me to jail."

"Chet's still an idiot, Duncan." She nibbled on another fry. She smelled as much as ate. If her nose almost rested on the food, the ammonia odour from the privy was momentarily blocked. She'd been hungry and had eaten peanut butter right out of the jar. Too much of the stuff, plus limited water rations, could be a bad combination. "Do you plan to let me out?"

"Nope. All this is too much fun!" He waved his arms into the expanse of darkness. "And Sheila, the tractor, thinks we're an item! Now, there's an idiot!"

"Sheila will kill you when she finds out the truth. I have every faith in Sheila." Ronny kept her voice flat and controlled.

"Listen, that woman is so starved for affection; she'll do whatever I ask. Like you, she would let me beat the shit out of her for fifteen years before she walked. You'll never be rid of me, Janine."

She could see his teeth reflected in the moonlight. You could always see Duncan's teeth, even when his mouth was closed. She opted to remain silent. This was always her default response when they were married. She hated how she automatically reverted back to her old coping mechanisms, like worn out slippers you should have thrown out but still manage to put on whenever you feel an emotional kind of cold.

"Have it your way. Pace yourself with that dinner. I might not be back for a couple of days. Forgot the lye. Maybe next time."

She heard a chortle when he pulled the door closed and rattled the key as he turned it in the lock. Two pieces of fish. One for today and one for tomorrow. She breathed a simple sigh of relief because he might not be back for a while.

****

By the time dawn begins to wiggle past the brambles and into her prison on Thursday morning, she has made peace with how she lost her anonymity, and an escape plan has managed to gel. She gives total credit to her brain, independent of her heart, mind, or good sense. For some reason, still a mystery, she thinks she should escape through the outhouse wall. This irrational plan must have been inspired by the lack of lye.

Not being an expert on outhouse construction and maintenance, she investigates. Ronny climbs off the cot and opens the privy door, compelled to peek down into the rough-cut hole now exposed after her removal of the toilet seat. Yes. Her logical brain was correct. She can see slivers of light down the hole in the back wall. She can see three strips of light shaped like a rectangle without the bottom long side. The bottom edge must be obscured by built up solids from over the years. *Could it be the clean-out door? Would somebody come along, open the door from the outside, and rake out the crap? This must be how Duncan expected to add lye.* She wiggles her nose, returns to the bed to get the seat which she positions strategically over the hole, and has a pee.

Would there be room to get through the clean-out hole if I can manage to push the cover off and out? It's likely nailed or screwed in from the outside. It could be loose like the toilet seat was. That would make life easier. What amount of force would I need to kick the clean-out door open? Can I climb into the box, force open the hatch for cleaning, and crawl out? Am I crazy?

The next necessary step would be to slide down on to the shit pile, kick the cover out, and hope the opening is big enough for her to get through, feet first.

Worst possible outcomes—she gets stuck and Duncan turns up; or she fails to get out and has to remain in her prison covered in crap; or even if she does get out, she has no idea where the hell she is.

Ronny shuts the door to the toilet behind her and returns to the cot. The taste of the smell remains in the back of her throat. She has time to work her plan through. He said he might not be back for a day or more. She gets up and stands at the window. There's a tiny breeze drifting through the holes, but no sounds of activity in the field although she knows there's canola out there. Despite her forced proximity to the shit house, she can still detect the unique and sweaty odour of ripe canola when she stands near the window. *Surely to God someone will turn up in the field and hear me scream so I can get rescued.* Her brain takes control. She cannot wait for such an elusive event to occur.

"Okay." She speaks aloud—a behaviour she has tried to avoid thus far. She thought, at first, if she talked to herself it might indicate some level of insanity. Now she has decided an assessment of her mental status matters very little. "Right now, we will see if these long legs of yours have any practical purpose. Can you reach the panel?"

She puts on her right sandal. The thought of where she bought these shoes, and how much she paid for them, flashes through her mind. "Those are wasted thoughts," she admonishes herself aloud.

She opens the door, removes the toilet seat and places it on the floor by the cot. She climbs up on the bench and drops her legs inside the hole. The cut edge is rough on the backs of her thighs, even through her chino capris. She hoists her body up with her hands, and uses her wrists as supports. She stretches her right leg down into the hole as far as she can reach and only grazes what she believes is the clean-out panel. It's impossible for her to kick with any force.

"Come on! I'm supposed to be tall—all legs! Fat lot of good they do me now! Okay! Elbows down!"

She lowers her body further into the hole by balancing precariously on her elbows and forearms. She finds it hard to keep her left leg bent. Her bare foot hits sticky sludge with no discernible bottom. She gives her right leg a swing and wallops the panel with considerably more force than she thought she would have. The pain searing the side of her foot is a surprise. Most of her motivation comes from her fear she will fall straight into the shit pile, old as most of the stuff is. She does not acknowledge the pain.

The damned cover moved a fraction. Elated, she kicks again. She ignores the slight tingle that starts to hum inside both her hands. Another tiny movement. The sweat pours off her brow and into her eyes. The smell makes her more nauseous than she has been in the last two days. Her stomach muscles haven't worked like this in years!

"Whack the boards again! You will get out of here or die with the effort!"

One more kick and she has to sit up on the side of the hole again. She shakes all over. She tries not to cry. Her feet are covered in crap, her right foot throbs, her hands are asleep, and she knows she must have lacerations right at her waistline from her attempts to balance against the sawn edge of the hole. She wants a drink, but wants to avoid dragging her shitty feet across the prison floor until her mission is accomplished.

She hears a truck motor. Deathly afraid Duncan has shown up to find her covered in crap with a hole half beaten through the side of the outhouse, she stops, stays quiet, and focuses all her attention on listening. The motor cuts out. After what seems like about a half hour, the rumble starts up again and drifts away. She remains still for another period of time, although she doesn't know exactly how long, before she resumes her task.

With breaks, the process takes her all day before she finally kicks the clean-out panel into submission; at least to the point where she's confident she can finish the job with both feet when she gets into the hole. The bottom is detached and tilted out about a half inch. She can determine the opening will be about eighteen inches wide by a bit more than a foot tall. She will be able to fit through. As long as Duncan doesn't reappear with the lye.

She uses toilet paper, and a good portion of the water he left her, to clean her feet off. She will leave in the morning. If she starts now, it will be dark before she gets out. Her biggest fear is that she wouldn't be able to manoeuvre herself inside the hole without the indirect light from the cabin window. To complicate matters, she is certain he is more likely to return after dark. Finally, she has not a clue as to where she is except probably not near town, so the light of day will help.

Her plan is set. Tomorrow, at first light, she will take the blanket from her cot and put it down the hole to give her some kind of separation from the crap. She will climb down inside, lie down on the blanket, kick open the panel with both feet, and go out feet first. There is insufficient room for her to turn around once she gets in the hole. She smirks. *Crawling out face first would be too easy. Might as well go the hard way.*

She clumps up a mound of toilet paper, the one item of which there is excess, and picks up the second piece of fish. She is filthy. She stinks to high heaven and she hasn't even been all the way inside yet. *Friday is going to be a great day.*

Chapter 18

Ava

Each day develops into one that's worse than the one before. Ava fears what might happen next. She is in her office on Thursday afternoon. Sheila sits across from her, head down, right knee bouncing to an unheard nervous rhythm. They wait for Fiona who has gone outside with Constable Wiley for some reason. Ava thinks, with what little she can see out her office window, the officer from Carter River might stick around.

"Are you gonna tell me what was said in the briefing yesterday?" Sheila's voice is whiny and child-like. She picks at her fingers and continues to bounce her knee.

"No." The gruffness manages to elbow its way into her tone. "We have to wait for Fiona. I wish she'd hurry up. I don't know what's taking her so long. We were scared witless today, Sheila. Maggie was beside herself. We have a new client here. I went to the hospital to interview her and when I came back you were gone. What is the matter with you? We're a team! You've been so secretive and defensive about this guy. We've all been worried sick."

They both turn toward the door as Fiona joins them. "Megan will wait for directions." Fiona is all business. "Sheila, I need to know where this person you call Devon Thompson lives and what he looks like. I have some descriptors from Maggie, but very few additional details."

"Devon stays at the Pimiskaw Tavern, up above the bar. I went there earlier, but he wasn't there."

"Describe him." Fiona sits poised with her notebook and a pen. Ava has never seen her so intense.

"Kinda' tall. Works out. He shaves his head and wears a ball cap most of the time, but I saw a funny tattoo on the back of his neck, up high and covered up by the cap. His teeth stick out a bit."

"What does he drive?"

"An old green Ford pickup, but he ditched it a couple of days ago. He drives a small grey beater truck now—a Datsun, I think. I used to know all the makes and models, but I have a hard time to remember most of them anymore."

"Okay. Back in a minute." She retreats to the parking lot. Ava observes both Fiona and Megan on their radios. Fiona, as sweet and amenable as she is most of the time, is angry and anxious. Ava sees fear in the constable's eyes. Everyone is scared Ronny has been killed.

"He was nice to me, Ava. He paid attention to me. He acted like he wanted to be with me! He even kissed me once—on the lips, like he meant it!"

Ava shakes her head. "You fell hard, my dear. I hope they can catch this guy, find out for sure if he's Duncan Taylor, and then locate Ronny. I have such a bad feeling, and find it hard not to think about Roz Dover gone more than three years. The time is fast approaching for Fiona's annual community meeting about Roz's disappearance." She holds her true thoughts in check, since she could, with no additional provocation, jump out of her office chair, walk around the desk, and shake Sheila Pasco until her teeth rattle!

Fiona returns. "We have cars on the way to both the Pimiskaw Tavern and the Four Corners Petro-Canada. If he is anywhere around, we'll pick him up today. Can you stay near the phone until you hear from me, Ava? Ask Maggie to stay, too, and keep all your current residents in the building. Nobody is to be out tonight, just in case a cornered guy gets ideas."

She returns her attention to Sheila, as she hurries to get underway. "Don't leave the shelter. If you think of any additional information, have Ava call the police station and they'll get in touch with me." With that, she is out of the building.

Ava makes her rounds and talks to everyone. June and her children will stay put. She is busy. The Family Counselling office has helped her find a place to rent in Edmonton and she expects to leave once the situation with Ronny is resolved. Marjorie answers the apartment door as she wipes her hands on her apron. "Chrissie and I are planning to sit down to a spaghetti dinner a little later. I thought she might appreciate a nutritious meal. Shall I carry the pot downstairs and we can all eat together? I even made French bread and all I have left to do is toss a salad and cook the noodles."

Ava is a little overwhelmed. This woman could be the matron for Segue House. She continues to talk about a move to her sister's, but she and her Lincoln are still here. "Spaghetti sounds wonderful, Marjorie. I will ensure the others are aware that you will, once again, host supper for everyone." Ava acknowledges her client with a respectful nod. "You, my friend, seem to find a way to take care of us all."

"In my own way, Ava." Marjorie's voice is soft, almost conspiratorial. "You care for people by your actions and words. I use food—the singular comfort I understand. We'll be down in a couple of minutes."

After she returns across the hall to June's apartment and invites the young woman and her daughters to join them, Ava makes her way back down to her office. Sheila is sitting beside Maggie's desk, tears flowing unchecked down her flushed and mottled face. Maggie peers up at her boss, desperation leaking from her round brown eyes.

"No need for tears, Sheila. Fiona will take care of Ronny, now. The police have requested that we stay here until they find Duncan—or Devon." Ava acknowledges the alias for Sheila's benefit.

Ava expects the night will be long. "Marjorie will be cooking us a spaghetti supper. Maggie. Would you and Sheila set the big table, get out the pot we use for cooking pasta, and take a peek at what we have for drinks?"

Maggie nods and jumps up but Sheila remains seated. "Water should be fine, but some people prefer a soda. I don't know what Chrissie likes. Poor thing. She must feel somewhat neglected after a day like today, but Marjorie has helped." Ava's shoulders sag.

"Let me call Rose, Ava, so she knows I won't be home. The boys—the cats," she smiles, "will want into my apartment."

"If Rose would like to come over after she tends to the cats, tell her she is more than welcome."

"Thanks, Ava, but I don't think she'll want to eat here tonight. And, Ava," Maggie focuses on her boss before she makes the call. "Chrissie will get my undivided attention tomorrow, even if developments get crazy around here." She refrains from stating their cumulative fears. "All we can do is talk, and call her parents. I imagine any appointments we might make wouldn't happen until next week. I can take care of Chrissie. She will spend the day with me. She has no immediate follow-up at the hospital, does she?"

"No, but I imagine her arm aches although she hasn't complained, at least not to me. She won't be much help to Marjorie in transporting supper downstairs. Sheila, how about you run up and help them. You need a chore."

Sheila swipes at her wet cheeks with the sleeve of her rumpled grey sweat shirt and leaves without a word.

"I've never seen Sheila cry before, Ava. She has always been so quiet and stern."

"I know, Maggie. You can learn something new about somebody every day." She turns toward her office. Maggie picks up the phone. Ava can hear her speak in a soft voice to her sister.

She enters her space alone for the first time in what seems like hours, sits down in the wingback chair wedged into the corner, and permits her tears to flow unchecked for a few precious moments. She will carry on for the rest of the evening after damp tension has run down her cheeks. She reaches for a tissue off her desk as she wanders to the window. *If they find this guy and he proves to be Duncan Taylor, will he tell the cops where Ronny can be found? Better to find her dead than not find her at all.*

Her breath catches in her throat. Has she come to grips with the realization Ronny could very well be dead? The tears start again—not the controlled, tension-releasing kind, but the unchecked flood of fear, dread, and clarity she seems to have uncovered.

****

Supper is a sombre affair. Even June's two daughters are more quiet than usual, if such a condition is even possible. Marjorie tries, in her own way, to give people hope and a sense of importance. Wrapped in an apron with a bib, the trim of red roses jump off the white cotton as she sets plates warmed from the oven down in front of each of them. After this, she magically produces a fresh loaf of bread liberally garnished with garlic butter. She tosses the spaghetti noodles and sauce in a huge metal mixing bowl before she places their supper, like an offering, in the centre of the table. Ava is aware Marjorie is trying, in her own way, to hold the house together.

Ava knows how everyone, except perhaps Sheila, is worried Duncan Taylor will show up at the shelter. She also knows an RCMP cruiser will glide past every fifteen minutes or so. When they stop, she expects the reason will be because they have Duncan in custody and she will get a call to say the shelter can rest easy. Then she and Maggie can go home. Until this happens, they are stuck.

She allows dinner to drag on a little. The activity absorbs time. By nine, dusk has begun to settle in. June thanks Marjorie and Ava as she scuttles her girls out the door and up the stairs to the apartment above. Maggie begins to clear the table. Chrissie helps. The two women seem to have hit it off. Ava overhears Maggie talking about tomorrow's plans with the new resident. Sheila nurses a mug of tea while she sits in the lounge area. She stared at her plate and mumbled but a few words all evening. She did manage to remember to thank Marjorie for supper.

Ava, once she sees the kitchen chores are well in hand, approaches Sheila with a measure of caution. "Are you okay? Do you want to have a chat?"

"I wish someone would call and say they found him. He has to be the one, but it would be better to know."

"There's always the hope he might not be Duncan and this is nothing but a big misunderstanding, Sheila." Ava makes a valiant attempt at kindness, but senses futility.

"What did Fiona say Ronny's real name is?"

"Not her real name, Sheila, but the name she used to have was Janine Taylor. Why?"

"I saw him with his jacket and ball cap off once. He has a lot of tattoos, but there is a tattoo of the name 'Janine' on his arm." She stares over at Ava who is incapable of preventing an expression of total surprise from enveloping her face. "I know it's him, Ava."

"Why didn't you tell Fiona this when we talked in my office? My God, Sheila, they are out there searching for a man who tried to kill Ronny. He took her. We don't know what he might have done, and now you tell me you're positive Devon is, in reality, Duncan. We have to call the detachment! Come with me."

She stomps across the apartment to her office in the back. "Come on!" She tries to contain her anger. How could Sheila have not told Fiona about the tattoo?

"Hayworth RCMP Detachment."

"Hi. Ava Burrway over at Segue House." She feels breathless as she tries to get her name out. "Can you get a message to Constable Fiona Werbowski for me? It's regarding the Ronny Étang case."

"I can try. They're pretty busy right now."

"Could you contact her and tell her to call me the first chance she gets? I promise, it is important. She has the number."

"I'll do what I can."

"I appreciate your efforts. Thanks so much."

She hangs up the phone and drops into the wingback. "Sit down, Sheila."

"No one told me Ronny had another name. I forgot to mention the tattoo, Ava. I'm sorry I'm so stupid. Can I go downstairs for a nap before they call, and you and Maggie leave? I am falling asleep in the chair, and I still have to be on duty all night."

"Of course, Shelia, and you're not stupid. Don't ever say that. We've had that conversation more than once." Ava glances at her watch. Almost ten. Fiona might call any time now. "You go downstairs for a rest. Someone will come get you if circumstances change."

"Ava, what did I do wrong? So...no guy will ever take an interest in somebody like me? Is that it? Everybody thinks 'why would ugly, fat old Sheila ever have a boyfriend?' 'Why would any guy ever take her out?' So... there will never be a chance for me with a guy? I wondered at first. What did he want? He asked a few questions about work, but he didn't seem to want much."

Ava opens her mouth to speak but Sheila keeps talking. "Should I have figured if a guy acts like he likes me and asks about my job.... I see the look on your face. I never told him anything. Should I figure there's a problem?"

She keeps her voice quiet and even. "Sit back down, Sheila. Let's think about some of the topics you talked about with Devon. Give my questions some thought and answer with as much detail as possible. Did he ever ask who worked here? Did you tell him?"

Sheila's face clouds as she recalls conversations. "Yes. I told him about you and your family place. I told him about Ronny and how she has a little house on Poplar Street. I never talked about clients or security stuff."

Ava's insides seethe, but she remains outwardly calm. "Did he ever ask about the investigation?"

Sheila's response is quick. She tries to please her boss, and her behaviour is obvious. Ava is shocked as she realizes Sheila still hasn't fully grasped the extent of her role in all this. The consequence of the head injury she suffered years ago has played a significant part in the situation.

"He asked about the cops all the time. I thought he was concerned. I wasn't here for the meeting they had, and he was a little pissed off I didn't have any inside info except they were workin' on the situation. He said over and over they never found Roz Dover so they would never find Ronny." Tears puddle into her eyes. "God, Ava. All he did was pump me for information! He probably didn't even like me! I'm a damned idiot! You guys must want to kill me!"

"No." Ava's voice is measured. "After this is all over, we will sit down as a team and talk about how important our personal information is, and how easy it is to betray someone's confidence without even realizing what we've done. We are always very careful to protect our clients, but I think we need a refresher course on protecting the privacy of one another. Fiona or Sean will be happy to come in and help me with a presentation. We've learned a lot this week, Sheila. I pray Ronny hasn't paid the price. You go rest. I can check on Maggie and the others. It's late. The cops must not be able to find him."

They both return to the main part of the apartment and Sheila continues on into the foyer and down the stairs to her rooms. Marjorie, Chrissie, and Maggie remain seated at the table. They all sip on mugs of fresh brewed tea. "Is there any more?" Before anyone responds, Marjorie jumps up, grabs a cup, and pours for Ava.

"I have been saying to the others that I would love to stay on here and be a house mother. I have an income. I can pay rent, or in lieu of rent, I can provide the food and cook the meals. If I need a day off, folks will be able to fend for themselves. Possibility?" She holds Ava's surprised gaze while she waits for a response.

"What about your sister and your move to Ontario?"

"Going east is merely an option. Listen, my husband couldn't care less about me. I expect he has one of his lady friends already moved in. Let me stay through the winter—same arrangement as now. I can keep the bedroom in the apartment upstairs, but there's still the hide-a-bed for another client. I will manage meals and even do some light housework. If you decide, in the spring, that my attempt to contribute hasn't worked out, I will tell my sister I am on the way." The other two at the table grin in unison, first at her and then at Ava. They appear to believe the idea has merit.

Faced with the three of them, Ava tries to sound supportive, but will not make a promise she'll be unable to keep. It is not the right time to say the idea has already crossed her mind. "Let's sit tight until we get Ronny back home, okay? No decisions right now. I want to avoid making any new commitments until we get Ronny home."

As if on cue, the phone jangles them all into a frantic alertness. Ava raises her hand to settle them down, and takes her tea into her office. She closes the door, panic-stricken in anticipation of what she might hear on the other end of the phone.

"Segue House. Ava Burrway."

"Hi, Ava. Fiona here. We have him. The investigators are questioning him now. I expect they will have a long night. We know, now, Devon Thompson is Duncan Taylor."

"How did you get him?"

"We did a little sting. Megan Wiley went to the Pimiskaw Tavern in street clothes and waited for him. The girl at the bar said she was certain he would be in at some point. He always arrived later in the evening. He seemed to like Megan right away. The rest was easy. He won't reveal any direct information about Ronny. Insists he just happened upon Hayworth and met Sheila. Pure coincidence, he says. Of course, we know the truth. I suspect it will take some time to get him to talk, though."

"Thanks for telling me about this, Fiona."

"No problem, but listen. Tomorrow I want to come over and interview Sheila again. I may have to deliver her down here and let one of the investigators have a run at her. We think Duncan might have let details slip about Ronny and her whereabouts."

"She told me tonight how he asked a lot of questions about the staff, where they live, and what was revealed to us about the search. Poor Sheila. She never once twigged she was his connection."

"You and Maggie go home. We will see you first thing tomorrow, and go from there. Good night, Ava." In a softer voice, she adds, "We'll find her."

Ava returns to the kitchen where the three women remain seated. "Maggie, how about I drive you home? Marjorie and Chrissie, you can go to bed. They have Duncan Taylor in custody and continue to question him as we speak.

Now I have to go wake up Sheila."

"Don't wake her," Marjorie pipes up. "I can stay awake tonight. Let her sleep. All I need is for you to explain to me what to do about security checks."

"Okay, Marjorie, if you're sure. We aren't operating exactly by the book here tonight."

"I thought I might bake. I bought some extra groceries, so I can watch Johnny Carson and make bread, maybe a pie. Tomorrow, they'll find Ronny." Her hand flutters up to smooth her hair as she trots behind Ava to learn the routine.

Chapter 19

~

Maggie

By the time Ava drops Maggie off in the front parking lot of The Station, the time is well past ten. Rose's light is still on. The main door is locked but Maggie has her key ready. She takes a moment to gaze up at the second and third story windows. Patrick's lights are on which is normal if he's not on shift at the diner. Joe's apartment is still empty for some reason. The owners haven't found a renter yet, or Joe still has the lease. Whatever. There are no lights at Cheryl's. She has probably gone to bed. Exhaustion wraps around Maggie's bones, but she knows she won't sleep. It pleases her to see Rose's apartment door ajar as she enters the building foyer.

She peeks through the opening. "I'm back." Her voice is barely above a whisper. The two cats wrap themselves around her legs in a welcoming ritual. She bends down to give each one an appreciative pat. Caesar and Caramel calm her, even when she treads closest to the edge.

Rose pops around the corner, wiping her hands on a tea towel. "My God, I thought you would never get here! I took care of the boys and I've been watching TV and knitting for what seems like hours." Her voice takes on a softened tone. "They haven't found her, have they?"

Maggie knows her sister can glean all the information she wants by careful inspection of her face. "No. They picked up Duncan Taylor, though. They have him down at the detachment, but Fiona told Ava he hasn't said much so far."

"Come in and have some tea. I've put the kettle on already. Tell me every detail."

"I want to go home and have a shower, Rose. Can I come back in twenty minutes for tea and a visit? I feel like I've been in these clothes for a week!" The pressure of the day hits with sudden force. Tears start to roll unchecked down her ivory cheeks. "Poor Ronny! Here I am complaining about clothes I put on this morning! She could be anywhere! Oh God, Rose. I have to go home for a few minutes!" She turns on her heel and dashes across the hall, fumbling with her keys as she goes. Caesar and Caramel thunder behind her, like participants in a parade.

When all three of them are inside her apartment, she turns on the lights, and prepares to have her shower. The cats curl up together on her bed.

She stands in the tub and permits the hot water to run through her long dark hair, down the back of her neck, around her shoulders, and across her breasts. The steamy fluid hardens her nipples, and she thinks of Sean. Within an instant, self-admonished and annoyed, she grabs the soap, completes a quick lather, and rinses down. She turns off the water and reaches for the towel hung on the hook near the tub. *How can I be so callous and think about Sean at a time like this? What is the matter with me?* The familiar tension, reduced by the hot water, starts to build again, especially in her neck and shoulders.

She pats dry and dons the soft cotton nightie she has hung behind the bathroom door. She pads on bare feet into her bedroom to retrieve her wrap and a pair of leather moccasins with fleecy lining. "Are you two coming or do you both want to stay here?" Her remarks go unheeded, so she assumes they will remain on her bed. She reaches for her keys, left on the kitchen peninsula, and returns to her sister's apartment. The door is still open. Unlike Maggie, who almost always locks her door, Rose quite often leaves hers ajar. The main door is always locked, for security. She assumes her neighbours will stop and say hello. Most do.

"Caesar and Caramel are the smart ones in this family and have gone to bed." She reaches behind her neck to grab her long hair and rolls the strands into a rope-like twist over her shoulder. "My straggly mop is still quite wet."

"Come have tea and tell me what's happened, Maggie."

Maggie nods but says nothing as she pulls out one of the matching three chairs and seats herself at Rose's orange lacquered, art deco dining room table. It was a deal she bought from Ben Tullis many years ago.

"You're exhausted. Have you eaten? All you told me on the phone was how circumstances were chaotic and you'd be late. I should have come over when you invited me."

"Like I told you, Rose, one of the residents, Marjorie—you met her yesterday—brought spaghetti downstairs once we realized the RCMP wanted us to sit tight for the evening." She wants to stay up for the night and do Sheila's job."

"What's Sheila doing that one of the clients is filling in for her?"

"Sheila's gone to bed—or at least she is down in the basement and out of sight. I don't know if she might be in trouble or not, but she sure as hell should be!" The sound of her voice is vicious, even to her own ears. Her sister's wide-eyed expression is difficult to avoid.

Even though the temperature has not turned cold yet at night, Rose is snuggled into a pink floral flannelette nightgown, with lace at the neck and cuffs. The fit is less than generous around the middle. Maggie thinks Rose should purchase a couple of new ones in a more suitable size. Oh well, Christmas is coming. She is aware her thoughts become more random with increased stress.

"So tell me what happened today. You can share with me, right?"

Maggie nods. "Ava told me I could tell you, since you were at the briefing. I called Sean this morning and told him about the old green pickup, after I told Ava. It was weird because Duncan was driving a grey compact truck yesterday and Ava said a small grey truck came into her yard about this time last night and sat there for a few minutes. She called the shelter after the driver left, I assume to hear a familiar voice, but the pieces of the puzzle must have started to come together for Sheila."

"What makes you think so?" Rose is on the edge of her seat. She has her short permed hair held back from her face with a plastic hair band. Her eyes are wide.

"Sheila borrowed Marjorie's car and took off this morning while Ava was at the hospital with a new client. She must have connected the truck in Ava's yard with her boyfriend's truck. In any event, I guess she went to find him, but couldn't.

"Ava called Fiona and she came over with Sean. I told Fiona every piece of information I could remember about the guy, while some other RCMP went out to search for Marjorie's Lincoln! Once they escorted Sheila home, they questioned her and she provided a physical description and told them where he was staying. They caught him. The stress has been awful, Rose!"

"Oh my, what a terrible time you all have had today! And, what about Ronny?"

Maggie starts to puddle up again. "Every time I think of Ronny, I start to cry. Fiona called tonight to tell us they located Taylor and we could all go home. He told the police he landed here by pure coincidence and happened to meet Sheila by chance. Ava said the investigators aren't buying any part of his story. My God, Rose, what if Ronny is hurt somewhere? What if he won't tell us where she is? What if Ronny's dead?"

Maggie starts to sob outright now, her tea untouched and cold on the coffee table. Rose wriggles out of her chair and settles in beside Maggie on the turquoise and yellow patterned couch. She puts her arm around her sister and squeezes a little. Overt displays of affection make Maggie uncomfortable, but she has managed to improve over the years. Rose's touch is no longer the annoyance and intrusion it once was. She pats Rose's knee as an expression of her gratitude.

"The pressure is unbelievable, Rose. I have never felt so hopeless; not since I was put in Forest Hills Institute." She meets her sister's stare. "Then, they gave me drugs and kept me comatose most of the time. Now, I'm here, and I don't know what to do. I hope I can avoid going to pieces."

Rose's voice is soft. "They will find Ronny. They will find her and you, my dear sister, will be fine. You are strong. After this is over, you can schedule a few extra appointments with Dr. Wilkerson if you want. We'll find a way to cover the bill. You do what you have to do, okay?"

Maggie nods. Rose always manages to work the budget into a conversation. She was so afraid Maggie wouldn't be able to make ends meet after she moved across the hall, but Maggie is good with money. "I think I'd better go to bed, Rose. I expect tomorrow will be a bad day, too, if Duncan continues to refuse to talk and they have no clue as to where to search for Ronny."

Stretched out in bed, with the pressure of a warm cat body curled up on either side of her, she is sure she hears Ronny's tears.

****

Maggie is up and at the shelter very early on Friday morning. Marjorie buzzes her in. It's just after seven-thirty. The shelter smells fabulous. Marjorie has spent the night baking brown bread and apple pie. Kitchen clean-up is complete and a big pot of coffee has been made. Maggie wishes she had skipped her cereal before she walked to work.

"The shelter was quiet, Maggie. Sheila came upstairs about midnight, all in a panic and we visited for a short time before I sent her back to bed. I told her I would wake her up this morning before I go upstairs for a rest. Does Chrissie think she will call her parents today?"

Maggie attempts a response but Marjorie continues. "She has been quite anxious but didn't want to impose. She knows she is safe; such a nice child." The older woman's report comes out in a rush, like she is in need of company after being alone and awake throughout the night.

Maggie drapes her yellow sweater, knit by her sister, over the back of her chair. Rose taught her how to knit after she arrived in Hayworth from Forest Hills Institute—after they returned to Penny Falls and made the final break with their parents—but she knows she will never be as good as Rose. She is unable to concentrate on the process for any length of time. "I will make sure Ava knows after she gets here. I hope to spend most of the day with Chrissie regardless. We can call her folks whenever she thinks she's ready. No outside calls overnight?"

"None. The phone was mercifully quiet. I knew I could go get Sheila if there was an incident or request, but I was fine."

"Okay. Brown bread toast all around, Marjorie! What did you make? Four loaves? Time to roust the others."

Ava arrives soon after. Maggie buzzes her in as Chrissie gallops down the stairs and Sheila trudges up from the basement like she is climbing one of the Rocky Mountains.

"Good morning, everyone." Ava begins once everyone standing in the foyer is paying attention. "Sheila, get some breakfast. Fiona will be here any time now. They want to go over every detail about Duncan with you. Be prepared. You may have to go down to the detachment."

She starts to bark a bit as she tries to take control. Maggie understands, but Sheila and Chrissie seem a little intimidated. "Chrissie, I think you need to at least make an attempt to call your parents. Maggie can go over with you what you want to say, before you call. If you're worried, come and talk to me first. Has anybody seen June? I expect she will want to have a conversation with me before the day's end."

The three women follow her like ducklings after their mother, as Ava enters the main apartment and goes through the various rooms to get to her office in the back.

"Marjorie made brown bread last night. Who wants toast?" Maggie attempts to smooth out the roughness left in the air by Ava.

Sheila thuds her ass into a chair at the dining table. "I guess I'd better eat before they come and haul me off."

Maggie offers her a cup of coffee. Sheila does not need to be waited on, but today will not be the day she chooses to fight over this particular recurring issue.

Fiona and Sean both arrive. Once they're through the foyer, Fiona goes straight into Ava's office and shuts the door. Maggie is sure Sean has remained outside in order to talk to her. She knows her cheeks are flushed and her tongue is tied in knots. She offers him coffee. "Have you eaten? Can I interest you in some homemade brown bread toast?" She tries not to sound coy. She has no flirtation skills.

Sean's eyes are soft and he pats her arm. Then he leans down and whispers in her ear. "I have to stand out here to make sure Sheila stays nearby. I shouldn't say so, though." His breath is hot on her neck as he bends down to her while she sits behind her desk. He straightens back up. "My job is to stand out there in the foyer until Fiona and Ava are ready for the interview." This comes out in a stern voice. He even frowns a little. Maggie attempts to be serious but the appearance of a tiny grin emerges.

After maybe ten minutes, Fiona opens Ava's door and asks Sheila if she will come inside for an interview. "Sean, will you come in, too? I think there should be two of us. Ava will stay so Sheila will have support." Maggie is unable to hear the remainder of the conversation between the two of them while they return to Ava's office. She understands the attempt at confidentiality, difficult in a place like this where doors are closed on rare occasions and residents often eat together.

Chrissie sits in the living room, sips her tea after her breakfast, and waits with patience for someone to pay attention to her. "Okay, it's eight o'clock in Vancouver right now. Are your parents early risers, or should we wait another hour before we call?" Maggie has approached Chrissie and taken a seat beside her.

"Mom takes Fridays off, so I expect she will be home. Dad will have left for work by now."

"Would you rather wait until supper time when they're both there, or would the conversation be better if your mother is alone?"

"I'd rather Mom deal with my dad. He will be so mad, Maggie." She trembles. Wisps of her long blond hair stick to the damp from the tears on her cheeks.

"Do you like your sneakers?" Maggie is unsure about how to move the conversation forward. Chrissie arrived from the hospital, yesterday, with her feet ensconced in paper slippers. Maggie helped her choose from the donated clothes kept over in the closet in Ronny's office. They wash or dry clean items donated. They have shoes and boots in boxes and clothes hung and covered in an old sheet. Chrissie found a pair of sneakers in her size. She also chose another pair of jeans, a T-shirt, and a large hooded sweat shirt with a zipper, big enough to accommodate her cast through the armhole. She was quite excited. Maggie also found her a small wallet-sized purse with a shoulder strap. Her cloth bag was about to fall apart.

"I love all the stuff you gave me, Maggie. I haven't felt so safe in a long time. Clean sheets and a cup of tea mean a lot when you've been living in somebody's dirty apartment. God, their place stunk."

Maggie does her best to stay focused. "What do you want to say to your mom when you call?"

"I want to tell her how sorry I am. I want to tell her I made a mistake and I want to come home. I don't have any money, so I need to ask her to send me money and I don't even know what to do to make that work!" She starts to puddle up again, and Maggie pats her arm.

"We can figure out the details. First order of business is to call the bus station and get all the particulars, so we know the cost of a ticket. Either of the two banks in town should be able to accept a transfer of funds. I will call and find out, so we can tell your mom what needs to be done. What else do you want to say?"

"I want to ask her if I can try to go back to school. I finished my first year at Capilano College. I know they would take me back. My grades were good last year."

"Is that all?"

"I want to ask her about my brother. He goes to university. He's older than me. He wants to be a lawyer!"

Maggie is struck by how Chrissie beams when she talks about her brother. "Okay. First thing is to call the bus station and both banks. We'll get ourselves some information, and then we'll call your mom. How does that sound?"

"Good, Maggie. Thanks so much to you and Ava for all your help. Mom would die if she knew someone had to give me shoes."

"Help works when a person is open to the idea, Chrissie. You wanted to make a change. That's all it takes!" She produces a confident smile, pats her on the shoulder one more time, and returns to her desk to do her telephone research. *As long as there are no new referrals.*

About ten minutes later, with Ava, Sheila, and the two RCMP officers still holed up in Ava's office, Maggie sets the phone back in the cradle after her chat with the bus station employee. June then appears with her kids. Maggie knows they'll soon be prepared to leave, but want to stay out of the way right now. June will try to linger at Segue House until the situation with Ronny is resolved.

"Good morning, everyone! Kelly, Amber say hello to Maggie and Chrissie." The girls, still shy and incredibly quiet, both mumble a muffled word or two to appease their mother. "Maggie, I have to update you. I have managed to find both an apartment and a job in St. Albert."

"That's wonderful, June! Are you leaving right away?" Maggie thinks June will want to stick around until Ronny is found, but perhaps circumstances won't permit that option.

"I want to stay here with the girls until there is some news about Ronny. I've told my new landlord we will be there next week since my job with the Canadian Cancer Foundation starts the twentieth—a contract position where I help with fundraising events. Part-time is better than no work at all and it will pay the bills for a while. What's the latest?"

"Congratulations, June! You have been busy despite the turmoil. I have no new information. The RCMP picked up Duncan Taylor last night and they're in Ava's office for an interview with Sheila right now. I thought maybe they would take her back to the detachment and let the investigators talk to her, but they haven't moved yet."

"Oh, I hope poor Sheila is okay. She must be scared."

Maggie nods. "I imagine she is."

"I want to stay for the weekend, Maggie, but I will make a donation to cover the non-emergency time, if that works. Now, what we need is for the cops to find Ronny."

Chapter 20

~

Ava

The air held a chill overnight. As a result, Ava dressed in dark trousers and a cotton sweater. Now, in the closeness of her office and confined with both Sheila and Fiona, she regrets her decision. She sits, rigid, in the second-hand wingback chair beside the office window. Sheila and Fiona are across from one another in the client chairs situated in front of her desk. Sean stands at the closed door. Her role is to act as support for Sheila. If the interview does not go well, Sheila will have to be questioned by the detectives down at the detachment.

Thursday night proved long. Even with Duncan Taylor in custody, they seem no further ahead in their search for Ronny. Ava lay in her big bed and stared at the ornate plaster ceiling medallion supporting the caramel glass light fixture illuminated by a slice of moon. The moon always makes more of an impression out in the country. She couldn't sleep and she couldn't keep her drifting mind away from the rocky shoals of bad outcomes. *Perhaps Duncan's cocky because he knows she is already dead but expects her body will never be found. That can happen. What if they can't find Ronny? Fiona will go crazy. They're good friends. Ronny's loss would rock the community, for sure. Hayworth would never recover. Neither would I.*

She attempts to focus on the task at hand. Fiona is assuring Sheila. "I want you to try and think of every conversation you've had with him, before and after Monday, Sheila." She leans over, puts her elbows on her knees, and gets as close to her witness as she can. "You haven't committed any crime, but we're sure you can help us. Let's go back over every detail once again."

"Take your time, Sheila. Review any conversations you had," Ava contributes. She knows Sheila spooks with little or no provocation, and her memory is worse when stressed. She doesn't want her to clam up, not now. There's a life at stake.

"I remember he asked me about the fundraiser dance and if someone named Ronny still worked at the shelter. I told him she did, but said we don't talk about staff or clients because of privacy rules." Sheila turns to search Ava's face for confirmation. "He already seemed to know she worked here. All I did was repeat what he already knew."

"He asked about the fundraiser?" Fiona is thoughtful for a minute. "Ava, do you recall if there was ever any publicity with Ronny included?"

"There were a couple of pictures in the paper, remember? Last year, she worried because one was published by the Edmonton Journal. We decided her own father wouldn't recognize her, so there was no need to be paranoid. No other issues." She raises her eyebrows at Fiona, behind Sheila's back.

"Did you give him any pictures, Sheila?"

The woman is aghast. "I wouldn't! Honest to God, you guys, I may be stupid, but not *that* stupid? He asked about her like he already knew somehow. I said she was here. All he had to do was hang around until she walked to or from work. She walks a lot! He didn't need me!"

"You are getting defensive, Sheila. Nobody thinks you're to blame." Ava forces her voice to be quiet and steady. Again, she wants to jump out of her chair, run over, and clobber Sheila. *How could she put Ronny in such jeopardy?* In her heart, she knows Sheila had no idea of Ronny's past and couldn't be expected to assume this guy was out to hurt Ronny. But still....

"Did he ever mention he knew where Ronny lived?" Fiona continues with her questions.

"I might have told him she lived on Poplar, and how she rents a little house." Her eyes are downcast and then she glances over at Ava. Sheila has begun to get upset. Ava knows she might well withdraw and they'll never get additional details from her.

"Tell me about your relationship, Sheila. Where did he take you? What did you do?" Fiona sounds genuinely interested and Sheila responds.

"We went for drives and to the diner to eat. I introduced him to Maggie and Rose at the diner. Night before last, Wednesday, he took me out to Pimiskaw, to the tavern for supper. He wasn't in a very good mood. I think, now, he was pissed because I didn't stay for your briefing. He asked me a couple of times if the cops had any clues. I told him over and over I didn't know. I was pretty sure he was mad at me. After we had supper, he brought me back here for work. He said he'd call the next day, after I talked to Ava about what happened at the meeting. Then, Ava, you called and talked about a grey truck so I borrowed Marjorie's car and tried to find him."

"Go on." Fiona encourages Sheila to talk. Ava aches to know precisely where Sheila went in Marjorie's Lincoln.

"I went out to the Pimiskaw Tavern but Penny said he wasn't there. After I left the bar, I went to the Petro-Can to get a sandwich. I called Maggie."

"Yes. Then we asked one of our officers to locate you and escort you back. That took a while. Constable Wiley was up and down the highway and couldn't seem to find you. Did you go someplace else?"

"Yes." Sheila's voice is almost a whisper. Ava sits up straighter in her chair and leans toward the other two women. "See, when I was at the service station, I went back to the car with my sandwich and he pulled into the lot right after. I watched him go inside and then come out with a coffee and a bag. I followed him. He went down some dirt and grass road. I couldn't go down there in the Lincoln. That would be wrong. I didn't dare drive Marjorie's car down that road, but now I doubt if I could find the turn-off."

Fiona is fidgety. Ava can tell right away. She attempts to stay calm, but Ava knows what will come next. "Tell me what happened, Sheila. Don't leave one detail out."

"He left the service station and crossed the highway. Is the direction east? Anyway, the road was gravel and dusty. I followed him and I let a grain truck pass me so he wouldn't see me at all, although I know he would never expect to see me in a big car like Marjorie's. Anyway, the grain truck pulled off into a field and he wasn't up ahead anymore. I turned around as soon as I found a spot and drove back toward the highway. I saw a cloud of dust way down one road. I stopped and watched, but stayed put. Maybe it was someone else and not him. Then I came back here. The lady cop stopped me on the way." She expels a puff of air and leans back into the chair, like she has just run a marathon.

Ava thinks Sheila remains oblivious to what she omitted in her discussion with the police the previous day. Fiona lifts her small frame, and all the gear she wears, out of the chair. "I have to talk with Sean for a minute. We will be right back."

Ava can hear murmurs on the other side of her closed office door. "Sheila!" It is a supreme challenge for Ava to keep her voice under control. "My God, did the thought not cross your mind Ronny could be down that road? Did you not think, for one minute, how it might be a good idea to tell the police about your wild goose chase?"

Sheila's eyes puddle up in an instant. "It just didn't seem important. Honest to God, Ava! When I followed him, I still felt he was who he said he was. I couldn't believe it. I hoped he went for a little drive to have his coffee. If you had told me what Fiona said at the meeting, I would have known." Her expression is suddenly defiant.

Ava scrapes hair off her moist brow as Fiona re-enters the room. "Sheila, we want you to come with us. We are going to retrace your steps from yesterday. We have other officers on their way to the area and the investigators will talk to Duncan Taylor again, to see if they can get more information out of him. You go outside with Sean. I want to talk to Ava."

After Sheila makes her way into the main part of the apartment, Fiona closes the door. "We're pretty sure Ronny is alive, Ava. Duncan finally admitted he grabbed her. He let slip about how we'll never find her and she'll starve to death. This is the fifth day and we have no idea how much she has had to eat. She was at least alive the last time he saw her. Keep this information confidential for now. I cannot reveal interrogation details, but intend to find Ronny today, if I have to take Sheila down every back road between here and Carter River."

"I know you will, Fiona. Keep a close eye on Sheila, though. She has had some bad experiences in a troubled past. If she gets too upset, she won't remember. She'll be of no use to you. She trusts me, Fiona, so if you have any trouble, call me. I might be able to talk to her."

Maggie is standing in the open doorway as Fiona rushes out. "What's up, Maggie? What's the trouble?" She can tell there's an issue by the expression on her face.

"I think we have a new client, Ava."

"What? Who is it?"

Maggie continues to report to Ava despite her anxious interruption. "I checked her identification and then tried to make her comfortable over in Ronny's office. She seems very young and has an exceptionally tiny baby in some sort of wrap tied around her shoulders. She said her name is Marta Sepp."

"How did she get here? Do you know?"

"Her baby is six months old and she came here on the bus from the Four Corners Petro-Can this morning. I found her a few diapers and some clean clothes for Jana—the baby. I made her some toast and tea. I told her the place is a little crazy today, but she would be safe here and could talk to you once you were free. Okay, Ava? What else could I do?"

"You did a fine job, Maggie, considering you happen to be the receptionist and bookkeeper. You're getting quite good at this social worker stuff." She reaches out and puts her arm around Maggie's shoulder—the merest of light touches.

In a move that surprises Ava, Maggie leans into her, almost as if she needs support from her boss. "Can you scare up a cup of coffee for me, before I go see this Marta-person and determine if we need to do an intake?"

"What happened with Sheila, Ava? Fiona and Sean took her with them. There were two more cop cars out front when they left. Sean's shoulder radio contraption never stopped. He said he'd call me later. I assume someone will drive Sheila back."

"Sheila's not in any trouble, but she may know more, even though she says she is unsure of what she saw. Keep your fingers crossed, Maggie. Come on. Let's find me some coffee and then I can go meet Marta."

****

Ava takes a couple of minutes to change gears and then crosses the hall to Ronny's office on the other side of the foyer. Two new referrals in one week is a lot for the shelter. Chrissie appears to be under control. Her parents will wire money to the bank so she can go home. She will take the bus to Edmonton on Monday and there's a plane ticket already purchased for her at the airport. New referrals have not been Ava's responsibility for some time. Ronny has done them all for so long, she had forgotten how exhausting they can be.

She gives the door a light tap and enters straight into the living room. The curtains are drawn, since Sheila most often spends her shift curled up in the lounger here, watching television through the night. Ava is shocked. Maggie was right. Marta Sepp seems like an adolescent at best, as she peers up through long blond hair desperate for a wash, and forces a polite smile supported by very sad, blue eyes.

"Hi, Marta? My name is Ava Burrway, the director here at Segue House. Please call me Ava."

The child, as that is what she appears to be—a child holding another child—lifts sad eyes toward Ava and responds. "Hello, Ava. This is Jana." She gazes with open affection back down at the baby.

"My, what a beautiful child. How old is she?"

The young woman cannot hide her worried expression. "Jana is six months, but she seems to stay so small. I've been breastfeeding her. Maybe I need to try some formula or whatever."

"We can help you, Marta. When was the last time you and Jana saw a doctor?"

"Not since I had the baby. Gustav, my husband, won't call a doctor. He wanted me to have the baby at home but I was too afraid."

"Let's start with what brought you here today."

Marta snuggles her remarkably quiet baby closer to her chest and begins. "Gustav has hit me before, but he stopped when I found out I was pregnant. He was so excited we would have a son! He made up his mind we would have a boy. A son is all he ever wanted. After I had Jana, he was angry all over again. He started to drink a lot more than he used to. Yesterday afternoon, while I was holding the baby and trying to feed her, he started to rant about who knows what. He threatened to hit me while I had her in my arms. All I could think of was how big her eyes were when he yelled and when he raised his fist. She never cries, even when the noise is very loud. I ducked. He stopped. He went outside and then later came in and went to bed."

Ava nods. "Go on, Marta."

"I waited until two this morning, dressed Jana, grabbed some money, and walked for four hours to the gas station where the bus comes. At seven, I caught the bus to the Hayworth Diner. I waited there for about an hour and then screwed up the nerve to ask the guy behind the counter if he could direct me to the shelter. He was kind." She seems breathless as the details of her story fill the space between them.

Ava is struck by how familiar Marta's tale is. "You must have talked to Patrick Hollinger. Yes, he is a very sweet young man. Do you have a plan? Do you have family nearby?"

"They're all in Saskatchewan. They wanted me to marry Gustav, even though he's twenty years older than me. It is rare when an Estonian immigrant family finds another Estonian to marry their daughter. They thought it would be a match made in heaven. I don't think they were right, do you?" Her tone holds the tiniest bit of sarcasm but her expression remains sad.

"Will your husband come after you?"

"Oh yes! He'll be wild. He'll probably call police and have them drag me home. I'm afraid for Jana."

"The police won't drag you home from here. You can be assured of that. For now, let's get you settled. We still have two empty units on the top floor. I think the one on the other side has a crib already in one of the rooms. You can stay there, but you have to be prepared to share. Maggie will do all the paperwork and the two of you can determine what you need for both yourself and Jana. We can supply everything from toiletries for you, to diapers and formula for your baby."

Marta's voice shakes as tears muffle the thank you she tries to say to Ava.

Ava smiles and pats Marta on the shoulder. "You just relax and finish your tea. You're safe. Give us a few minutes, and then Maggie will settle you in. Think about your next move, Marta. We begin to plan discharges from Segue House the minute you start to receive our services. Everyone has to have a plan to move forward."

She remembers Marjorie and June. Sometimes an exit strategy works. Sometimes the process takes longer than one expects. She might even take Marjorie up on her offer to stay on.

Ava finds Maggie at her desk, her eyes focused on a smudge on the opposite wall. She jumps a little when Ava rounds the corner. "Hi! Sorry, Ava, I guess I was wool-gathering about Ronny. Do you think maybe Duncan will tell them where she is?"

"I have my doubts, but I have every faith in Fiona and the Hayworth detachment. They will find her, Maggie. I know they'll find her. Now…about Marta. I need you to settle her up in Number Six, above June. She needs essentials. She has some money but no vehicle and no real plans. Is Marjorie cooking again tonight? If I'm not careful, she will be an employee before I know what's happened!"

"Yes, she gave strict instructions this morning for us not to eat the pie while she was napping because she wants to serve it for dessert with supper tonight."

"Okay. See what we have in supplies for baby stuff and if we need formula, or diapers. I can run downtown and get whatever we might need. Make me a list. I managed to avoid the paperwork." She graces Maggie with an indulgent, motherly grin.

"That's okay, Ava. I can take care of it. You have enough to do."

Maggie is stepping up. Ava couldn't be more proud of her. "I knew you'd want to fill in the forms so they're done properly."

Maggie is out from behind her desk and gone before Ava gets into her own office. How Maggie has changed since she presented for her interview as a part-time bookkeeper. Back then, Ava had no other staff. Maggie was so excited. She promised she could do the job, regardless of her history. Maggie has always been open about her past. Ava is at a loss to know how the place would run without her. As an aside, it would be nice if she and Sean went out. He's such a nice young man and Ava suspects Maggie is quite smitten.

Marta will have to decide if she will go back to Saskatchewan or try and start again someplace else, like maybe Edmonton or Calgary. Ava has not asked about her education, or if she thinks she could find a job. The size of the baby is suspicious. Ava has seen a few "failure to thrive" babies in her time—babies who don't seem to follow the standard growth charts. Perhaps there is a physical problem with the child, or perhaps the condition is linked to emotional issues. Marta said her baby never cries. Ava decides not to rush her new client. June and her kids will be gone the first of the week. Chrissie is only here for a couple more days. During this crisis, Marjorie has seemed to emerge as a member of the staff. A formal decision about Marjorie will have to wait. The one issue remaining is to get Ronny home.

Chapter 21

Shelia

Fiona opens the back door of the squad car and Sheila climbs in with a familiar reluctance she hasn't felt in some time. Back in the day, cops weren't your friends. Cops, on the move toward you, meant trouble. All the old images return. Even the smell of air freshener, meant to camouflage stale sweat and urine, is familiar.

Sean navigates the big Caprice from the back lot to the street where two other cars, one marked and one not, idle. They all take off out of Hayworth, toward the highway and Carter River.

"Once we get to the Petro-Can, we turn left. Am I right, Sheila?" Fiona sits sideways in the front seat and peers through the partition. Her face looks like it has been in some horrific accident, dissected a dozen times by the wire mesh.

"Yup. I followed him across the road, so from this direction it would be left, but I can't remember where he went. I never saw where he turned!" Sheila is scared their expectations of her are too high. She forgets things. The more anxious she gets, the less able she is to remember. She becomes confused. She has managed to learn enough self-awareness over the last few years with Ava, to know she has to be careful and not let her emotions get a grip on her thoughts.

"We'll travel down every side road, every driveway, and every cut line we can find, Sheila. All you have to do is tell us when the fields and roads start to look familiar."

Sheila nods but keeps her face down and her hands folded in her lap. The air inside the cruiser is hot. She dressed in a sweat shirt and corduroy pants this morning because the days start with a chill in the air, but now the sun's out and she feels dizzy with the August heat. "Can you crack a window for me, Fiona? I'm about to faint back here."

She sees Fiona glance over at Sean and he lowers the back window on the opposite side from where Sheila sits, but only by about an inch. Perhaps they think she plans to try and jump out.

She attempts to calm down, but all she can think of is the last time she was in the back of a police car. She was in Edmonton, before her return to Hayworth.

****

She tried her damndest to find a job after she and her father fought for the last time and she left. She had worked hard for him. She ran the farm with little assistance from him after her brother went to work in Fort McMurray. Her father, a burly Ukrainian immigrant, who believed all women should be in the kitchen and having babies, needed a hand but was always mad at her anyway. Ava suggested he was angry because he resented getting help from his daughter, and so he took it out on her. He hit her and beat her up so many times, she lost count. Once, he grabbed her by the foot and pulled her off the tractor while the wheels were still moving. She was almost run over. Her mother never said a word. Frederick, Sheila's brother, was the family favourite; had always been the favourite. Her mother made no apologies. Sheila was mannish in her appearance, would never get married, and therefore would never provide her parents with grandchildren. They hated her. She understood this from the time she was young.

In the end, she left and went to Edmonton after her father took after her with a pitch fork. He hit her across the back with the prongs. She could have grabbed the weapon from him but she was scared of what might happen then. She left in the afternoon, with just a kit bag. She walked to Hayworth, about five miles away, and took the bus out to the city.

Her plan for an independent life did not work out. Instead, she lived two years of pure hell. She couldn't get a job because she had no specific training and no schooling after grade eleven. She could manage machinery—any piece of equipment on the farm that moved—but this wasn't good enough at the job fairs where they searched for people to work in the oil patch. They all said she would have to go back to school. Fat chance.

She couch-surfed, sleeping on the battered furniture of friends, and friends of friends. She knew very few people and none of them well. She stayed in homeless shelters when the weather turned cold. She shoveled walks to earn money. She thinks about her past, and wonders how she stayed alive. At the time, she couldn't have cared less.

****

Her mind jumps back to the present when the police radio kicks into gear and a voice from the detachment crackles through the speaker. "Are you near Four Corners, yet? What's your ETA? We have members from Carter River there to meet you."

"Ten minutes from the turn."

"Stop in at the Petro-Can to coordinate with our officers there."

"Right oh. On our way."

"Did Devon, I mean Duncan, talk about her, Fiona? Do you know for sure he took her?"

Fiona turns around to face Sheila slouched in the back. "We know for sure he took her. He also indicated he would never reveal her location and she would starve to death before we ever found her...so we know she is likely alive."

Fiona turns back to face the front, as Sean adds, "Our plan is to have her home today, Sheila, and we expect you to help us."

"But I can't remember, Sean. Stuff gets cloudy for me. When I'm upset, my memory gets worse."

"We know, Sheila." Fiona's voice is soft. "But today is the day you will rise to the occasion." Fiona's tone seems to leave Sheila no other option.

The boat-like Caprice turns off the highway into the gravel parking lot of the service station. Both of the police vehicles accompanying them turn in as well. Constable Megan Wiley leans against the front fender of one dusty patrol car while she waits with her colleagues from Carter River. Another cop is in the passenger seat, talking on the radio. There's a second car parked beside, with two more members standing outside.

"Stay put, Sheila. We'll talk to everyone and then start out." Fiona gets out of the car as Megan unrolls a map on the hood of her cruiser.

With locked rear doors, Sheila has no choice but to follow instructions. Her frustration clouds her brain because she has no idea how far she went down the road. She knows a grain truck with an odd coloured door passed her and then she lost sight of Devon. Then she remembers dust down a long road but then the plume went out of sight—another grain truck for all she knows, or can remember.

****

The last summer she lived in Edmonton, she spent most of her time outside. There were groups of people who camped in the parks of the river valley. She stayed there, made some friends, and drank more than ever. They all begged for money. She found the very idea disgusting. Sheila considered herself to be a good worker, so she would offer to weed gardens and mow lawns for residents in the subdivisions nearby. Her work netted her a sleeping bag and a warmer jacket, but lots of people considered her some kind of traitor because she worked. Maybe he was high on some chemical shit. Maybe he resented that she chose not to panhandle like the rest of them, but some guy beat her within an inch of her life one night. He stole the pint of rum she made the mistake of leaving in plain sight. She would have given him the bottle if he'd asked.

She was in the hospital for three days. They said she had a concussion and called Social Services, but after forty-eight hours, she checked herself out and went back to the river valley. The blackouts and the memory loss started then. Staying drunk seemed to take the edge off. She worried less about what she forgot, if she was drunk.

Then the "Edmonton Sweep" happened. The city decided squatters couldn't stay in the park anymore. Families were scared to take their children for a picnic because of all the people in tents and under blankets. Winter would soon arrive and Social Services said they would make sure everybody had a roof over their head or a bus ticket back where they came from. It was the last time Sheila was in a squad car.

She was at the police station a long time. There must have been fifty people to be processed through the system. Not much time had passed since she was in the hospital, so Social Services located her file. The social worker thought she should go home and work on the farm again. She preferred not to go, but the other choice was a shelter and there was no future in that option, either. She took the ticket.

****

All the units left the Petro-Can parking lot at once. After they crossed the road, some stayed straight, like Sheila did yesterday. Others took off down cut lines and field roads. Farmers were out, starting to swath the canola. Farm implements seemed to dot the landscape. "What's everybody going to do, Fiona?"

"Our goal is to talk to the people in the area who are out on the land today. You keep your eyes peeled for a familiar side road."

"Is this my fault?" Sheila's voice is soft. She can hear the tremor. She has always refused to cry, but her insides seem to have forgotten this rule.

"According to what you've already told us, Sheila, you never gave Duncan Taylor much in the way of confidential material. He already knew she was in the area and worked at the shelter. The one piece of information you might have let slip was about her trip to Carter River for a meeting. He would have had no trouble identifying her vehicle. Her old Buick funeral car is easy to spot."

Sheila starts to blubber in spite of her attempts at control.

"Now, come on. Look out the window! Examine every detail. We will find her today and then we can go back to normal. You might have been Duncan Taylor's connection, Sheila, but this is most definitely not your fault. He was bound and determined to grab her. That's his doing, but you can help us."

The countryside all runs together. She could be on the way down the lane to her parents' farm. Flat lands and gravel roads all look alike.

****

She arrived back at the Hayworth Diner, after her botched attempt at a new life in Edmonton, with the sum of ten dollars in her possession. She made do with a cup of coffee before she started to trudge the five miles to the Pasco homestead.

She recalls the walk up the driveway. Her mother was in the backyard, taking bed sheets off the clothes line. Sheila approached her. "Hi, Ma. How you doin'?"

Her mother continued to remove clothes pins from the corners of the white sheets. Sheila remembers how they flapped against the dark blue fall sky. She never turned around. "I doubt if you're gonna' be welcome. Your father's in the barn."

Sheila walked across the dusty yard to the dilapidated outbuilding with the sagging roof. The big door was closed but the small side door stood open. The space was dark and murky. She took one step in and hollered. "Dad, are you in here? I've come home, and Ma said to come and see you."

No answer. She took another step further inside. The gloom enveloped her. She felt smothered. "Dad?"

"Over here." He appeared out of the darkness at the back. "We don't want you around, Sheila. Now, git!"

Sheila tried not to jump, but knows she did. "I thought I could come home to help. Don't you need some help on the farm, Dad?"

"We hired a fella'. Now git! Outta' my yard. No need for you around here upsettin' the apple cart."

Sheila left the shadows for the October sunshine. She retraced her steps down the gravel driveway. Her mother stood on the porch with the basket of sheets balanced against the railing. She made no move toward her daughter. Sheila snuck one more glimpse of her as she turned back on to the road.

She was out of choices. Once she returned to the diner, she asked Nancy, the waitress, if she knew somewhere she could stay for the night. Instead, Nancy called Segue House and Ava Burrway came to get her.

Sheila knows she never qualified as a client for the shelter. She hadn't run away from an abusive situation, in the strictest sense, but Ava took her in anyway and let her stay. She worked hard and proved she could handle the night job. Marjorie Westerman appears to be in a similar position. She had no emergency need to come to the shelter. She has money and a big car. She could have gone anywhere, but Ava knew she needed support and people around her, so she took her in. Now, maybe Marjorie might stay.

After all this is over, Sheila is afraid Ava likely won't want her there anymore. Maybe they will all tell her she was the reason Ronny was grabbed, and now she'll have to go. Her fear churns inside her brain and makes it hard to focus.

****

They turn down yet another dirt and grass path. The big patrol car lumbers over the bumps and slides with little grace through the ruts. Sean is a pretty good driver, though. He makes good time.

"Do you remember any of this, Sheila?"

She squints out the side windows, as the dust billows around the ass end of the car. "No, but Fiona, I never went down the road!" They don't seem to understand she has no idea where he went.

Sean turns around in the field and they return to the gravel road and continue. Sheila tries hard to determine if there might be a familiar land mark around. They go down two more lanes. One is a driveway that leads to a little house, not much bigger than a granary, tucked into some trees. He stops the car.

"You stay here."

Her heart beats so fast she has to swallow to keep the thing from rising into her throat. She watches through the grill as they walk toward the building. Fiona has her hand on her gun. Sean approaches the door, steps to the left, and reaches for the handle on the right. He opens it and the old hinges start to give way. The door almost falls off in his hands. Fiona enters. The place is empty.

They return to the car. "She could have been in there," Sheila sighs as a means of explanation. "I don't know if I went this far or not, Sean. This seems like we've been driving for a long time."

"We'll keep going down different side roads, Sheila. You never know. He might have gone down a road and then cut across the back. We have to keep trying."

Sheila is desperate to help. She focuses her attention out the passenger side of the patrol car because she knows it was this side of the road where he turned. She almost misses the grain truck with the blue door parked in the field on the other side. It has to be the same truck that passed her yesterday.

"Fiona! Fiona! There's the grain truck I let pass me yesterday. When I let him go by, I followed him until he turned in here. Devon's truck was gone and when I turned around, I saw dust down a road, a path, behind us." Sheila almost leaps out of the seat.

Sean turns into the field. By the time they stop, the farmer is approaching the squad car. "Can I help you folks? Must be somethin' goin' on. There's RCMP everywhere."

"Did you pass a dark blue Lincoln on this road yesterday morning, sir?"

"Sure did. Nice car. Turned around up the road a piece, and then came back. The driver stopped and parked further down."

"Can you show us where the Lincoln stopped?" Sean sounds like he is struggling to control the excitement in his voice.

"Sure. You want me to get in? It would take a while for me to walk." He leans over and peers in the back window.

"No need to worry. Sheila is not a prisoner. She happens to be a witness, here to help us out." Fiona is around the car in no time. The farmer avoids touching the door handle, as if he has to wait for instructions.

Introductions are quickly made. His name is Homer. Sheila doesn't catch his last name.

Sheila sizes up her back seat companion. He must be mid-fifties. His white hair sticks out from under a ball cap with a picture of the local grain elevator. He is dressed in overalls and big boots. The former are well-worn and have seen better days. The latter smell like they've been in the presence of lots of cow shit. Sheila wrinkles her nose. Her sensibilities have improved since she moved into Segue House.

Homer points out the road after less than five minutes. "Can you wait here, Homer, while I radio another car to take you back to your field?"

"Not necessary, Constable. The walk is pleasant enough when there's no hurry." Fiona opens the back door and he unfolds his lean frame to get out. "Hope you folks find what you're lookin' for. John Fitzpatrick is probably out swathing his canola today. You'll see him when you get about eight miles straight down the road. He owns over three hundred acres of canola back there."

Chapter 22

~

Ronny

Light started to crawl through the bushes outside the window. The time must have been about five in the morning. In the stillness, she heard the wings of birds as they left the trees to start their own daily routine. Life would change forever today, and it began with the rhythmic flap of a bird's wings.

Last evening was cool. Ronny was up all night. She wanted to make her escape but was afraid to leave in the dark—afraid he might be lurking somewhere. She convinced herself that daylight would be her friend; that if she could get to a road, someone would surely see her; that if she could see a ranch in the distance, she would be able to get there.

She sat in the murky shadows of dawn and reviewed her plan. The precious blanket off her cot would serve as her basic protection from years of outhouse crap including her most recent deposits. She feared the ammonia smell, and wondered if it would be more than she could bear. She dithered about her sandals and decided, in the end, sandals covered in crap would be better protection for a run through a field than bare feet. Funny what comes to mind and seems essential.

Today, she decided, she would focus on all the positives in her life. She would not be afraid of what might happen. She would think about the good and anticipate a bright future.

****

Her mother's name was Eleanor but everyone called her Ellie. She was a wonderful woman who loved her daughter, Janine, with every fiber of her being. Ronny knew this truth from the time she was a very young. Her father was a gruff character. He cared for his wife and daughter in his own way, but never exhibited love until after Ellie died and he married Sophia within the year. They had two boys. Ronny watched, from afar, the father she wished she could have had.

After she gets out of here, she will reconnect with her father. She will talk with Chet. Forgiveness will be a challenge, but she will forgive her half-brother who provided Duncan with enough information to find her.

After she gets out of here, she will be more committed to her work and entertain the idea of taking over from Ava, as she knows this is what her boss wants. She will accept more responsibility. With her fears of Duncan abated, she will be able to forge ahead with her life.

After she gets out of here, she will be more social. Her freedom will enable her to open up to those who care about her. Besides Ava and Maggie, she will show her true self to Cheryl, Fiona, and Rose. She will tell her story to Gaby and Joe. She will convince Gaby to sell 15 Poplar Street to her, and she will make Hayworth her home forever. There will be no more thoughts of escaping from the past. She will keep her new name. She has become Ronny Étang and expects to stay Ronny Étang.

At this point, she squared her shoulders, hugged her ragged blanket to her chest, and wiggled her filthy feet into her sandals.

****

The blanket, dirty and threadbare, will become the great sacrifice. She cannot permit thoughts of failure. The blanket is her most valuable object as she carefully lays the fabric out across the pile of composted solids and recent personal waste. The ammonia smell of fresh urine, as it ferments on top of years of decayed matter, makes her eyes water. She can taste the smell and her empty stomach churns. She gags. The thought of uncontrollable gagging, or maybe even throwing up, hadn't entered her mind until now. She has taken all this time to plan an escape through a mound of shit. To hurl would be the final insult. She steels her emotions and starts her descent into the hole. Her back scrapes the rough edges of the wood. She can sense the fabric of her blouse as it starts to shred.

The blanket may cover all the crap, but proves to be an insignificant barrier against the wet which starts to seep through the wool the instant Ronny puts any kind of weight down. Maybe this will be like pulling off a Band-Aid. She needs to make a move, jump down in, kick the clean-out door as hard as she can, and get the hell out.

She has no idea how long she has remained on the prison side of the open hole. The cabin has warmed up. She has a headache from the smell. *You have to do this. Come on! Think about him coming back!* She hauls her ass back up on to the edge of the hole one last time and runs a finger over the scar on her neck. *He could hurt me again. He could kill me this time!*

When her butt, with a soft thud, settles on top of the blanket, the wet ooze of urine and shit soaks straight through. Ironically, the toilet paper probably could have provided as much protection. For a moment she thinks she might sink right out of sight. She panics and starts to kick the panel with a force she is surprised she possesses. After four good kicks, each one serving to force her further into the pile, the wood gives way and opens with a rush of fresh air. The door flaps back and forth. She catches momentary views of the outstretched field and a scrap of blue sky. For the first time since her abduction, she hears some sort of machinery. Too late, now. She has to get out.

She must lie back far enough to get her feet out the hole in the wall. Then, she will need to pull on the sides, and while the door, inconveniently hinged at the top, bangs with unpredictable force on her thighs, she will hoist her hips through the hole. The process takes time—more time than she wants—longer than she ever imagined.

Her long legs are out. She touches grass as she tries to dig her heels in and get more traction. Her bum is balanced on the sharp wooden frame of the cut-out. She pushes again and her back bears the impact of the raw wood through her blouse. The shitty flap whacks her stomach. A random thought sprints across her mind. In a moment of clarity, she understands why nature does not permit the recollection of one's birth.

"Do you need some help?"

Panic flies through every cell of her body. For a split second, she thinks she will have to try and get back inside the privy. Then she starts to kick. If Duncan is out there, she will have no other option but to fight.

"Get the hell out of my way!"

"Easy, miss. I want to help you. Hold still. I can hold the door and pull your ankles." Through the edges of the flapping clean-out door, she catches a glimpse of coveralls. She does not resist. Duncan most definitely does not wear coveralls.

The process is not without pain. She braces in anticipation, thinking about the lacerations on her back. He grabs her knees. With one last shove by her and pull by him, she manages to prevent the clean-out door from striking her in the face, as her ass lands without ceremony or dignity on the stubbly grass surrounding the cabin. She squints up at him as her eyes adjust to the bright sunshine.

"Can I help you up? Whatever made you decide to use the clean-out door of the old privy instead of the front door like everybody else? And I'm John, by the way, John Fitzpatrick. I own all this property and I believe you have been makin' use of my grandparents' homestead."

"Yes, you can help me, if having crap all over your hands is okay." He shows her his hands. Since he pulled her free from the outhouse, the idea of clean hands is no longer a priority. "Oh, okay. Thanks." She struggles to her feet.

"To answer your question, my name is Ronny Étang. My ex-husband grabbed me on Monday morning and I've been locked in your grandparents' house since then. There are bars on the inside of both the door and the window. My only way out was through the clean-out hole. I expect there are a lot of people searching for me." She sees the swather about three hundred feet away. "How far are we from a telephone, John?"

"My wife will be here in a few minutes with my lunch. You can go back to the house with her and call the cops from there." He purses his lips for a second. "And you'll be more than welcome to have a bath while you're there, Ronny."

John goes around to the front of the cabin and forces open the door. Apparently, he wants to determine, for himself, whether or not the place has been turned into a cell. By the time he returns to Ronny's side, a baby blue Mercury Rideau has bounced into the field. A burly woman in blue jeans and a yellow polka-dot blouse climbs out. She waves over at John and retrieves a brown paper bag from the back seat. "I brought lunch, John. You didn't tell me you'd have company." She wrinkles her nose a tiny bit as she approaches Ronny.

"Hi, I'm Ronny. Your husband helped me escape through the shitter. I've been stuck in the shack since Monday. I'd shake your hand, but…you know."

"This is my wife, Kay. Kay, this is Ronny with a funny last name." He turns back to Ronny. "We never heard nothin' on the news about a woman bein' missin'. When that woman who worked at the hospital disappeared in '81, everybody from Hayworth to Carter River was lookin' for her."

"I have no idea, John. The RCMP has its own way of conducting a search. I know a couple of them quite well, because I work at the women's shelter."

"Well nobody's been around askin' questions."

Ronny finds this hard to believe. "I expect they're anxious to find me. They would not want to spook my ex with a lot of publicity."

She turns her attention to Kay. "Lovely to meet you." Graciousness and manners are a stretch when one is covered in crap. "Any chance I can come back to the house and use the phone? It's urgent I call the cops and tell them where I am."

"We'll go right now, honey. I happen to have some garbage bags in the car. You can sit on those."

As Kay unfurls big green plastic bags, a dust ball the size of the shack appears out of nowhere. There has to be more than one vehicle to create such a cloud, so she is certain that Duncan is not about to turn up. Two police cruisers and another unidentified dark car emerge. *After all this time, all I needed to do was start to yell when I heard the swather, and between John and Fiona, they would have found me. Talk about bad timing!*

She watches her good friend, Fiona, along with Sean get out of the first car. "Ronny, are you okay? We've taken Duncan into custody. You're going to be fine."

Fiona races across the yard and wraps her arms around Ronny. She backs up. "Has anybody told you that you're covered in shit? Were these nice people too polite to point this out?" She and Ronny start to laugh and cry at the same time.

The other officers stand back, but Sean approaches with Sheila. "Sheila!" Ronny exclaims. "What are you doing here?"

Sheila's eyes puddle with tears as Fiona chimes in. "Sheila helped us find you, Ronny. We'll tell you the whole story after we get you back to Hayworth and to the hospital. Did you know you have blood on your back?"

"How did you find me?"

"Duncan Taylor was no help. He said he'd let you starve first. We'll explain everything, Ronny."

At this point, John seems anxious to contribute. "I pulled her out through the clean-out door of the privy—like birthin' a calf. She was a breech—feet first!" He places his big, weathered paw on Ronny's shoulder. Kay, here, was about to take her home so she could call you and have a bath. I guess you won't be needin' us now."

In an instant, Fiona is all business. "Officers will take statements and go over the shack with a fine-tooth comb. Ronny, you will come with Sean and me. Sheila will return with the other officers. John? If you and your wife would be so kind as to provide statements. Tell them about the property and what happened here when you helped Ronny. I think we need to get this girl to the hospital."

****

On the ride back to town, her deplorable condition is never mentioned. Ronny has lots of questions about who knows what about her, now, but Fiona makes it clear they will talk once she has been assessed by a doctor. Ronny gazes out the window of the speeding police car, and marvels at how far the little house is from the main road; a distance of almost ten miles, as reported by Sean.

Fiona radios dispatch to tell them they have Ronny and will transport her straight to the outpatient department of Hayworth Community Hospital.

Hospital staff waits for her. Fiona manages the paperwork while Ronny has an initial conversation with an attending physician. A nurse, who looks like a teenager—*are they younger, now?*—ushers her into a room with a walk-in shower stall. She peels off her clothes while the nurse bags each item in a clear plastic version with the word EVIDENCE printed on the side. Ronny avoids unnecessary conversation or questions, although she has already told the doctor she wasn't sexually assaulted. Her primary goal is to climb into the shower. "We'll find some clothes for you until your friends collect you some from home. You'll need antibiotic cream for your back. The scrapes will be pretty sore when…"

Ronny interrupts with an anxious nod. "Once I get out of the shower, you can look at my back. I'm not in much pain."

The nurse nods and waits. When the hot water hits Ronny's bare skin, she almost passes out.

Fiona is there when she is escorted into a private room down the hall from the outpatient department. They hug once again. Ronny notices, with appreciation, how Fiona has changed clothes, too.

To Ronny, the young police officer and her friend, is making a valiant attempt to maintain control. "Crying is inappropriate while I'm in uniform, Ronny. Give a gal a break! Come sit down. How's your back? Can you tell me every detail about what happened?"

"I can, Fiona, but what about Duncan? You said you have him, and Sheila helped find me. I am failing to connect the dots."

"We have Duncan and he will be charged with kidnapping, forcible confinement, and assault." Her voice drops. "I need to know if there will be other charges, Ronny."

"If you're referring to rape, he never laid a hand on me, except when he grabbed me and shot me up with some chemical. I've already told the doctor. I think everyone was grateful I didn't require a pelvic exam before I had a shower." She sits down on the side of the bed. "He never even came inside the cabin. All he did was hand me water and food through the hole in the bars. He said he wanted me to be stuck in a box and suffer like he did for the last forty months. Speaking of food, the nurse said they would send up soup and a sandwich."

Right on cue, someone from the cafeteria arrives at the door with a tray. Fiona jumps up to grab it and set it on the bed-table. Ronny is ravenous. To be clean and have a meal is like a dream come true. She directs her gratefulness toward the young worker whose name tag indicates she is Audrey Baranski. "Thanks for this."

The nervous creature raises shy eyes in Ronny's direction and then gives a nod of respect to Fiona, before making a speedy retreat. Ronny guesses she will become the talk of the hospital.

"So, what did Sheila have to do with this mess?"

"Listen. I'm supposed to ask the questions, but since you'll have your mouth full for the next few minutes, I will go first. Duncan befriended Sheila. She thought they were becoming a couple, but his plan was already in place. He used her to obtain details about the shelter staff, and then she let slip about your meeting in Carter River."

Between slurps of soup and bites of the most delicious turkey sandwich she has ever eaten, Ronny tells Fiona about her younger brother and the picture of the fundraiser in the paper. "By the time Duncan was paroled, he was bound and determined he would find me. It was only a matter of time. The picture moved the whole process along." Ronny knows she sounds philosophical, but she is free now and he has returned to jail. She can afford to be generous in both thought and deed. "Poor Sheila. She must feel awful."

"She does. Thinks the situation is all her fault. Keeps repeating she must be the connection."

Ronny wipes her lips with the paper napkin and sips on her tea. "Let me talk to her. I feel bad for poor Sheila. So what else do you need to know?"

"Give me a detailed account of what happened, Ronny. We will have to go over this about a dozen times. The investigators want to talk to you, too. Your statement will be recorded once you are able to come down to the detachment, but for right now, I need to know what happened and get an indication of whether or not there will have to be more charges."

"He approached me when I stopped for coffee at the Petro-Can on my way to my meeting in Carter River. He remarked on my transformation but he found me anyway. You are not aware of this, but I have very dark, very thick, very curly black hair. I have always let my mane go wild. When I decided to move out here and assume a new identity, I cut my hair off so short my head felt shaved. Then I dyed it as platinum as I could without burning my scalp. I *do* appear quite different, but a fat lot of good the makeover did me. I tried to get out of the picture at the fundraiser. Even Ava tried to make an excuse for me, but the publicity people wouldn't cooperate. There you go."

"For an attractive woman, you did seem oddly reluctant about a photo. I just chalked it up to you being humble." Ronny sees her friend grin and accepts the tease.

She sighs, shakes her head, and continues. "I thought he was gone when I left the restaurant. He grabbed me from behind, told me to throw my keys and purse into my car, and lock the door. I did as I was told. When he slammed me into the front seat of his truck, he jabbed me with a needle. When I woke up, I was in what turned out to be John Fitzpatrick's grandparents' homestead. I had no idea where I was.

"Duncan appeared a few times, with food and water, but never very much of either. He never unlocked the bars installed behind the door, so he never came in. I knew you would search high and low for me. I also listened for the sound of farm machinery. I know enough to figure out farmers have started to swath since the weather's been good. Today was John Fitzpatrick's day to get started and I managed to have my great crapper caper in time for him to haul me out. If I had waited another couple of hours, you would have found me. God, Fiona, I'm glad there was nobody around with a camera!"

"Listen! You persevered. You did what was necessary. You're all right and safe. Nothing else matters. The hospital wants to keep you until tomorrow morning. We'll park your car in your driveway. I will come back with your purse and ask Ava to go to your house and get you some clothes. I hope the chief investigator will let Duncan stew for a couple more days so we can get you home and settled. What else can I do, Ronny? Will you want us to call you Janine now?"

"Nope. I legally changed my name and Ronny Étang is who I am. Are you able to come and get me tomorrow?"

"I can, but I imagine one Miss Ava Burrway will be here by dawn to pick you up. No need to worry, now. Relax. The office has called her to say you're all right. Maybe you should have a nap…do I sound like your nurse now?" She gives Ronny a gentle hug before she leaves.

Chapter 23

Ava

She replaces the telephone in the cradle with such care and determination, an observer would think the object was made of glass. The dispatcher reported a simple statement. Miss Ronny Étang was found safe and has been transported to Hayworth Community Hospital. Ava was asked to remain at Segue House to receive a call from Constable Fiona Werbowski within the hour. Also, Sheila Pasco would be dropped off at the shelter shortly. She was asked if she understood. She said yes, thanked the voice on the other end, and now, here she sits.

The crisis is over. Ronny is okay. She is stunned in her relief. She struggles to take a deep breath. She wants to shout, to cry, to laugh, to run and tell everyone. She has never felt like this before, so she sits and stares at the wall. Her emotions tumble over each other. She is delighted as tears roll down her cheeks and she smiles from ear to ear.

Her door is ajar, but not open. She knows Maggie waits on the other side, to hear what the RCMP detachment called about. The phone bleats again. "I'll get it," she practically screams through the open wedge of doorway. She is sure the caller is Fiona.

"Segue House. Ava Burrway."

"Hi. Fiona here. Did the office call?"

"Yes, Fiona. Tell me what happened. Is she okay? Did he hurt her?"

"Ronny's okay. They want to keep her in the hospital overnight. I told her you would go to her house and get her some clothes and shoes for tomorrow for her discharge. I also told her you would pick her up. I am going to try and hold the investigative unit off until Monday morning."

"When can I go over?"

"Give her another hour or so. When I left, I suggested she shut her eyes for a little while. I expect everybody will turn up tonight."

"I will be able to manage the influx from this end, Fiona. I can get Maggie to make some phone calls but tell people not to go to the hospital or to her house tomorrow. Okay?"

"Good idea. She will tell you details when you take her stuff this afternoon. Sheila should be back anytime. She rode in another car after they took statements from a neighbour where we found her. Gotta' run. Lots of paperwork, now." In a much less official voice, she adds, "I am so relieved, Ava. This could have been a very bad outcome."

"Me too, Fiona." Tears start to run unchecked, again, as she says good bye.

The second the phone light goes out, Maggie is at the door. "What's happened, Ava? Have they found her? Is she okay?"

"Gather everyone around, Maggie." The expression of horror on the young woman's face compels Ava to change her plan. "Ronny is fine. She is at the hospital. Go get everyone. I want to make a few announcements. Sheila should be here anytime. I need to talk to her, too."

While Maggie rounds residents up, Ava runs through the clients in her mind. Plans appear to have progressed for each one in their own way. Marjorie Westerman wants very much to stay as a kind of glorified housekeeper, and the more Ava thinks about the arrangement, the more appealing the idea becomes. They will have to formalize the position with some paperwork next week. June and her children will leave for St. Albert now that Ronny has been found. She expects them to be gone by Monday. Chrissie's parents are sending money, so she will be on a bus next week as well. Marta and her baby remain without a plan, but all in good time. Ava wonders how long before Ronny comes back to work. Ronny will no doubt want to return on Monday, but there are a few bridges to cross yet. She'll talk to her later today, when she takes her clothes to the hospital.

****

Ava is standing in the kitchen making tea as Maggie returns with all the current residents of the shelter. "Still no sign of Sheila."

The words are no sooner out of Maggie's mouth than the buzzer sounds. Maggie nods to Ava, turns on her heel, and enters the foyer to follow security protocols. A minute or so later, Sheila joins the group in the reception room.

Marjorie appears quite jaunty in wide legged lounging pants and a printed top. She delivers tea to June, Chrissie, and Marta. Baby Jana is asleep in a wicker bassinet-affair Maggie found in the basement storage room. Kelly and Amber are curled up in a corner, colouring in new books picked up by Marjorie when she went to the grocery store. In response to Ava's raised brows, she declares, "They were to be a going away gift, but I thought today would be a good day for them to have a special treat." The gentle challenge in her eyes speaks volumes. They need a focus besides a missing woman and another move. Ava nods her support. Marjorie has the potential to be a real asset to the shelter.

Sheila fills the doorway. She stands mute, dishevelled, and with a dark expression that defies description. If thunder clouds took on human form, they would be Sheila.

"Everybody come in and sit down. Sheila, I know you'd like to go downstairs and relax, but I'd like you to join us for a few minutes. We can have a conversation together afterward."

Sheila sits down on a dining room chair at the edge of the assembled group. She does not make eye contact with anyone in the room.

"Okay!" Ava claps her hands for effect. "I will attempt to say this without puddling up. First, the detachment called and then Fiona called. Ronny has been found. She is okay, in so far as she was not physically hurt in any way. We can only imagine the state of her emotions. She will spend the night at the hospital. I have been asked to go to her house and get her some clothes and pick her up when she is discharged tomorrow morning. I will offer to take her to my house for the weekend, but I know Ronny. She will want to go home, and I wouldn't blame her."

Ava surveys the room. Maggie blubbers unabashedly. Marjorie sits on the arm of Maggie's chair and softly pats her back. June is bent over, whispering to her children who hug their mother as she tries to keep them quiet. Marta stares wide-eyed and remains silent. Sheila has her elbows on her knees and her head bowed. "Let me continue. Fiona has suggested we not all plunge into her hospital room tonight. As a result, I am tasking Maggie with calling everyone else who has been involved in this case—Rose, Patrick Hollinger,

Cheryl Nadler, as well as Joe Dodd and Gaby Ridgway—to let them know she is safe and sound, as well as inform them not to race to the hospital. I understand everyone wants to lay their eyes on her; to see for themselves that she is safe." She provides the assembled group with an expression of indulgence.

"Any questions?"

The room is quiet for a minute and then Maggie whimpers a response. "Ronny lived across from my sister and me for a long while. If she goes home tomorrow, I will never be able to keep Rose from visiting her on Sunday, Ava, no matter what I say."

"I imagine, by Sunday, she will be ready to see people, Maggie. I will alert Ronny when I go to the hospital later. I can also tell her how much she means to everyone. That's all for now. Enjoy your tea. I understand Marjorie has supper all planned. I can smell a pot roast simmering on the stove as we speak! Sheila, come into my office for a few minutes, so you and I can have a visit."

****

"I suppose you want me to quit." Her words thud into the room. She focuses on a carpet stain and avoids eye contact.

"Sit down, Sheila, and what the hell are you talking about? No one wants you to quit!"

She releases her gaze from the carpet and trains hooded eyes on her boss. "I figured you would give me the boot since this is my fault." She crashes down into the chair in front of Ava's desk.

"You were naive, and not as cautious as you could have been, Sheila, but you should not lose your job. Duncan Taylor is the bad person here, not you. Want to tell me what happened today?"

Sheila is a wreck. She has aged ten years. Ava notices her puffy cheeks and the bags under her eyes. Her hair needs a comb and her clothes are rumpled like they came out of the hamper. Her sigh fills the room. "I followed Devon, uh, Duncan, down a gravel road yesterday. I let a grain truck go past me so he wouldn't suspect a car was following him. When the truck turned into a field, he was gone. I started back to the highway and saw dust down a side road. It was more like a track through a field. Then the dust disappeared. I parked there for a while, but whatever went down the road never came back, so I came home. I couldn't find the road when I went looking with the police today, but I recognized the grain truck. It had one blue door and it was out in the field again. The farmer knew where I had parked the Lincoln. I expect he sees very few Lincolns on that road."

She stops to catch her breath and perhaps gain some composure. Sheila shakes and her cheeks twitch as she talks. Ava suddenly realizes she is trying desperately hard not to cry. A wave of empathy passes through her. How sad for Sheila that the situation came to this. "Go on. It sounds like you helped the RCMP, since you recognized the farm truck."

"If the truck hadn't been back in the field, we might not have found her. We went down this gravel and grassy track, at least ten miles. I had forgotten you could go so far into the middle of nowhere and still find people. The land is so flat out there, like you could drive until you drop off the edge. Not a bit of wonder people used to think the world was flat. They must have been to Northern Alberta." She lifts her sad face toward her boss and attempts to respond to her own little joke. Her lips turn up a fraction, but her eyes still hold their tortured expression.

"By the time we pulled up in front of this little hut, or old house, or whatever, Ronny was standing in the yard with some farmer. She was all covered in shit and stunk to high heaven. His wife was there, too. I don't know all they said. Fiona hustled me into another cruiser and I had to wait until they finished talking to the farmer and his wife before we came back."

"Did you speak to Ronny?"

"Not so much. Fiona told her I helped find her. The farmer said he pulled her out through the outhouse hatch on the side of the little house. He said he felt like he was birthing a calf! That's all I heard, Ava. I was happy I didn't have to come back with Fiona and Sean, who brought Ronny. Fiona hugged her, so they were both covered in crap. Ronny's back was bleeding through her blouse. She seemed okay, though. Maybe because she crawled out through the hole." Sheila wiggles her nose in disgust. "Can I go downstairs now?"

"Of course you can. Get cleaned up, have a rest, get a bite to eat—whatever you want to do. Do not repeat your story to anybody else. Information will come out in due course, okay?"

"No problem, Ava. Everybody knows I'm an idiot, anyway. I thought the guy liked me! How stupid am I? I thought somebody liked me, for me. How could I be so stupid?" She lifts her solid frame out of the chair and turns toward the door.

Ava is afraid for Sheila's mental well-being so changes her mind. She should not be alone down in her basement rooms. "Sheila, wait. I think you need to have some company for a while. Come with me into the kitchen. Maybe we can scare up another cup of tea." She puts an arm around Sheila's shoulder. "There are many people who think the world of you, Sheila. Duncan is a bad man. This whole incident had little to do with you, in the direct sense. He could have picked anybody who would be vulnerable. You know, any one of us would be in the same circumstance. You are not to blame."

****

Later in the afternoon, Ava leaves the office and returns to 15 Poplar Street. Maggie has called and talked to all the significant others who were involved in the case. As she parks her car in the driveway, she imagines Ronny will be anxious to see her own vehicle back in the yard. She expects Fiona will ensure the old Buick is returned.

As she unlocks the front door and steps inside, the little house seems to have an entirely different atmosphere compared to when she entered on Monday. What a difference five days can make. She takes a moment to peek at the framed photograph by the front door. Now, when people ask Ronny about the setting, instead of her standard response of: "just some picture", she'll be able to tell them about the cottage her family used to have on Lake Superior. Ava remembers how pleased Ronny was when she first showed that small reflection of her personal self to Ava. The poor girl probably felt the same way when she shared the photo reflecting the time when she had dark and curly hair to Maggie. She will be able to be her real self from now on.

She makes her way into Ronny's bedroom and slides open the closet door. She chooses jersey trousers with big pockets and an elastic waist. She finds a short navy sweater. It matches the pants. Could this be one of Rose's creations? She locates underwear and, since the weather still warms up during the day, she roots out a pair of sandals from the back of the closet. She places all the clothes in a large rattan shopping bag she brought from the shelter. In the bathroom, she locates the basic necessities and puts them in a cosmetic bag she finds in the linen closet.

Ava is struck by the quiet. What a sweet little house. It would be nice to have a little house like this instead of the rambling, talkative, and drafty old homeplace. She returns to the living room and sits down in one of Ronny's mismatched chairs. Ava thinks she might need to shake up her life a bit. Ronny will be fine. Marjorie has decided to volunteer and live at the shelter for the foreseeable future. Ava's neighbour wants the homestead property and will no doubt pay her a fair price. Life can kick you in the ass when you least expect it. *Perhaps the time for a change has come, Ava. Perhaps the time for a change has come.*

****

On this particular occasion, when she walks into the Hayworth Community Hospital late Friday afternoon and stops at reception, Millie and Karen both beam as Millie rushes to provide Ronny's room number. Ava nods her thanks, settles her bundle over her arm, and trots with a no-nonsense determination down the hall to the private room at the end of the corridor.

Ava stands at the doorway. Ronny is stretched out on the bed. She may be asleep, so Ava stands there for a moment. She needs her sleep, so maybe she will have to come back. Slowly, Ronny's eyes open and she turns toward the sound of rustling rattan. "I hoped it was you."

Ava rushes to Ronny's bedside. "My God, my friend, we were all so scared! Are you okay? Fiona said you were okay, but I need you to tell me for sure."

Ronny sits up and reaches out to embrace her boss and friend. "I am okay. He didn't hurt me. It was a long and scary four days, but he didn't hurt me—not in a physical sense—at least. Sit down. Do you have clothes for me? Fiona stopped back with my purse. She said they would drop off my car tomorrow and you would be here with clothes."

Ava places the bag down on the foot of the bed and then plops her tired body in the brown naugahyde lounge chair strategically positioned in the corner of the small room. "I brought you clothes and toiletries. Check them over. If you want or need a particular item, I will go back to your house and get whatever you need. I want to stare at you for a few minutes, though. Do you mind?" She giggles as she teases her.

Ronny, like a child at Christmas, peeks into the bag. "Oh, you brought me my favourite around-the-house pants and the sweater Rose made me a year ago! Perfect! As luck would have it, I ruined every piece of clothing I had on when I made my 'unnecessary' escape." She shrugs her thin shoulders. "I understand you want to hear all the details, and you will, but not until tomorrow, okay? You will come and fetch me, won't you?" All of a sudden she appears nervous.

"Of course. I will pick you up early tomorrow. And you can tell me whatever you want, whenever you want to tell me. Let me share with you the people who know the details, though. We told Fiona about your history. Sheila has more information now, of course. The RCMP provided a briefing, including your background, to the staff and residents as well as Rose Woodward and Gaby and Joe."

"The whole town will know in no time, but no matter. No more secrets, eh Ava?" Ronny smiles at her boss.

"Your disappearance was never made public, Ronny, so you may decide who else you tell at this point. There were only a few other people who were given basic information—new residents at the shelter, plus Patrick, and Cheryl. No one else. Maggie has called them all to give them the good news and tell them no visitors here at the hospital or at your house tomorrow, but I expect you will be inundated on Sunday."

"Fiona said the police investigator would want to see me at some point on Monday. I hope that after that is over, I can come to work."

"Maybe Monday is too soon and too fast for work, Ronny. What would be wonderful, though, is if you dropped by the shelter for a visit. June is all ready to leave. They are off to St. Albert soon, but she is anxious to share the details with you. Also, we have a couple of other clients for you to meet. You might be interested to know Marjorie and I have decided she will stay on for at least the short term. She is excited to tell you about our decision. No need for more information today."

Ava notices how Ronny has started to flag a bit. "I am going to leave now and let you get some rest. See you around ten tomorrow morning. You know you can come out to my place if you would prefer."

Ronny stands up with Ava and puts both arms around her boss. "Thanks for your help, Ava. Thanks for the offer, but I want to go home in the morning. You understand."

"Get some rest. See you at ten." Ava tries her best to be brusque and pragmatic, but the damn tears start to roll once more.

Chapter 24

~

Ronny

"Yes, I'll be fine. See you tomorrow. Thanks again for the lift home." Ronny latches the screen and sinks into the door as she pushes it closed and turns the bolt. The silence wraps around her—not like the silence she experienced when imprisoned. This kind of quiet provides walls of solitude and comfort, of safety and freedom you love when you want to be utterly alone. She pads across the hardwood in bare feet and thinks about the rough floors in the shack. She will shower in her own bathroom. She will go to bed in the middle of the day in her own bed. Despite the risk someone might think her rude, she will unplug her phone.

****

Ava arrived at her hospital door at exactly ten, like she said. They stopped at the grocery store and then made their way to 15 Poplar Street. Ronny sat in the passenger seat of the Le Baron and gazed at her little house. Yes, she discovered she thinks of the place as hers. She feared, at one point, she might never see her home again. She took a moment, as she climbed the steps up to the tiny porch, and stood in silence while Ava employed the spare keys from her office to unlock the front door.

Ronny breathed in the smells—old hardwood and the musty scent of a place closed up for a while. "I emptied the garbage and put the bag out on the back step, Ronny. I find it hard to believe a full week hasn't passed since

197

you started out for Carter River." She put a protective arm around Ronny's shoulders. "It is not necessary that you stay here alone. I can stay. Or you can come out to the farm for the weekend with me."

Ronny was appreciative, but more than the support or company, she wanted to be alone. She knew she needed time to decompress. She felt like she was holding back a dam—of what, she wasn't certain. The doctor told her they could refer her to Rachel Wilkerson if she wanted to seek some professional guidance. Dr. Wilkerson is a great person and a good shrink, but she told the doctor she would wait and see. "I'll be fine, Ava. I need today to regroup, though. By tomorrow, I should be ready to see people. Come for a visit then. Tell the others. I am fine, really." She put on her best expression of confidence—a well-honed smile perfected from years of experience covering up episodes of abuse.

Ava bought her story, although she waited until after the Buick was delivered before she left. They had coffee in the meantime. Fiona didn't stay when they brought the car back and parked it in the driveway up near the fence. Sean waited in the squad car, since they were on duty. Fiona handed her the keys, patted her shoulder, and said she was off the next day and would pop by.

Ava wanted to know what happened, so Ronny told her the basics. The abject hopelessness she felt much of the time was hard to explain. Her escape through the clean-out hole in the privy, and John Fitzpatrick, the farmer who came to her rescue, were easier topics to share. She made the story seem funny. She left out the bits about gagging and almost throwing up. She left out the hysteria she felt rip through every bone when she first thought it was Duncan who arrived on the scene and saw her legs. She did not mention how she discovered a power within her quite capable of killing him, given the opportunity. Instead, she mixed humour with bravado. Her boss was pacified.

Ava took forever to drink her coffee. Ronny knew she wanted to stay. Suspicious and observant because of years of practise, Ronny could tell Ava was worried for her well-being if left to her own devices for very long. Ronny felt compelled to convince the woman she was fine. "I want to have a shower in my own bathroom, and go to bed in my own bed."

"What about supper? Shall I come and get you to come out to my house for supper?"

"Ava, I'm fine. I think I could sleep for a week, and there's more than enough food. Tomorrow, I will 'receive' visitors." She tilted her head and produced a grin to convince the older woman her fears were unfounded.

"Okay. Okay. I will take off, but whatever you might need, all you have to do is call me. I'll make sure people know they can visit you tomorrow. Will the afternoon work?"

Ronny sighed with the effort to cooperate. She was well aware of how terrified people were, their anxiety compounded by the disappearance of Roz Dover a few years ago, but she needed her space. "Perfect, Ava. I will be open for business tomorrow afternoon and then stop at the shelter Monday, at some point, for a visit. Fiona said the investigators could come here, but I would sooner go there. Duncan's invoked presence in my house is not welcome. At least, if I go down there, I can walk away. The doctor said I could go back to work whenever I want, so I want to be there, for sure, on Tuesday."

****

In the shower, the flood gates release and she cries like she has never cried before. She cries with relief. She cries with gratitude, with amazement, and with hope. Her tears flow as fast as the water pours over her abrasion-covered back. She allows her fears to swirl and disappear down the drain. Her anxieties about her identity flow away. She wonders if she will ever be able to stop the tears, but she does.

Ronny stretches out on cool sheets in her blind-darkened bedroom. She sinks deeper and deeper into the comfort of the mattress. A warm breeze drifts across her arms and chest. She appreciates the fresh air, the light she can control, and the silence she now welcomes. She sniffs the air and revels in the smells of home. She clutches the soft blue chenille bedspread and thinks about her sacrificial blanket in the bottom of the outhouse.

She sleeps until after midnight and wakens in the dark. For a second she is back in the cabin and her escape was all a dream. In a panic she sits bolt upright. She stretches out her hand. The bedside lamp is there. She will be okay.

****

The first person to appear on her doorstep is Patrick Hollinger. He beams with unconcealed joy when she opens her front door. He extends a lanky arm as he offers her a pie encased in tinfoil. "I thought I should show up first, since I was the first person you ever met in Hayworth, Ronny. I brought pie."

She opens the door, takes the pie, and wraps her arms around the young man who has made such progress in his personal life over the past few years. "Come in, my friend. Thanks for the pie, but you didn't have to, you know."

"Oh, I think I did. You know, everybody will be here this afternoon. You'll be hosting a party whether you want to or not!"

He no sooner sits down on one of Ronny's many arm chairs, when the doorbell rings. Joe and Gaby tumble in, while Ronny holds the screen open for them. "We are both over the moon that you're all right!" Gaby wraps her arms around her tenant as if she never intends to let go.

Joe drops one heavy hand on to Ronny's shoulder. "I'll put this in the kitchen." He knows his way around. He renovated the place, after all, so Ronny defers.

Gaby gushes with excitement. "I brought a tray of sandwiches, Ronny. I suspect there'll be a crowd. Joe has beer and wine he'll tuck into the fridge. Are you okay?"

"I'm fine, Gaby. Really, really fine. Just tired. I am so happy you are here."

"Good! You seem a little baffled. Did I not understand you told Ava you would be here for everyone this afternoon? Well…everyone plans on showing up! I think I had better find you some wine." She tosses her head back and laughs. Wispy hair disengages from the clip employed to hold the strands in place. She raises a yellow cotton sweater-clad arm to push the mess back where it belongs. "Sit down and relax. We all want to feast our eyes on you."

Rose and Maggie turn up a moment or two later. Cheryl, along with her daughter Amy, who happens to be visiting from the Maritimes, both appear. Ava and Sheila arrive, too. They present a glazed ham, sliced and ready to serve with slabs of homemade bread. They report how Marjorie sends her love and will see her tomorrow.

Ronny makes it a point to approach Sheila, hug her hard, and whisper in her ear. "None of this was your fault, Sheila. Duncan Taylor is a terrible man and abused you like he abused me. We're good, okay?" As she peeks over Sheila's shoulder at Ava, she can see tears in her boss' eyes.

Shelia returns the hug, for just a second, then steps back and nods. "I'm sorry, Ronny."

"I know, Sheila. Come on. Let's see what everyone's brought to eat."

As she is about to give up hope that Fiona will be able to get away from work, there she is—framed on the other side of the screen, dressed in real people clothes. Behind her looms Sean Knox, in uniform so obviously still on duty. Overwhelmed by all the attention, and the volume in the little house, she struggles to welcome them with "Come in!" and "Glad you could come."

"Sean's here on both some personal and some professional business, Ronny. We need to determine a time when you can meet with investigators tomorrow."

Ronny addresses her response to Sean. "Whatever time is convenient, but I want to come down to the detachment."

Sean glances over at Fiona, who simply nods. "The detachment is fine. How about early, say nine in the morning?"

"Do you have any idea how long we'll be?" Ronny's thoughts are on Segue House and how she would like to see June and her children before they leave.

"Could be a couple of hours."

"Maggie. Do you know if June plans on leaving tomorrow?"

"Not until Tuesday. Ava said you might drop in tomorrow, and she won't leave until she sees you."

"Okay, Sean." She turns her attention back to the constable. "See you tomorrow."

Before Ronny has a chance to tell Maggie she'll be over to the shelter after she goes to the police station, Sean has crossed the room. He and Maggie mutter together. Maggie's face has turned a bright pink and Rose tries to discreetly find someone else to sit beside.

Ava approaches Ronny. "I'll tell folks you'll be in after lunch, okay? Plan to stay for supper. Marjorie, of course, wants to cook."

"What's the story with Marjorie? I thought she had plans to live with her sister in Ontario."

"Yes, yes, I know. You can get every detail from her tomorrow, but she appears to have carved out the role of house mother. The basic cost to the shelter is one space, and she proposes that she pay rent through grocery purchases and housekeeping duties. I think we have a good deal." She leans over closer to Ronny's ear, "When you're the boss, you can send her to her sister's if you want." She straightens up and winks at Ronny.

Director of Segue House. A distinct possibility. Speculation for another day, but one task she wants to accomplish this afternoon is to have a talk with Gaby about the house. Gaby and Joe are busy setting out food and dishes on her kitchen table, so people can help themselves to sandwiches and pie. She will speak to them later.

Cheryl and Amy approach. Ronny acknowledges the young woman, perhaps eighteen, very petite, and a mirror image of Cheryl.

"You remember Amy, here in Hayworth with me for a visit. We are celebrating her birthday early. She starts university next month, and will turn eighteen on September 30."

Ronny extends her hand. "Nice to see you again, Amy. I hope this business about me has not ruined your visit with Cheryl."

Cheryl shakes her head. She beams at her daughter with a pride Ronny finds difficult to describe. "We've enjoyed a wonderful couple of weeks and this is the perfect end—to know you're okay and home safe and sound." In a spontaneous move quite out of character, Cheryl reaches up and hugs Ronny around the neck. Then she blushes a bit and suggests to Amy they go see if Gaby and Joe need any help in the kitchen.

Fiona and Ava are huddled in the corner, each with a glass of wine. When Ronny gets within earshot, Fiona frowns at Ava but Ronny clearly understands the message. "Don't worry about me, you two. I will be fine. Glad to be home. Glad to know Duncan is in jail—but it no longer matters, even if he gets out. He will never hurt me now. He wouldn't dare. Duncan's a coward."

"He will most definitely not be released anytime soon, Ronny. I doubt he'll even get bail." Fiona is pragmatic to a fault. "Oh, and by the way, having our annual community meeting around Roz Dover's disappearance will be delayed this year, thanks to you."

"Sorry I messed up your schedule, Fiona." Ronny leans over and nudges her friend's shoulder.

"And…we've made an executive decision to postpone the annual fundraiser ball until early in the New Year. We all need some breathing space." She smiles up at Ronny. "I am awfully glad the rescheduling is because of finding you, and not because…." The unfinished sentence floats like stale smoke in the air between them.

"You know, you two, I do not feel any need to apologize." Ronny leans over and hugs each woman in turn. All the fears of what might have been are gradually slipping away.

Sean has left and Maggie has taken a seat near Rose and Sheila. When she sees Ronny cross the tiny living room, she jumps up to get her attention. "Sean asked me out, Ronny," she whispers hard into Ronny's ear. "I haven't told anybody because Sheila's so upset about Duncan. I wanted to spare her, but I knew you would be happy for me!"

Ronny puts her arm around her friend's shoulder. Maggie is a different woman than the insecure waif who walked with her to Segue House on that first day. Back then, Maggie worked three days a week as the bookkeeper. "Good for you, Maggie. He seems like a nice guy."

Maggie moves off and proceeds to hustle Rose, Sheila, and Patrick into the kitchen. She overhears Patrick tell his neighbours how Margo Johnson, his boss and the owner of the Hayworth Diner, may have just sold the business. She has threatened to get rid of the place for years. Amanda and Chester Wolski, the current managers at The Station, are in the process of buying it.

"Gaby, can I talk to you?" Ronny tries to make her voice casual and not nervous sounding.

"Sure. The food is all organized. We can stay to help clean up, too."

"Thanks. Once the place quiets down, can we talk about the house?"

"Sure. Is there a problem we need to fix?"

"No, not at all. I want to know if you might entertain the thought of selling. I think I need to put down permanent roots. Before this all happened, I never knew when I might have to run. That's over now."

Joe calls from the other side of the room and Gaby turns to see what he wants. "We'll talk. I am most certainly open to the idea," she whispers as she moves off.

The afternoon is memorable, although she begins to fade within a couple of hours. She imagines the din of conversation as objects flying around the room. After living in silence for so long, the constant barrage of words is a challenge. All of her favourite people arrived to wish her well. She had a chance to talk to Sheila, so she knows all is forgiven. Her fall into the trap that is Duncan Taylor was not her fault. Duncan would have committed some act against her, regardless of Sheila's involvement. As she stands at the door, makes her goodbyes and assures each and every one in turn she'll be fine, she wonders if she really will be.

By the time all have departed but Gaby and Joe, they have managed to tidy the kitchen, pack away leftover food, and clear the dishes. "Shall I put the kettle on for tea while we have a chat?" Ronny wants them to relax, and for Gaby to agree.

The couple glance at one another—communication with no words. "Sure, Ronny. We have time for tea. Martha should be okay for another hour." Gaby is always so preoccupied with her dog, now the mascot for Dodd's Contracting and Interiors. She takes Martha to work with her every day.

Once tea is served, they sit in arm chairs in the front room. "I've never asked before, Ronny, but does the picture have any significance?" She points to the photograph, of a tiny island and small building, hung on the wall by the front door.

"Yes, as a matter of fact, the photo is personal—the one connection to my past I ever dared display, Gaby. The view is of our family cottage, when I was a kid. My mother took it from the shore. I've described the image to people before, when they've asked, as a random scene. I won't have to lie anymore." She takes a sip of tea.

"I would very much like to buy this house, Gaby. If you're interested, and I can afford the payments, I want to make 15 Poplar Street my own. What do you think?"

Gaby meets Joe's eyes and thoughts are exchanged. It's incredible how they don't have to talk at all. "Funny. Joe and I discussed the idea a couple of weeks ago, before this all happened." She seems reluctant to use a word like kidnapped, grabbed, or abducted. "I said I wouldn't mind selling, but I would put off the idea as long as you wanted to live here. This might be the perfect solution. The house is yours if you decide you're able to buy. We'll talk about price and details next week after you get reoriented and the investigators are out of the way. Drop into the store and we can put some numbers together, okay?" She turns to Joe. "I think we had better start for home. Somebody needs a walk and I don't mean Martha." She rolls her eyes at Ronny, tips her head back, and roars.

Joe raises his eyebrows. "Do you think she might mean me, Ronny?" He grins from ear to ear.

After they leave, Ronny makes another cup of tea and curls up in her favourite overstuffed chair. The future will no doubt be bright. Ava is thinking about retirement, or at least semi-retiring, and has openly expressed her desire for Ronny to take on more responsibility. She'll be able to accept, now. Gaby has agreed to sell the house, and Ronny is quite sure she'll be able to make the purchase.

Maybe John Fitzpatrick was right, and her escape through the hole in the outhouse wall was like a birth of sorts; for her, a rebirth. Thanks to the likes of Duncan, she can restore the parts of her past she has missed and put the remainder of Janine Taylor to rest forever. Her hand absently touches her short platinum locks. Perhaps she'll let her hair grow back.

About the Author

L. P. Suzanne Atkinson was born in New Brunswick, Canada and lived in both Alberta and Quebec before settling in Nova Scotia in 1991. She has a BA in Psychology from Mount Allison University, a Bachelor of Social Work from McGill University, and an MA in Sociology from Acadia University. Suzanne spent her professional career in the fields of mental health and home care as both a therapist and trainer. She also owned and operated, with her husband, both an antique business and a construction business for more than twenty-five years.

Her philosophy of life is based on two qualities for which she continually strives. They are her benchmarks. First: there is no better descriptor than to be called a kind person and good friend. Second: a lesson learned and not shared is information squandered.

Suzanne writes about the challenges inherent in aging and about the unavoidable consequences of relationships. She uses her life and work experiences to weave timeless stories that cross many boundaries. She and her husband, David Weintraub, continue to make Nova Scotia their home.

Email – lpsa.books@eastlink.ca
Website – http://lpsabooks.wix.com/lpsabooks#
Facebook – L. P. Suzanne Atkinson – Author

Watch for:

Diner Revelations: Regarding Hayworth Book IV

The final installment in the Regarding Hayworth series
Coming in the spring / summer of 2018